KITCHENER PUBLIC LIBRARY

Y0-AWH-917

SWEET JESUS

SWEET JESUS

CHRISTINE POUNTNEY

McCLELLAND & STEWART

Copyright © 2012 by Christine Pountney

All rights reserved. The use of any part of this publication reproduced,
transmitted in any form or by any means, electronic, mechanical,
photocopying, recording, or otherwise, or stored in a retrieval system,
without the prior written consent of the publisher – or, in case of
photocopying or other reprographic copying, a licence from the Canadian
Copyright Licensing Agency – is an infringement of the copyright law.

Library and Archives Canada Cataloguing in Publication

Pountney, Christine, 1971–
Sweet Jesus / Christine Pountney.

ISBN 978-0-7710-7123-2

I. Title.

PS8631.O8356S84 2012   C813'.6   C2012-900967-9

The author acknowledges the financial support of the Canada Council for
the Arts, the Ontario Arts Council, and the Toronto Arts Council.

Typeset in Bembo
Printed and bound in the United States of America

McClelland & Stewart,
a division of Random House of Canada Limited
One Toronto Street
Suite 300
Toronto, Ontario
M5C 2V6
www.mcclelland.com

1   2   3   4   5   16   15   14   13   12

For Michael and Leo

1

Zeus Ortega closed the door and leaned back against it, giving his weight over to its solidity. He wore his clown costume. With the inside of his wrist he held a warm flat pizza box propped against his hip. He shouted, Someone order an extra-large quattro formaggio?

His boyfriend, Fenton Murch, was in the bedroom, sitting up on the waterbed, a thick fall issue of *Vogue* open on his lap. Look at this stunning photograph, he said, smacking the magazine with the back of his hand. The woman on the page swung around to glance over her shoulder, as if in flight, pursued through an Italian cemetery. She wore a voluminous mauve dress with a silver-grey taffeta waistband tied in a hefty bow that sat like a gargoyle on her lower back. Brown hair pinned up in a large heart-shaped chignon, teased to look like a bird's nest. The problem with being sick, Fenton said, is it takes all the fun out of being shallow.

Zeus put the pizza on the waterbed and Fenton flipped the box lid and yanked off a slice, considered it for a moment,

3

then took a small bite. He licked a finger and flicked to the next page of his magazine. He hardly even looked at Zeus these days. He'd lost all of his tenderness.

Zeus went into the bathroom, peeled off his wig, and scratched his head furiously. He looked under his fingernails — a whitish paste of dead skin. Even in the midst of life, we are in death. Tucked into the frame of the bathroom mirror were two quotes. The first was from Groucho Marx — *A clown is like aspirin, only he works twice as fast.* The second was Samuel Beckett — *No matter, try again, fail again, fail better.* Zeus reread them now and pledged his allegiance, once again, to the likelihood that no plan he made would ever come to fruition.

He woke the next morning to the radio. Someone was conducting an interview next to his head. There had been violent protests against an upcoming gay pride parade in Jerusalem and the reporter was asking a rabbi for his opinion. This is not the *homo* land, the rabbi said, this is the *holy* land. The rabbi was taking a blithe dismissive stance in contrast to the reporter's earnest concern. Zeus didn't like his tone. He rolled over — as well as you can roll over in a waterbed — and brought his hand down on the alarm clock. The interview was cut short. Silence bloomed. The bedroom smouldered with dirty-grey urban daylight.

There was comedy in the rabbi's line, but Zeus didn't appreciate the sarcasm. Shouldn't a rabbi show more decorum? Or was it true, as Fenton's father had once told him over dinner, that a line is a line is a line. Don't fuck with the joke, Fenton. Sometimes it's all you've got.

What? Fenton had said. You think belligerence is some kind of protection?

You prefer I should be meek? His father was piling mashed

potatoes onto his plate. Don't be such a putz. It's balls, Fenton. That's what you've got to have if you want to get anywhere in this life. You think the meek will inherit the earth? Since when did my son convert? And you'll pardon my *blunt Jewish belligerence*, but do you see the Christians behaving meekly today? Hell no, dropping bombs all over the Middle East.

So are the Jews, Fenton said.

The meek shall inherit nothing, his father said, but their own demise.

And so it had gone, a typical Sabbath meal at Fenton's parents' place.

Thing is, thinking back to the rabbi, Zeus couldn't understand what all the fuss was about. He made an irritated noise with his tongue, and Fenton — who was lying on his stomach beside him with his head sideways on the pillow — said, I know, I know, without opening his eyes. He lives in a country where his neighbours want to kill him, and he doesn't have anything better to do than worry about a frivolous gay parade of men in leather chaps and feather boas.

Leather chaps and yarmulkes, Zeus corrected him.

Bare bums, but thine head shall be covered.

You get two skull caps with every pair, and Zeus held up his hands like bear paws to imply the buttocks.

Fenton snorted, then started to cough and rolled onto his back. Zeus leaned against him to kiss him.

Get off me, Fenton snapped in a voice that suggested he was in some kind of pain.

Zeus backed off. He'd never known Fenton to be so fragile. The truth was, Fenton had never been one to readily give into weakness. The idea of weakness had never impressed him, never sidled up to him or bowled him over, so it astonished Zeus to realize that weakness had snuck into his lover's body.

Fenton pushed the duvet down to reveal his thin, pale chest. He was slight, but his body had always been strong. He had milky white skin and cinnamon-coloured hair. He was older than Zeus by twenty years and beginning to show signs of aging, but everything about him, to Zeus, still epitomized beauty. Zeus wanted to help but he didn't know how. Fenton had gone to see the doctor a few weeks ago and come home saying that the only thing he needed was a little more bedrest. They'd always given each other a lot of freedom, but there seemed to be other short absences recently that Zeus couldn't account for.

He sat up and sank deeper into the mattress. Maybe you should go see the doctor again, he said, and Fenton grunted a small, stubborn refusal into the air.

Don't you have to go to work or something? Fenton said, and eventually Zeus stood up. The mattress sloshed, rocking Fenton like a canoe. Zeus went over to the antique vanity with the oval mirror and sat down on the low upholstered stool that was faded and threadbare. He contemplated the pots of makeup, the wigs, the noses. A child's black tutu that Fenton sometimes wore around his neck.

It was Zeus who had wanted to be the sad clown – mute, naive, pining for love, the butt of jokes – with a white face and tears painted down his cheeks. He'd wanted to mime with exaggerated pathos all the suffering he understood with his prodigious talent for empathy – which more often felt like a burden than a gift. But, at the age of twenty-two, he was too good at the physical humour. He had to ham it up, be jolly, do somersaults, and trip over trolleys. He took off his sleeping shirt and began tucking his black hair under a nylon cap. Then he pulled on his wig with the rubber bald top, making its ring of smoky orange hair sway and hover around his head. Leaning towards the mirror, he painted on his elaborate dark eyebrows, like the silhouette of two birds facing each other, then the big white sausage of a grin, around which he dabbed a grey five o'clock shadow. Lastly, he applied the glue and, holding it in place for a moment, affixed his red latex nose, slightly oblong and shaped like a big toe.

He stood up and double-checked his wig and makeup, thinking again how boyish he looked for his age. He walked over to the bed in his underwear and sat down and stroked Fenton's curly hair. For the last three years, the two of them had been working as therapeutic clowns at the children's hospital in Chicago – for the last year or so, almost exclusively in palliative care, where their characters had begun to take on an otherworldly aspect, as if they belonged somewhere outside the normal standards of decorum and their purpose was to soften the transition between worlds by messing with the rules. You sure you can't come to work today? Zeus felt a bit fragile himself.

I'm working on a part, Fenton said. It's called the invalid.

Zeus shook his head. Too close to the bone, he said.

That's all I know, too close to the bone.

And it was true. Fenton played the bleeding heart, the melancholic. He was the one who got to paint his face white and put inverted triangles under his eyes and make a fetish of his sadness. His wig also had a bald spot, but the hair was grey and he wore a loose white satin jumpsuit. The kids took one look at him and felt their lot improve. He'd curl up in a fetal position on the colourful carpet in the common room and they'd go up to him and put their tiny hands on his shoulder and intone the mantras they'd heard all their short lives. It's gonna be okay. Don't be sad.

C'mon, Fenton. We still haven't done the baby swap.

They had worked out a routine. They would take the babies out of the parents' hands, the babies who weren't hooked up to IVs or life support systems, maybe even a healthy visiting sibling, and switch them around. It was a variation of the hat trick. You take one man's hat and give it to another, take his hat and give it to a third. You take that man's hat and give it to the first. Fenton and Zeus had wondered how it would play out. Even if it was unnerving, they found the riskier the skit, the greater the catharsis – the more release it offered by way of coming crash-bang head-on with the wretched injustice these parents faced, having brought a baby lovingly into the world only to see it succumb to some virus, heart deformity, organ failure, car wreck.

You'll have to settle for the country house, Fenton said. The country house was a small painted wooden house on wheels that blew bubbles out of the chimney. Zeus would pull it down the hall on a string and pretend not to notice how the kids came to their doors or sat up in their beds to watch his progress. Then he would disappear into a closet and maybe come out riding a stretcher.

Zeus got dressed, then came back to the bed. He wore high-top sneakers, an old-fashioned black morning jacket with tails, and a pale yellow shirt with a polka-dot tie. His pants were tapered and grey, six inches too short, and patched with velvet squares of ruby and plum. Can I get you anything? he asked, bending to fill Fenton's ear with his warm breath. I hate to see you like this.

Fenton was silent, then he adjusted himself on the bed, and Zeus got up and poured him a glass of water from the kitchen tap, placing it on the bedside table. Then he put on his beige trench coat, tossed a red wool scarf around his neck. He felt scared for the first time.

Outside, the world felt unknowable, incomprehensible. Zeus bought a bottle of apple juice at the corner store and headed for the train station. How do you sift through the memory of so much history to explain the moment you have arrived at? Fenton had introduced him to clowning not long after they met, five years ago, when Zeus was hanging out on the university campus. He was seventeen and working as a bike courier and used to eat lunch at the student union cafeteria. The food was cheap and he liked the boisterous atmosphere and the cozy feeling he got from infiltrating the sanctuary of a more privileged class of people. He'd get a burrito and a rice pudding, and sometimes even sit in on a class, clicking up and down the lecture hall stairs in his bike shoes and leggings, carrying his filthy canvas bag.

One day Zeus reached for a bowl of rice pudding inside one of the cafeteria's refrigerated glass cases and took hold of someone's hand. It was Fenton's hand and the last portion of rice pudding on campus and they'd both glared at each other like gunslingers, then broke out laughing. Zeus tossed a coin and lost, but then Fenton invited him to share it. Fenton must have sensed an outsider and started to vent. Can you even tolerate what these people take for granted? he said, waving his spoon at the room. Rugby and cheerleading and overpriced textbooks?

Fenton was back at school, attempting to please his father by doing a law degree. He already had an MA in art history and been halfway around the world. They arranged to meet for lunch the next day. They sat and talked for hours. Fenton told him later he'd loved Zeus's curiosity and determined independence, a lightness about things that seemed to cover something needy and sad. After a while, their friendship took a romantic turn.

It would be hard, years later, to separate the birth of their romance from their initiation into the world of clowning because it was around this time that Fenton was walking through a park in Chicago's West Town and came across a small crowd gathered to watch a short film projected on the cement wall of an old warehouse. It was black-and-white footage from the 1950s, a brief skit of two clowns, dressed like tramps, trying to share, with as much exaggerated dignity as they can muster, a bottle of vodka in the open air, under the watchful eye of a policeman. When at last the bottle is empty and all the vodka gone – after using it first to wash their hands, then gargle with and spit on the ground, to prove to the policeman that it's just water – they still haven't drunk a drop. In the end, all they have to share is a crust of bread. Fenton discovered later it was a clip of Yuri Nikulin, the famous Russian clown, and his partner, performing with the Moscow Circus, but at the time, he had simply been entranced. He told Zeus that nothing he'd ever seen had so thoroughly captured the struggle between pleasure and authority, or expressed the poignant and humiliating nature of life, and what could be more noble – or more representative of his own truest feelings – than to become a clown?

The movie haunted Fenton for days. He seemed constantly distracted. Then he seemed to reach a state of contentment that was almost conceited. He stopped going to class. Zeus didn't know where he was spending his days. What the hell's the matter with you? he yelled.

I've joined the Chi-Town Clown Academy, if you must know, Fenton said. And he knocked Zeus between the eyes with the heel of his hand. Who's the comedian now, eh?

Clown academy? It seemed like the most outlandish place for a man of Fenton's temperament and background.

That's right, Fenton said. I'm studying to be a clown.

You're already a clown, Zeus said with a sneer.

You should come with me.

Ha ha.

Fenton shoved his hands into his pockets. I think it's a good fit.

And if the shoe fits.

The shoe will never fit! Fenton said, throwing his hands into the air. That's the whole point. Fitting implies a level of comfort and respectability this profession will never allow, or even endorse. And I happen to be in full agreement with this line of thinking. Wear your underwear on the outside of your pants the next time you go to the corner store to get a carton of milk and you'll see what I'm talking about. I'm talking about the soul here, Zeus! The power to transform lives, provide relief, to point out the silly path towards decency. I'm talking about being an outcast, a social critic. I'm talking about saving lives!

Okay, okay, Zeus said. Take it easy. You're freaking me out. Zeus chewed his lip.

You have to come with me, Fenton had said. I know you have this in you too.

And so Zeus had gone with him and fallen, as Fenton predicted, under the academy's spell. He loved the crazy antics and the open expressiveness of clowning, and finding a place to belong, where loyalties were formed around common goals and common opinions, and not because of blood ties, or the lack of them. Besides, it's where Fenton was spending his time, and Zeus wanted to be with him. As he did now. But, over the last few months, Fenton had grown so listless he seemed indifferent to everything, even to his art. He'd lost muscle mass. His movements had become rigid and tentative. About a month ago, Zeus had seen Fenton cry on the shoulder of a bald child with a tube coming out of her nose and both arms wrapped in bandages. Her mouth had a mashed look and her eyes were too big for their sockets. They'd sat side by side on the edge of her bed, his head on her shoulder, while she held a pale hand to his white cheek. It was like being comforted in hell.

Or maybe this had been a dream.

It was as if only a thin membrane separated him from his subconscious these days. He'd woken up two days ago and heard himself say, Where's the other man? Lately, his dreams had become very ordinary. One night he dreamt about sharing a doughnut with Fenton, and the next day didn't know whether or not this had actually happened.

The L-train was coming.

He saw the silver square of its flat face shift slightly from one side to the other and knew that it was barrelling down the tracks. The screech of its brakes as it came into the station was an angry lament that reminded him of his own frustration. Zeus got on the train and stood by the doors. Dressed even as he was, most people didn't seem to notice him. He was always stunned by what other people ignored. He tried to cheer himself up by pulling a pocket watch, the size of a cup saucer, out of his pants and opening it up. A small brown terrycloth dog, perched on top of a flexible wire and attached at the base to a wind-up mechanism, sprung up and flew around in circles, chasing its own tail. Zeus shrugged and closed the lid and wound it up again. He leaned away from his pocket and, holding it open, lowered the watch by its chain back into his pants. This normally got a laugh. Sometimes someone would throw a few coins at his feet and he would make a show of fawning over the money, clasping his hands together against his chest like an ardent suitor in a silent film, but never stooped to pick it up.

Halfway to the hospital, a man got up from his seat and lumbered towards the doors. When the train stopped, he swung out onto the platform, hesitated, then swung back into the train. Zeus thought the man must be drunk, but he smelled reassuringly of aftershave. The man sat down again. His dark hair was pulled back into a short comma at the base of his skull, and he wore a gold corduroy jacket over a white shirt with a maroon tie. He removed a bottle of cologne from his pocket. A cut-glass bottle with a German label in blue and gold. He yanked off the atomizer nozzle and took a swig. Now Zeus realized the man's hands were dirty, his fingernails cracked. His clothes were scruffy and stained. Zeus had let his sense of smell obscure his eyes. This was an observation Fenton would normally appreciate, but Zeus wondered if he'd even bother telling him when he got back home tonight. He felt a pang of something like feeling sorry for Fenton, but then he recoiled. You can't pity a clown. As soon as you pity a clown, he's done for.

Zeus was two stops from the hospital now and an argument had broken out between the guy drunk on German cologne and a wiry young man with an enormous gym bag. The young man jumped up and yanked the older guy's corduroy sleeve. Come on, he said, that's enough. Get the hell outta here. The drunk man was pressing his cologne bottle against the collarbone of a dark-eyed woman sitting next to him. She looked frightened and harassed. Put some of this on your pussy, he said. Might freshen you up.

The young man said, That's it, and pulled the older man up and dragged him to the doors and pushed him out as soon as they opened. The man braced himself in the doorway, one last arc of protest, his gold jacket flaring open like the wings of a moth. The young man kicked him in the back of the legs and he fell out of the train. Zeus saw him land on his shoulder, his face like a wedge, shoved between his momentum and the platform. That's gotta hurt, someone said. The man lay still for a moment amid the indifferent traffic of busy feet. Then he picked himself up proudly and made his way to the exit. He lifted his leg as if his foot was encased in cement and, listing backwards – his hand shooting out for the railing – descended onto the first step of the stairwell. Zeus heard a whole stadium applaud. The doors slid shut and the L-train moved down the track. The young fitness enthusiast who had thrown the man out turned around. He had sweat on his upper lip. He looked at Zeus – the wig, the wide eyes. Got a staring problem?

You talking to me? Zeus said and raised his eyebrows.

You look ridiculous.

Thank you very much, Zeus said politely, and the painted birds relaxed back onto their perches.

What's with *this* guy? the young man said, looking around. His chivalry was all defensive bravado now.

Pick on the clown, tough guy, Zeus thought.

What an idiot, the guy said, walking back to his seat. Fucking clown suit, he said under his breath.

L ast year, Norman Peach had gone hunting in Newfoundland and come back to Toronto with a hundred pounds of frozen caribou meat. Hannah Crowe had never known anyone to hunt. He'd left her the keys to his apartment and two hundred dollars and called her halfway through the week. Go get me a chest freezer. So Hannah had gone around the corner from where she lived to a secondhand appliance store on Queen Street West and chosen a little freezer that had been painted white on the inside to cover its imperfections. Two middle-aged men, one Jamaican, grey at the temples, and the other a thin Ukrainian in flat dress shoes, carried it up the steep fire escape to Norm's apartment. When the Jamaican man heard what it was for, he joked, I'll bring a two-four round, man, in a couple of weeks and we'll have carry-bou steaks on the barbie.

Hannah was impressed that Norm had gone into the woods alone, found a caribou, shot it down, gutted and quartered it, then carried the quarters to where his old Toyota Tercel was parked, somewhere on a woods road. He was only about half a mile from his car, but it took him five hours to lug the meat out. This was proof of a kind of courage, self-reliance, and physical endurance that she admired. She wanted to admire herself for the same reasons – so, this time, she'd gone with him. They'd flown to Norm's hometown of St. John's, rented a car, and picked up the keys to the house of a friend who was away on vacation. In the morning, they drove to a quarry forty-five minutes outside the city, to sight in the rifle and take a few practice shots. Hannah was nervous about the kickback. She'd seen a picture of Norm with a dark bruise on one side of his chest, just below the shoulder.

They got out of the car and Hannah lifted the gun out of the trunk and slung the strap over her head so the rifle hung diagonally across her back. She'd never carried a gun before and it was thrilling. Wearing the first warm clothing of the year, she felt like some glamorous Russian spy from an old Bond film, about to ski down an alpine slope in a tight, white one piece, with fake fir trees bouncing behind her in the background. She had an accent. *You know nussing about me, you only sink you do.*

Coming? Norm said.

You know, Hannah said, we could turn around and go home now and I'd still feel like we'd been on a pretty satisfying adventure.

Yeah, but there's shootin' to be done.

Norm was drawing a circle the size of an eyeball in the centre of a square of cardboard. He paced off fifty yards, set the cardboard at the far end of the quarry, and walked back. He showed her how to flick the safety on and off and check the barrel for cartridges. The bullet's going to arc, he said, and there's a bit of wind from the south, so aim higher than the crosshairs in your scope and a bit to the right. Norm could sense that Hannah was stalling.

Do you want me to take the first shot?

No, I'll do it, she said.

She planted her feet and aimed, but looking through the scope was like looking through a blurry magnifying glass. A little juniper growing out of the gravel exploded into focus. Okay, I got it, she said. It was like binoculars. You had to get the angle right. Hannah panned an inch to the right and the target slid out of sight. She panned back and caught the cardboard in the crosshairs. It looked small. The bull's-eye smaller. Her arm was trembling from the weight of the rifle.

You can crouch, Norm said. Like this.

Hannah squatted, put her elbow on her knee. The Lee-Enfield was sighted to hit dead square at both fifty and two hundred yards. The target was fifty yards away so all Hannah had to do was centre it, but the view through the scope still floated.

Breathe out, Norm said. And squeeze.

Now the picture sat still. She had the bull's-eye lined up. She hesitated, just to be sure, then ran out of breath. She lowered the gun and yawned.

Take your time.

She glanced back at him. Norm had his fingers in his ears and his eyes were wide open.

She tried again – concentrated, aimed, held the butt firmly against her shoulder, and squeezed the trigger. Holy fuck. The noise shocked her. It was very loud and very fast. You almost doubted it after you heard it. Now she understood how a gunshot in a movie sounded fake. It sure ain't cracked celery in a sound studio, that's for sure.

Norm said, That's gunpowder for you.

Hannah's ears were ringing and adrenalin was prickling in her fingertips. There had been no kickback. Her heart was racing. She put the gun down as if denouncing the power of it.

She shook her hands loose at the wrists. I have no idea, she said, whether I hit that or not.

They started off at a walk, then Hannah broke into a run. Not only had she hit the cardboard, she was two inches shy of the bull's-eye at fifty paces.

Norm said, I think you'll be fine.

Hannah took two more shots. Neither shot was as close, but good enough in Norm's opinion and closer than both of his, though he took his standing.

They got into the car and headed back for the city, where Norm's friends were expecting them for dinner. But then Norm pulled over at a spot where the trees thinned out and you could see the long clearing of a run of power lines. I've seen caribou in here before, he said, so they stood at the edge of the highway and got geared up. It was mid-October and they had rubber boots and rain pants and rain jackets and sweaters. They had orange toques and Hannah had bought a cheap plastic orange safety vest that was so large she had to tie it in a knot at the front. How do I look?

You look like you don't want to get shot.

Norm tossed her a pair of thin white cotton gloves.

What are these for?

So you don't cut your hands when you're gutting the animal, he said.

You think we'll get one now?

You never know.

Norm carried the rifle and a cracked waxed army surplus bag that was heavy for its size. Inside were bandages and a lighter in an old tobacco tin, a compass, topographical map, a small axe, hunting knife, whetstone, disassembled handsaw, and a yellow cardboard pack of rifle cartridges. The shells were for a Lee-Enfield .303 – an English rifle made in 1943. When

Hannah called home before leaving and happened to mention to her father what kind of gun they'd be hunting with, Tim Crowe had said, That's the same gun I used as a fifteen-year-old cadet in the British Army. I used to win sharpshooting competitions. And Hannah had said, I wonder if it's in the blood.

They followed the razed path beneath the power lines, then headed into the woods. Norm gave Hannah the gun and she didn't hand it back. They saw nothing, and after a while the shooting and the anticipation and the physical exertion of carrying a twelve-pound rifle and the joyful privacy of walking where there were no trails and the clarity of the bright sunshine on the red grass and the brittle grey branches of dead trees and the dark green fur of the stunted junipers made them feel very alive.

We haven't talked about you beating me up for a long time, Hannah said.

Norm had come up behind her. He was unbuckling his belt.

They had got lost inside a fantasy, in the early days of their relationship, born of a desire to merge, to obliterate and dominate each other. It was, for Hannah, a way of exploring the rare temptation to surrender, of wanting to be broken open, but not knowing how, short of an act of violence. I wanted you to drag me through the woods by my hair, she said, remember? We talked about coming to a place like this and doing it.

Norm dropped his pants and Hannah heard the clink of .303 cartridges in the front pocket of his jeans. She had her hands on the scratchy bark of a fallen tree.

I wanted you to yank me over logs, and the sound of breaking twigs. I wanted my skin to be cold and scratched and streaked with dirt and pine needles.

You'd be naked, Norm said, but I'd have my clothes on. Like in that film by Buñuel.

Naked and tied to a tree and totally vulnerable, Hannah said, breathing heavily through her mouth. She was getting close and then Norm pulled out and came on the ground and it was like pulling a trampoline out from under someone in mid-air and, *God*, why won't he come in me? And then the frustration and the unachieved climax and the throbbing nub of her arousal pulsing furiously.

Hannah sank to her knees and rolled over onto her back. The faint warmth of the sun on her belly. Legs bound at the ankles by her pants. One hand above her head. I wanted you to bring a couple of friends, she said, arching her back and pressing her ass into the moss. Couple of guys just sitting around smoking roll-ups and spitting tobacco on the ground. Gorgeous young men in parkas, with fur-lined hoods.

They could take turns, Norm said, picking up the rifle.

C onnie Foster wanted to wear white. That's why she was on her knees, digging through a laundry basket full of clean clothes, trying to find her yoga pants, when Mary-Beth arrived after the vestry meeting – a meeting she was supposed to have been at, but her husband still hadn't come home. He was staying out later and later these days and it was making Connie nervous – nervous and short-tempered – when all she really wanted was to be patient and caring and wise.

She'd put the kids to bed and was trying to get focused before Mary-Beth arrived to watch a rerun of the second presidential debate that had aired earlier. She wanted to clear her head, and getting into something clean and white was part of that. The situation in the world right now was so dire that, in the last six months, she and Mary-Beth had watched more CNN than they thought they could bear. On top of it all was the three-ring circus of the Republican Party. While they shared many of the belief practices of their charismatic brethren south of the border, they were convinced they were being politically misled. They knew how the Christian right had voted during the primaries in the spring, and were now praying for God to give those people discernment in the upcoming election.

Connie had been raised in the Anglican Church and loved how cerebral and rational it was, with its emphasis on the power of words and metaphor and ritual. She felt there was a mysticism in the Anglican liturgy that could erupt at any moment by its sheer recitation every week. It wasn't until she met Mary-Beth that she found somebody who shared, in her own way, a profound spirituality. Mary-Beth was open to all sorts of manifestations of God. She'd been to charismatic gatherings and been hurled to the floor by the power of the Holy Spirit, but also loved the quiet, dignified poetry of the Book of Common Prayer.

Mary-Beth had moved to Vancouver Island sixteen months earlier because she'd found an excellent special-needs school in Mill Bay for her teenaged handicapped son, and could afford to open up a hair salon and live nearby. She catered mainly to the wealthy high-school students at the local private boarding school, and had done about thirty up-do's last spring at graduation and twice as many manicures and pedicures. She would sometimes witness to the girls as they sat getting their hair dyed or nails done, especially if it was a quiet afternoon and the salon cosy with the heat from the hair dryers, the windows fogged up like milky stained glass. The girls are in their own element, she told Connie, so it makes the gospel seem more friendly, more accessible. I tell the story of Mary Magdalene washing Jesus' feet with her hair.

Her salon was called The Beauty Ministry – *Making Women Beautiful Inside and Out* – and it was there that the two women met. To Connie, Mary-Beth was like a breath of fresh air. She'd led a secular life until her conversion four years earlier at the airport in Seattle, where she'd been visiting an old flame. Her return flight was cancelled because of a snowstorm, so she'd sought out the chapel, thinking it might be a quiet place to sleep. She told Connie she was curled up on the carpet when a woman walked in, kneeled, and started to cry. Mary-Beth offered her a small pack of kleenex she had in her purse. The woman's son had recently drowned. Mary-Beth told her, I have a son too. He's got MS. He's in a wheelchair. I understand what it's like to feel angry, to want to rail. But the woman had said, I'm not railing. I'm thanking my saviour for walking beside me through this terrible journey.

It was at that moment Mary-Beth felt compelled to commit her life to Jesus. She didn't bristle or judge at the news of somebody's drug addiction or delinquent child, she was honestly forgiving. And it wasn't until she'd experienced Mary-Beth's compassion first-hand that Connie realized intimate friendship and genuine acceptance were two things sadly lacking in her own life.

There's no such thing as a scandal, Mary-Beth once said. Look at me? Divorced, a single mother, a handicapped son most people refuse to make eye contact with. I probably used to have a bit of a drinking problem too.

She was so open that Connie trusted her opinions unreservedly, though there were those who thought of her as vain, that her profession indicated a weakness for the adornments of the flesh.

Connie opened the door and her friend walked in, billowing a waft of Estée Lauder. What a day, she said. How are you, darling?

Oh fine, Connie said, taking Mary-Beth's leopard-print coat. How was the vestry meeting?

We argued for thirty-five minutes about whether or not the worship band should have a dress code, she said and poked her long fingernails into her hair.

I made walnut brownies, Connie said, offering up a tray in the kitchen and nodding towards the living room.

You're such an angel, Mary-Beth said and followed her down the marble hallway. Nothing like a vestry meeting to work up the appetite, she said and plucked at the corner of one of Connie's elbows with her fake nails, and it gave Connie a shiver.

Connie pushed the French doors to the living room open with her foot and carried the tray in. Her living room was white and she found it helped. A cut-glass bowl with five pink marble eggs, one for each member of the family. The coffee table was white and the carpet oatmeal. What a bland, pale room this was, she thought, but it was how she liked it.

Mary-Beth stood at the huge picture window. You really do have the best view of the water, she said even though it was dark outside and the window a perfect duplicate of the living room. She crossed the room and collapsed onto the sofa. I'd be more jealous if I didn't know I could never keep a house this clean with Jay around, she said, referring to her son.

Well, I don't let the children in here except for birthdays and holidays, Connie confessed. And I told Harl I want a fibre-optic Christmas tree this year, as an eco-decision, but it's really because I don't want pine needles worming their way into the carpet again. Connie was kneeling next to the coffee table. She flashed Mary-Beth one of her furtive looks while pouring out the tea, but Mary-Beth wasn't looking. She was flicking the TV on with the remote.

You know, Mary-Beth suddenly said in a passionate voice, I just wish I could grab Obama by the wrists and drag him to his knees and force him to pray for his soul, the whole soul of

America. I mean, he made all these promises four years ago, that's what he was voted in on. And what did he do? Protected the interests of the rich, that's what. And is he going to invade North Korea now? You start that kind of thing and it's hard to get out. Look at Iraq. It took him a lot longer to get the army out of there than what he assured everybody in his campaign.

But that war was started, Connie said, well before Obama got into office.

Exactly, but he was supposed to put an end to it.

Connie handed Mary-Beth a cup of tea. The sad thing is, after 9/11, people thought they were fighting a righteous war.

Even if it *was* a righteous war, Mary-Beth said, deflated after her short outburst, it'd still be hard to contemplate. War should be the last resort. I'll never forget how excited Bush looked, addressing his troops on that navy ship, in one of those leather bomber jackets with the sheepskin collar. Like he was announcing the start of a football game. He made it seem like some kind of party.

And now they have the Tea Party, Connie said.

Mary-Beth raised her cup and lifted her pinkie off the handle.

It's not like we're having a field day up here either, Connie said. As they chip away at all our social institutions. What's it going to be next? And she reached up and felt the solidity of her jaw bone beneath her skin.

Ever since Theo had been born, life seemed more precarious. Her first two had slipped out slick as seal pups, but Theo had come into the world blue and screaming, in an explosion of blood that covered the doctor. Connie saw the doctor wince, as if she'd never been covered in blood before. She'd been sawing the handle of the suction cup up and down in the air between Connie's knees with such force that it made her husband think of a construction site, he told her afterwards. The way an electrician might pull a bundle of wires through a tight pliable rubber hose, slippery with dish soap, out of a hole in the wall, one foot braced against something solid. Those were his words. The blood gushed and in the air she heard – *hemorrhage*. For six whole minutes people rushed around the room. The nurses pulled blue masks up over their noses. Harlan's face was so close. There was sleep in the corner of his eye and this outraged her. And then she panicked, Where's my baby?

He's okay, Harlan said. Ten fingers, ten toes.

You must take care of him, Connie said. If.

Excuse me, a nurse had said, pushing the father aside, and then a grey needle shrank against the yellow skin on the inside of Connie's arm. Between the pale V of her knees the sudden red of the doctor's gloves when she raised them, like a child's pair of winter mittens. Pain again. Connie didn't think she could feel any more pain. She rolled her head. Something large, a wrecking ball, swung down and entered her vagina, smashing her innards. What was left of them. Or so it felt. God help me, she thought. I don't want to die.

They were going to call the baby Andrew, after his grandfather, but they decided on Theo. The name for God.

You know, Connie said to Mary-Beth, ever since Theo's birth, I've been so aware of the possibility of a sudden extinction.

Well, every year the world gets more dangerous, Mary-Beth said. Remember that murder in Langley?

I think so.

A woman was killed in her car while her four-year-old son sat in the back seat.

That was so terrible.

They shot the car full of bullets, and she drove into a tree. Fortunately, the boy was unharmed.

Thank *God*, Connie said.

Apparently, she had some connection with a gang.

How can you do that to a child?

So, of course, you're *worried*, Mary-Beth said. We're all worried.

Well, you and *I* are worried, Connie said, and they let the melodrama of their concerns open for a moment like a window, then close again.

I just don't want to smother my children by being over-protective, Connie said, leaning back against the sofa and hold-ing her brownie over a small china plate.

No parent should worry about smothering their children in a world like this.

But I had such freedom growing up. I would like them to know that freedom.

Well, you give them some freedom, of course.

And then you hold them close and will a conviction that God will take care of them?

He *does* take care of them, Mary-Beth said, stressing the present tense.

With my own vigilance and God's love.

They'll be fine.

But that life persists at all, such a tiny flame, seems like such a miracle to me.

It *is* a miracle.

I've just had my doubts, you know? I mean, maybe we've got it all wrong, Mary-Beth. Maybe life is just a brutal rat race to succeed, after all, without higher purpose or redemption, and I've just dragged three more unsuspecting victims into the fray.

I think your fears are wildly exaggerated, Mary-Beth said, and need a little dose of reality.

I'm up to my eyeballs in reality, Connie said. What I need is a dose of the mystical.

Mary-Beth put her plate down, wiped her mouth, and tucked her feet up onto the couch. I fear, she said, that our evangelical Anglican isn't getting enough Pentecostal on her Sunday mornings.

Just *something* to bolster my faith, Connie said, looking baffled and resigned.

Mary-Beth picked up the remote and pointed it at the TV. When's the debate supposed to come on again? she asked and started blinking through the channels.

In about fifteen minutes, Connie said and stared at her watch longer than it took to tell the time. She realized, at that moment, that she could imagine a life in which she had no faith.

There had been a period in her youth when she'd lost her focus, turned her eyes away from God. Her parents never knew, it wasn't radical, but she'd had a quiet rebellion. At seventeen, she had a boyfriend. They'd done cocaine. Connie thought about it now – it didn't make her cringe, she wasn't ashamed – two tiny white envelopes in a small ziplock bag hidden among her underclothes. Her younger sister had found it one day. How triumphant and betrayed Hannah had looked, brandishing the bag like some proof of heresy, grateful for once of being spared the burden of being bad, but hurt too, by the exclusion of Connie's secrecy. Hannah had acted as if she took Connie's privacy as an indictment of her own character, and it pained Connie to know that this might have been true. She felt her sister wasn't to be trusted. She was too moody, and prone to bouts of anger that left everyone in its wake toppled like palm trees after a hurricane. In fact, Connie had, on more than one occasion, thanked God explicitly for not endowing her with Hannah's temperament and her ambiguous, unreligious life. It seemed chaotic and unhappy to her.

They'd been raised Christian, and Connie had never really strayed. Her faith was an inheritance from her parents, but she'd also made it her own by a decision of intellect. She'd decided to believe in Christ's message. It struck her as truthful and it suited her. Connie had been married for nine years. If someone asked her, are you happy? she would probably respond that happiness is not the point. The point is to live in accordance with God's will, and by the fruit of your actions will you be judged. Only then do you reap the rewards, and so far – Connie couldn't help but think – things were looking pretty good in that respect.

She had always wanted a view of the ocean and now there it was, right outside her window. At the bottom of the sloping landscaped lawn, you took a narrow path of red-brown wood chips through the rhododendrons to a grey pebble beach upon whose shores lapped the cold waters of the Pacific. Her husband, Harlan Foster, had bought her this house. It had been built by a highly sought-after Vancouver architect, on a hectare of oceanfront property, for a man whose marriage collapsed before he and his wife had a chance to move in. The price was more than Harlan thought they could afford, but Connie was thrilled. The house had a state-of-the-art kitchen, two stone fireplaces – one in the living room, one in the split-level family room – and the dining room had a vaulted cathedral ceiling with a chandelier four feet across. There were six bedrooms, four bathrooms, two ensuites with jacuzzi tubs, a finished basement with a snooker table, and a three-car garage.

At least my husband's a good provider, Connie said, almost to herself, as if Mary-Beth wasn't there.

That must make you feel safe.

Well, sometimes it makes me feel like we're on the right track.

Though I don't think the Midas touch ever saved a soul, Mary-Beth said. Harder for a camel to pass through the eye of a needle than for a rich man to enter.

Yes, yes, I know, Connie said. It's moral scrupulousness that ensures the resurrection of the flesh.

That and a good skin-care regime, Mary-Beth joked. I'm using straight olive oil now. Apparently it's the new fountain of youth.

Earlier, Connie said wistfully, the ocean was the colour of olive oil. The sun came out just as it was setting. The clouds were purple and pink and orange. There was a hawk sitting at the top of a tree. Maybe a hundred feet up. White breast with a grey back. Just sitting up there and swivelling its head around. How suddenly the air changes when the sun goes down at this time of year. I felt the chill and melancholy of it. The maples were still wet from the rain and black. Just a handful of yellow leaves hanging from their branches like paper stars. Do you know what they reminded me of?

I know you'll tell me, Mary-Beth said, wincing slightly at Connie's morbid tone.

The yellow stars the Jews were forced to wear, and Mary-Beth shook her head sorrowfully.

Connie told her how she'd been to Dachau when she was twelve years old, as a tourist on a family trip to Europe. Her parents had taken her there. She'd held her sister's hand and they'd walked through the white enamel shower rooms and saw the ovens and watched the black-and-white film footage of rooms piled to the ceiling with glasses, leather shoes, dark wool coats. The piles sloped down from the highest point like grain in a silo, as if poured from above and not accumulated from the floor up. That night, Connie had woken up on the floor of a French hotel scared stiff. She'd seen Nazis under the bed where her parents lay sleeping. They were crouched there with their black stovepipe boots in their hands. Her fear was visceral. It had circled the rug and settled in for good, resting at the centre of things ever since. Connie got so used to her fear she forgot what had caused it in the first place. It was company. She mistook it for truth.

Sometimes I think you're half in love with the idea of disaster, Mary-Beth said, but I'm not sure why. Look, she said, suddenly pointing with the remote. They're doing some kind of follow-up story on that awful incident again.

Four years ago, a man on a Greyhound bus had stabbed a fellow passenger – a young man asleep with his headphones on. The guy was schizophrenic. He hacked the young man's head off with a knife and held it up by the hair to taunt the other passengers, who'd all fled the bus and were standing outside on the edge of a dark highway. In the rush to get off, a mother had thrown her toddler over several rows of seats to get her away from him. Then the man on the bus started cutting up his victim's body with a pair of scissors and eating it.

I can't even begin to comprehend, Connie said. How long ago was it that she'd seen that al-Qaeda footage of a hostage on his knees in an orange jumpsuit? A man in a black hood standing above him. A large knife is raised into the air. These televised beheadings, direct from Baghdad, birthplace of the ancient world – such a biblical place. Birthplace of a whole new style of crime.

The depth of misery, Mary-Beth said, that could drive a person to such a thing.

Why can't people learn to control themselves! Connie slapped the empty plates back on the tray and stood up. I mean, people everywhere just seem to be giving into their own worst natures. There's no restraint. We're not animals, you know. We can't just go around doing whatever the frig we like.

Mary-Beth glanced up from the TV to give Connie a sympathetic look. Connie's occasional outbursts of muted profanity encouraged her. As she'd once told her, they were a reassuring sign of defiance in an otherwise obedient life.

Whatever happened, Connie said with regained composure, to the private interior reward of virtue?

The private interior reward of virtue? Mary-Beth repeated.

Well, you know what I mean, Connie said and carried the tray out to the kitchen.

Connie ran the hot water and squeezed some lavender dish soap into the sink. She didn't mind washing the dishes because a frugal upbringing had taught her to spare the appliances. Besides, it was an excuse to warm her hands. Connie held her wrists under the warm flow from the tap and prayed. *Oh God, Father Almighty, maker of heaven and earth, of all things visible and invisible, very God of very God, begotten not made, being of one substance with the Father – and from whom all good things flow.*

Sometimes a string of religious words would pearl through Connie's mind, like beads dragged through her fingers. It wasn't quite prayer, it was too unbidden, and it made her a little nervous, but she dearly loved the sound of the words she heard in church and so her mind poured them forth, only she knew on these occasions it was out of a love of their sound and not their meaning. Sometimes she wished she had Mary-Beth's fearless evangelical faith. They had run the Vancouver half-marathon together last spring, and the night before, Mary-Beth had had a vision and felt called to testify. To the back of her t-shirt, under her runner's number, she'd pinned a handwritten sign – *Jesus is my Coach, I am running with my Saviour, to the finish line.*

Connie was cautious, however, that these proclamations should be uttered in a spirit of absolute sincerity. Faith without vigilance made you an easy target for hypocrisy. The devil will want to get you, Connie's parish priest had once told her, because your parents are such Godly people. He will want to win you over to his camp. And Connie had understood that there was a power to be harnessed in God's name, that it required a reverence and a sanctity. It was something she admired about the Jews and the Muslims, how they refused to spell out the names of their gods in full. The way the Muslims wove flaws into their carpets so they wouldn't be committing idolatry or mimicking God's perfection on earth.

The floodlights came on outside, giving the reflection in the dark window above the sink an eerie depth, at exactly the same moment Mary-Beth yelled from the living room, It's on! The sudden interruption gave Connie's body a jolt. She answered, Coming! and wondered why these kinds of collisions seemed to happen so often. It was like being jolted out of sleep by a noise that coincides with a dream, the way a car on the street can squeal at the very moment someone taps you on the shoulder in a dream. Connie looked at the clock. Her husband should've been home by now. Where are you, Harlan?

Connie dried her hands and left the kitchen. She leaned through the French doors into the living room. I'm just going to go check on the kids.

Okay, Mary-Beth said without turning away from the TV. It's just the preliminaries. You haven't missed anything yet.

Connie went upstairs and looked into Emma's bedroom – her eldest at eight years old, mouth open, hair like caramel sauce. A storybook was jammed between her mattress and the headboard. Connie carefully pulled it out like a sliver, then put the book back on the shelf and went into Theo's room. He lay on top of his covers like a starfish, with his head at the foot of the bed. She could hear the surrender in his breathing, his complete trust in the moment. She picked him up, turned him around, and tucked him in again. She went into Simon's room across the hall. Si was six years old, three years older than Theo, and he lay curled up on his side with his arms around a soft, black, stuffed gorilla. Connie sat down and touched his warm head. She tucked the covers around his body and stroked his dark hair. His cheeks glowed pink in the light from the hall, like sunlight through magnolia petals. Connie felt the sharp pangs of love. How blessed I am in my children, she thought and walked into her own room – she felt expansive, more free in her own house now that her friend was over – and sat down on the edge of the bed, the bed in which all three of her children had been conceived. Maybe one had been made on the sofa, or in a sleeping bag on a camping trip, but mainly she and Harlan restricted their lovemaking to the queen-sized bed they'd bought after their honeymoon nine years ago, with money Harlan made from the sale of his first patent.

Harlan Douglas Foster. As reliable a husband as Connie could have ever hoped for. He had a master's in engineering from UBC and ran his own security systems company, sold mostly household burglar alarms. He specialized in security, and the symbolism was not lost on either of them. It was something they both wanted, especially while their children were young.

Once the kids get past their vulnerable stage, Harlan was fond of saying to guests at dinner parties, then we'll encourage a healthy curiosity in the opportunities that life might present. Adventure is a concept we want to encourage, he'd say, but only in its potential to offer wholesome, character-building experiences.

Both of them valued the lessons to be learned from a physical challenge, and Harlan especially was an avid outdoorsman. They were the kind of people who took their children camping and sailing and hiking and biking. Once, Connie had even jumped out of a plane, but that was before she was married, and although she would never consider doing it again, it was exhilarating at the time.

There was something reckless about falling in love too. She had met Harlan when her doorbell broke. She'd taken a summer job at a plant nursery outside Mill Bay and was living in an apartment at the top of a large house with a steep interior staircase that led up to her door. Connie unscrewed the buzzer next to the door and gathered up all the wire that ran to the heavy black receiver at the top of the stairs. She put it all in a cardboard box and took it to a store on the highway she must have noticed unconsciously because now she knew where to go – Home Protection Plus. A cheerful electronic ding-ding sounded as she walked through the door and Connie felt she'd come to the right place.

Harlan Foster was in the work area when his assistant came back and told him there was a woman at the counter with a broken doorbell. Should I tell her to go to Canadian Tire?

What's wrong with it? Harlan asked.

Well, it's busted, the assistant said. I don't know, we don't do doorbells.

Harlan checked the wall clock. It was ten to six. He lay down the web of wires he was holding in such a way that they would retain their shape, walked out from behind his work-table, and looked over at the counter. He told her later how he'd noticed her standing at the counter, with her hands resting on the rim of an open cardboard box that could have been holding a litter of kittens, that there was something fragile about her features, and that he was moved.

I'll get this, he'd said to his assistant and walked out to greet her.

They shook hands. Their eyes lingered. I don't know what the problem is, Connie said, tucking a slip of hair behind her ear, the movement of her arm giving off the clean scent of laundry soap. So I brought the whole apparatus.

I can see that.

Was that silly of me?

No, not at all, Harlan said. Let me have a look.

He took the box back to his worktable. A small fuse had blown. Two wires had heated up and melded. Harlan fixed the wires and replaced the fuse with a used one — a fuse he knew would blow again in a couple of weeks. Twelve minutes later, Harlan returned with the box, explained what the problem had been, charged her eight dollars, and shook her hand once more. She smiled and Harlan said he wanted to see her smile that way at him twenty years down the road.

Ten days later, Connie was back with the same doorbell. This time Harlan didn't scheme or plot. He simply asked her if she would allow him the privilege of taking her out to dinner. Connie put a hand to her cheek and looked down at the counter. It wasn't like she never got asked this sort of thing, it was that she wasn't used to feeling shy. Besides, she liked the way he looked at her so intently, with such interest. I'd like that, she said in a small voice. I'll leave you my number.

Thirteen months later, after they'd announced their engagement, Harlan told Connie how he'd fixed her doorbell to break so that he would see her again. He told the story at a family dinner in front of Connie's parents and her sister,

Hannah. Hannah had congratulated Harlan. It had seemed to make him more interesting in her eyes, more complex, as if the best thing a person could show you about themselves was something you didn't already know or hadn't guessed. It was a romantic gesture, and Hannah told her she liked him more for it, which made Connie feel uneasy. She didn't want Hannah thinking about whether or not Harlan was romantic. But even her parents applauded the story. They took this small ambush as a measure of Harlan's love for Connie and they approved of that. The family devoured the story like it was part of the meal they were sharing. It became part of their joint public history, and yet it still made Connie uncomfortable. She worried just a little that their relationship should be founded on a deception.

But I'm not complaining, Connie thought, smoothing the quilt under her hands, the snow-white quilt of her matrimonial bed. I have everything a woman could ask for. She reached for her leather Bible on the bedside table, unzipped it, flopped it open, and hit the page with her fingertip. Job 6, verse 6. *Can that which is unsavoury be eaten without salt? or is there any taste in the white of an egg?*

It's starting! Connie heard Mary-Beth shout again and went downstairs to watch the debate.

A friend of Norm's — Hannah couldn't remember her name — twirled into the dining room, pushing the door open with her shoulder. She was wearing oven mitts and carried a roasted leg of lamb on an oblong dish. She had the graceful beauty of a poster girl for the proletariat. She could have been welding in a shipyard with her sleeves rolled up, singing rousing and patriotic songs to Newfoundland. She had a rosy hue to her cheeks and an inclusive nature. The lamb was steaming and crusted with rosemary and garlic. She put it down on the table and someone said, Look at that. Now *that's* a work of art. The woman's husband, Roger, followed with an aluminum bowl of crispy roast potatoes. He lifted the bowl to his face and used the back of his wrist to push his glasses up his nose.

Flo! Norman said.

Florence was her name, Hannah thought.

This looks fabulous!

Help yourself, Florence said with obvious pleasure. There was homemade mint sauce and yellow squash with nutmeg and brown sugar, and a salad of spinach and roasted pecans with crumblings of blue cheese.

Roger put two more bottles of red wine on the table, already open and inhaling the North Atlantic air. Norman Peach sat down diagonally across from Hannah. She watched him reach forward and scoop a bottle by the neck and start topping up glasses with the ease of someone entitled. He often took charge of the celebrations, confirmed or initiated them. People enjoyed it, it put them at ease. His enthusiasm was the honey glaze on an evening.

To the hunt, Norm said, raising his glass.

To the hunt! everyone cheered.

Hannah took a sip and savoured the spicy vanilla sweetness on the sides of her tongue.

Norm's friend Mona Terrance was telling a story about a couple who were not present but had attended a garden party in the fall. Mona was wearing a red sweater with gold thread in it and her skin glowed like bone china. Her face was framed by a halo of jet black curls that bounced as she talked. She was animated, almost manic. It was riveting and slightly distressing to watch her talk.

She was standing at the opposite end of the pool, Mona said, holding a small plate of sandwiches. She saw her seven-year-old son sink into the deep end, a foot away from her husband, who was engrossed in conversation with this really beautiful young woman who works at Auntie Crae's. She flung her plate onto the grass and literally dove into the pool in her little blue dress! Mona shook her head as if her own black curls had just got wet. The whole party stopped dead in its tracks. Her husband was standing right there by the edge of the pool and he was seething. He was *furious*, Mona said, smacking the table and pitching forward. He glared at her and said, I could have done that. Mona narrowed her eyes and tightened her lips against her teeth.

Florence said, Now you're just exaggerating. I was there. The front of her dress was wet, but that was from picking him up.

She jumped in! Mona protested.

She yanked him out by the shorts!

Hannah thought, these Newfoundland women have such a bold confidence. They're outspoken and aggressive and pre-occupied with the huge melodrama of their lives. It offended her inbred puritan humility. In truth, it made her jealous. But to celebrate the importance of your own life – there was a difference between that and vanity. She felt uptight and repressed. Of course, she knew that wasn't how other people saw her. When Norm looked across the table, what he saw was a good-looking and adventurous woman who spoke two languages, rode a motorcycle, had lived in seven different cities, and had a wild past but still kept a heart that was soft and sentimental.

You know, it's the women who overreact in situations like that, Roger said. It's not that the men are indifferent.

The men are more self-conscious, Mona said. They have a higher breaking point for composure. That's why it takes them longer to react. They're like chicks that have to hatch out of their monumental composure before they can come to anyone's assistance.

Men like it when their sons take risks, Florence said, joining forces with Mona to take sides against the men. They see a boy climbing out on a limb and they think, Go on, my son. Attaboy.

Exactly, Mona said. It makes them proud.

Do you think so? Norm said. In my experience, it's the women who push the envelope. They're the crazy ones. And they admire craziness in others.

Six people turned to look at Hannah. She shrugged. The conversation moved on. Hannah looked around the room for an excuse to seem distracted. The friendship around the table was a river in which she was standing hip-deep, braced against the current. It was all so heady – the palpable giddy conspiracy of old friendship – and she felt excluded. There was something antagonistic about this evening too, a teasing she couldn't participate in because it was the property of knowledge and trust. It was the careless treatment of someone you love. The way Norm would attack Mona on a point of no significance was a lot like flirting, a public intimacy. So Hannah sulked a little, even as she chided herself for the sulking.

The dining room was large and square and wood-panelled. Old plates salvaged from the sea were propped on the wainscoting and gleamed like moons. There were small clay pipes, tossed overboard two hundred years ago and covered now in barnacles or lime scale or white coral. An empty iron candelabra hung from the ceiling like a black fishhook and on the table were red candles in baby food jars half-filled with sand. Outside, the rain was slashing the windows with a sound like shuffled cards, as if a game was being dealt against the house. Mona laughed and put her arm around Norm and leaned into him. A candle flame slid into view on the window behind her. The room was so hot and humid. The music from the living room was thick and heavy too. An old blues man's voice. This was the Newfoundland tropical effect. They were expert, it seemed, at creating artificial weather systems and had sealed, within this clapboard house, all the warm fecundity of a greenhouse.

The woman sitting across from Hannah had a pale wide face and the rich red luxurious hair of a chow. So remind me, she said, how long have you two been together?

41

Bernice McFaddon and Norman Peach went way back. She had once given him advice when a lesbian couple wanted Norm to father their child. They wanted his sperm and no other commitment. She listened and said, What, are you fucking crazy? In this town? The child would be walking down the street in fifteen years and see you coming and buckle at the knees. In a moment, it would destroy the both of you.

Almost two years, Hannah said.

Is that *it*? Bernice said. Christ, I thought it was longer than that. You know, I don't know anything about you. You're a nurse, aren't you?

Hannah's head jerked back, her chin tucked into her neck.

I thought I heard.

A nurse? Hannah said.

I don't know, Bernice said. You seem. So what is it you do?

I'm a writer.

Oh God, Bernice said, not another writer. And she showed her vexation by resting her wrists on the table and looking sideways at Norm, but he didn't notice her. A car passed and silver raindrops flashed on the black windows like beads of mercury.

So, what do *you* do? Hannah asked.

Bernice took a mouthful of lamb. She rolled her eyes and waved her fork, chewing gallantly. It's too complicated, she said.

What do you mean?

Bernice said, It's hard to explain. She was cleaning her lips with her tongue.

Try me, Hannah said. She couldn't tell whether this evasion on Bernice's part was self-effacing or supercilious. She was still bristling about being called a nurse.

She's a sometimes-academic, the man to Hannah's right said, a sometimes-chef, and a full-time mom. This was Mona

Terrance's dashing husband and he sat at the head of the table. He wore a thin red bandana twisted and tied around his neck like a Spaniard. He was smiling with apparent delight, but on whose behalf or at whose expense Hannah couldn't tell. She was starting to feel a little persecuted.

See? Bernice said modestly. It's not important.

But that sounds interesting to me, Hannah said and reached for one of the bottles. If she had to admit, she was a bit afraid of people. She feared that they would always, ultimately, reject her. Norm and I went to Bell Island yesterday, she told Bernice, rallying herself. It's such a beautiful place. We met this old guy on the ferry and his accent was so thick I could hardly understand him.

Yeah, and I've met a lot of mainlanders I couldn't understand either, Bernice said, tossing her napkin onto her plate and giving it a small push.

Really?

She nodded.

Like who.

People from Toronto.

Come on.

I'm serious.

But it was like this guy was speaking a completely different language, Hannah said. Even his expressions were foreign to me.

Maybe that's what he was thinking about you too.

But I speak so obviously. I don't think he was having any difficulty understanding *me*.

How do you know?

I live in a big city. It's a pool for accents. They all get watered down. He's living in a remote place. Language evolves idiosyncratically in isolation.

43

Maybe he doesn't appreciate you coming along and making him feel idiosyncratic.

Hannah stared at Bernice.

Maybe he doesn't think where he comes from is so remote or so isolated.

I'm not trying to, I mean, this is an island. Take any island. It's like the Irish.

We're not Irish.

But it's similar. Have you ever been?

No, why would I want to go there? As if I could afford to go travelling, she said, turning to Mona's husband and appealing to him for sympathy. You know what it's like.

We should all get honorary degrees in parenting, he said, in addition to the ones in our specialized fields.

But instead what you've got is a small-town superiority complex, Hannah thought, concentrating on the act of slipping her fork underneath a shiny mottled spinach leaf. If this party were bundled under furs, galloping across the Russian steppes in a horse-drawn sled, Hannah knew she'd be the first one thrown to the wolves. And this certainty made her dwell on all the things that set her apart, until she alighted on her own childlessness.

Everyone at the table was married with kids, except for her and Norm, and Hannah wanted so badly to be a mother – the constant, gentle, protective presence in a child's life. They all had a reason to rush importantly away from the dinner party at a single phone call, and Hannah yearned to be that crucial to someone, to have the clarity of being indispensable, of having that one responsibility above all others, to have that sweet, hard relationship with a child, all those tender, casual caresses, navigating the small urgent dramas of childhood, to have her own chosen family. And she'd be good at it, felt there was a talent there, untapped. She'd be tolerant and fun, make time and take an interest, be patient and adventurous, with an easy, generous affection. She would adore without smothering. Ask very little in return. She was already preparing for the inevitable separation. Taking the high road. Sending her child off to college. Hope is so reckless, it can actually catapult you ahead of the incident you are wishing for so you can practise feeling nostalgic about it.

Hannah looked at Norm. He was leaning close to Florence's face with an expression of rapt interest. Hannah couldn't feel jealous. It didn't mean anything. That was his way. It's what people loved about him – the intense quality of his attention. And she loved it too. How could you not? In fact, Hannah was enjoying this new, unaccustomed feeling of possessiveness. She'd been married, but she'd had an allergic reaction to the semantics of it, the smug confidence of the vows. She'd never known how much she prized a mystery, but now she appreciated a little uncertainty with her love, maybe even the painful thrill of being ignored.

Norm rose off his chair to lean forward and stab the last potato in the bowl. He looked across at Hannah, but his gaze didn't linger. His face didn't soften, nor did he give her a conspiratorial wink with the private knowledge of what they'd got up to earlier that evening in the shower. It made her feel lonely. When they first met, Hannah had been frightened by the intensity with which her heart clamped onto him. After a month, she told him she couldn't do it anymore – couldn't keep making love if it wasn't exclusive. That was her ultimatum and Norm was enjoying his freedom. He was attractive and popular. Women all over Toronto wanted to sleep with him. Some men bloom later in life after going quietly unnoticed through their youth. He had said, I don't think I've ever misled you into thinking this was something exclusive. Besides, Norm had told her he wasn't sure if he could trust her. She'd told him about the naked parties in London, and that was a wildness he was suspicious of. She had an adventurous sexuality and a past unlike his own – messy and decadent. And so they had said goodbye. And yet, four days later, he showed up at her apartment. I missed you, he said. I didn't know how much I would.

So what are you saying?

I'm saying let's be an item, he said, and Hannah fell into a swoon that lasted for months. Even her sister began to hear a change in her. A contentment that was uncharacteristic. I finally understand the whole point of compatibility, she'd told Connie over the phone. When you're unhappy, your life is an open book. But for the first time I'm actually starting to value my privacy. And her sister had made some noise of relief.

Hannah was staring down at her empty plate and now Mona Terrence's soft white arm was slowly reaching across her lap. Hannah almost caressed it before she realized Mona was after her plate. Let me help you with that, Hannah said, pushing back on her chair.

You have to believe the fact that you're loveable, Norm had said earlier. They'd been walking to the dinner party, and Hannah had her finger hooked through one of his belt loops.

But it's the hardest thing for me to do.

Why? he said. People like you, I can tell.

I have a history of failed relationships.

How come, Norm said, when a bad thing happens, it cancels out all the other times when good things happen?

As soon as they had arrived at Florence's, Mona Terrence said, Did Norm's sister make that?

What, this? Hannah asked, touching a brooch made of small black feathers she'd pinned to her blazer.

Looks like something his sister would make.

Norm doesn't like it, Hannah said.

Well, *I* think it's gorgeous, Mona said, apparently enjoying the flagrant trumping of Norm's opinion. Mona Terrence was Norman Peach's closest friend and they were like bear cubs, cuffing each other constantly about the ears. Already tonight she'd asked Norm twice in front of Hannah when he was moving back home, as if his life with Hannah in Toronto wasn't even a consideration.

Hannah followed Mona into Florence's bright yellow kitchen. Mona's running shoes were making a kissing noise on the linoleum. So, how are things these days? Hannah sounded falsely optimistic.

Mona swung around to face her. Well, I'm putting a lot of work into Kinshasa, she practically shouted.

Who?

The Congo.

Oh, Hannah said.

It's a humanitarian crisis! Mona raised her eyebrows at the obviousness of what should not have been missed. Thousands of children are being accused of witchcraft?

I didn't know that, Hannah said.

They're being thrown out of their homes and tortured, Mona said. This one girl, her mother got sick, then the generator broke down, and they blamed her for it. They tried to drown her in a sack, and when she escaped, they took her to a priest who performed an exorcism that included branding her with an iron and forcing her to eat a bar of soap.

That's *terrible*, Hannah said.

She's only nine years old. There's going to be a nationwide charity drive next week. I'm organizing the whole event. It's the biggest thing I've ever done in my life.

Big as in size? Hannah said. Or big as in important?

Both, Mona said and turned to Florence, who was staring into her fridge. Flo, do you need help with dessert?

I had a salmon-coloured fridge once, Florence said dreamily, that lit up from the bottom. It made everything glow like a Gilbert and Sullivan production. And Flo crossed her hands like fans under her chin and batted her eyelashes.

There was whisky in the living room after dessert. Hannah felt unlaced and drunk. What time was it? She was sitting on the floor facing the sofa, talking to Mona's husband. His face reflected a certain curiosity. He was taking an interest and it was encouraging her.

I was in Venice a few weeks ago, she said, half-reclined on her elbow. For my friend Ursula Bishop's wedding? We took a boat to the reception, just stepped off this boat, right into this medieval palazzo, and all the Italian men with their shaved heads, wearing sunglasses and beautiful suits. The groom gave a speech and halfway through, this guy he's known since he was like, six years old, started heckling him and said, go fuck your mother, in Italian.

Mona's husband said, What's go fuck your mother in Italian?

Mona turned and said, What is this, a joke?

It was a wedding, Hannah said. *Via tua madre.*

What did you say?

She said, go fuck your mother.

That's what the guy said. And they came down hard on him, so he got his coat, as they say, and left.

That's so great, Mona said and looked away.

It was a little freaky, Hannah said. I was running back to my hotel room at three in the morning with absolutely no one around. From the reception to my hotel, it was like I was the only person in Venice. Just the clack of my high heels. And corner after corner of old rock and cement and brick. Nothing alive, not a blade of grass, and the little tickle of water, the little lap of water, and all the shutters shut fast, and a thin strip of sky with stars overhead. I was laughing because I was wearing this silver fox-fur stole and to a half-British wedding. I mean, I wasn't even *trying* to be provocative.

Hannah heard Norm laugh in another part of the house. Florence ran into the living room as if running across the deck of a listing ship and collapsed onto Mona's lap. She crossed her legs and cupped a hand to Mona's ear and started whispering.

Excuse me, Hannah said and swayed out of the room. She started up the stairs. It felt like climbing an escalator that was slowly coming down. When she came out of the bathroom she couldn't remember if she had flushed. God, she was drunk. Norm was there. Where have you been?

In the kitchen, he said, with Bernice.

Hannah looked at her feet. Can we *please* leave now?

I never get to see these people, Norm said. They're my friends. I just want to enjoy myself.

So maybe you'd prefer it if *I* left.

If you have to leave, that's fine by me.

She wasn't expecting this. Norm reached into his pocket and pulled out the key to the house they were staying in. He handed it to her and went downstairs. He said something in the living room, which was greeted with laughter and cheering. Hannah walked into the master bedroom. She sat down on the queen-sized bed for a few minutes. Somebody outside rumbled past the house on a skateboard. An image of the boy her parents had adopted, laughing and falling backwards off a flipped-up skateboard, arms windmilling over his head, flared in her mind, then faded. Zeus was eight years old when he came to live with her parents. Hannah was living at home as well. She hadn't for years, but she'd just finished her BA and gone home for a few months to save some money. It was weird to see her parents looking after an eight-year-old. He was almost too unbearably cute, although what happened in the end was all wrong. Hannah always felt bad that, at the time, she'd never tried to do anything about it. He left when he was fifteen, without saying goodbye, and no one really knew where he was for a while. They thought he might have gone back to New Mexico, to look for his family, but then he called one day from Chicago. And that's where he was living now, with his boyfriend, some older guy apparently, and working as a clown with kids in a hospital there, which she thought was pretty remarkable. Suddenly, she wanted to talk to Norm. She went back downstairs to the living room.

Mona's husband was saying, It's what Gertrude Stein told Hemingway *not* to be. Like Modigliani's nudes. They were *inaccrochables*.

Modigliani was born in Venice, Hannah said, standing in the doorway. Where had she recently learned this?

We were *all* born in Venice, Roger said.

No, no, listen. His family was Jewish and they went bank-rupt, she said. But there was this law, if the mother was about to give birth, the family was allowed to keep whatever they could pile onto the birthing bed. So Modigliani was born on a four-poster bed piled high with candelabras and clocks and silver spoons.

There was a dreamy silence. It's true, she said, then Mona's husband laughed briefly at something totally unrelated. It sounded like a cough. Mona swung around to scold him and spilled red wine on the carpet and ran to the kitchen to get a cloth. Hannah sat down on the floor again and felt the wild horses of her own drunkenness move in dizzying circles.

How long was it before they were struggling to push their arms into the sleeves of their coats. Norm and Hannah stood in the foyer. It was foggy outside, and the rain had stopped. The trees were still dripping and the road was shiny and black as a canal.

Be careful, Florence hollered at their backs as Norm and Hannah took off down the hill. They walked as if carrying heavy suitcases. They crossed a spongy field to get to a street of tight rowhouses. At a spot on the sidewalk, Hannah stopped. I'm just gonna lie down here for a minute.

Norman stood above her and held his arms out. He bent forward and almost fell. He was swaying. Aw, come on, babe!

The cold was seeping into her, but Hannah felt so tired. She understood the only way she'd get home was if she ran. She leapt to her feet and took off.

Hey! Norm shouted after her. Wait for me!

When he got to the house, she was curled up on the front stoop like a cat. He dug in her pockets for the key. Up you get, he said.

Hey baby, she said.

Hey.

I'm so wasted.

I know you are.

I love you, baby.

I love you too.

I wanna spend the rest of my life.

I know you do, baby. I do too. Now give me a hand. The screen door hit Hannah's forehead with an aluminum twang. Sorry, Norm said.

Didn't feel a thing, she said.

That's good.

Can we get a puppy, Norm?

Okay, he said.

And a little baby? Just a teeny one?

Norm didn't say anything to that but folded her carefully over his shoulder and took her upstairs, all the burden he wanted in the world for the moment.

Harlan Douglas Foster locked up and left Home Protection Plus at twelve-fifteen in the morning with the last two of a six-pack of beer he'd bought earlier that evening. They were swinging by the neck from their soft plastic nooses. Something about those plastic rings made him think of lingerie, a drawer full of Connie's bras. He bleeped the car alarm and slung his briefcase and the two cans onto the passenger seat and got inside his Cherokee Jeep.

For a moment he contemplated suicide.

Harlan had deceived his wife. He knew that much. What he didn't know was how he'd allowed things to unravel to such an extent in the first place. He was a ruined man. And he still hadn't told Connie.

How does a thing like this happen? All he wanted to do was please her. Show her how lucky he was, how lucky she was to have him, get that high and hold on to it, that cosy high like a cocoon or a womb where nothing can touch you – not failure or futility, or the fear of death, or the devil himself. That's how a thing like this happens. The devil has crept in, but you don't know it. You start with a simple equation. A stock that's breaking through its fifty-day average, verging on parabolic. A ten-bagger. The next Voisey Bay. But then it plummets. They call it a falling knife.

He couldn't get away from the thought that it had all begun so promisingly. He was having a slow season in the security business, time on his hands, and started checking his stocks online. He tried his hand at making a trade, enjoyed it, then made another one. He got lucky that year and made fifty thousand dollars off a quarter of a million dollars' worth of trading. It was a rush, but he should never have fired his accountant and taken over his own investments. Why had he been so stupid? He started playing futures and shorting stocks. He adjusted his account so he could trade on margin.

Three years ago, he'd tried to take advantage of the depressed American economy. He waited for the equity market to correct itself, but it took another downturn. His investments bottomed out and he found himself in a desperate situation. He started borrowing to pay his mortgage and expenses, and that's when the calls began. He changed his cell number three times to escape the debt collectors, each time inventing a new explanation to give Connie. He couldn't bring himself to file for bankruptcy, and then, a few days ago, a collection agency finally sent their repo men to clear out his business effects. Now his lender had a court order to seize all his assets, the house and its contents, both vehicles, a speedboat he had docked in the Mill Bay Marina, all of which he'd agreed to put a lien on at the time of borrowing, as collateral for what was supposed to be his final consolidating loan. He was, he realized now, sitting in an SUV that technically he no longer owned, while Connie, at this very moment, was sleeping in a bed that wasn't hers, under a roof that no longer protected her, dreaming of a future for her children she would no longer be able to afford.

Harlan accelerated down a stretch of highway so familiar he had it memorized. How awful it was to have a life that finally resembled what his father's life had been – recklessly irresponsible. What memories he had of him, they'd been surfacing more and more of late, and less damningly so than ever before. He thought about how, when he was eleven years old, his father just up and left him to fend for himself in an apartment full of women, and while he never grew accustomed to the painful longing in his heart, he did over time forget the cause of it. Besides, the women in his life had long ago cornered the market on displays of emotion and expected him to be strong, not needy, but to show manly composure, even offer assistance.

His mother was so reliant. She started helping herself to his money when he was just a boy. At the age of twelve, he got a paper route. One evening, at the end of his first month, he left the apartment – with his shiny new hole-punch and a stack of customer cards held together by a big silver ring – and went to collect payment. He met the grumpy, fat housewives and the sweet young mothers, and found out who had dogs and whose house smelled bad and what people ate for dinner. When he got home and tallied it all up, he'd made forty-seven dollars, including tips. His first earnings! He ran into his mother's bedroom and waved the bills in the air.

Let me see that, his mother said, transferring the cigarette to her mouth and holding out her hand. Harlan gave her the money and she said, Boy, you must be the smartest kid on the block, look at all this dough. Am I ever lucky or what? She kept twenty and handed him the rest.

What? she asked with her chin, tucking the bill into the bosom of her bright yellow nightgown, between soft papery breasts that were, when his mother hugged him, the source of either delirious comfort or smothering panic. She rolled over onto her other side like a huge caterpillar and resumed her reading. A magic beanstalk of smoke tendrilled up from her hip. The ceiling was beginning to turn yellow. He could still see her now, clutching one of her thick, corner-store paperbacks, with the black-and-crimson covers, embossed with gold lettering – a woman in a scarlet bodice, holding on to some long-haired, bare-chested pirate, on top of a windswept cliff somewhere in the Caribbean, a plume of black smoke rising from the burning topsails of a full-rigged ship on the horizon.

Like his wife, Harlan's mother always feared the worst, but she had none of Connie's good intentions or energetic willfulness. Misery is fond of company, and the bitterness Harlan's mother felt at her own failed wish for love in the dancehalls of the Okanagan Valley resurfaced as the implied wish that everyone else in her life should fail as well.

There were tears on his cheeks. Harlan was crying again and this annoyed him no end. He flicked them off with a finger. How many times had he cried today? He couldn't remember, but it was a lot. When he cried as a boy, his sisters made fun of him. They hugged him too, lavishly, almost sexually – they were very expressive, very indulgent – but not before making him feel like a sissy. Shame on you for crying, Harley. Have you ever seen a boy cry like this, Jodes?

No, and if I did, I'd kick him where it counts.

They laughed into their cans of root beer and rye. Everything was a joke to them. They made him feel ridiculous.

When a parade of undeserving boyfriends started traipsing through the apartment, expecting nothing less than the fawning submission of his older sisters and trampling on his instinct to be protective, Harlan was too young to object, too powerless to stop it. When they spoke in lewd terms about his sisters, Harlan felt a thing subside in him like an exhausted muscle, a blueness spreading out. What's more, his desire to protect his sisters was matched by the embarrassment he suffered, the shame he felt over their poor taste. He couldn't help confusing good taste with moral superiority, and so there was disdain for his family mixed in with his jealousy and pity, and all of this sat heavy on his love.

He remembered how his sisters would squeeze into the hall mirror, popping their mouths with last-minute lip gloss, while a V8 engine revved at the curb. At least they have each other, he'd think, as they fluttered blue eye shadow and kissed him on the head. He could smell their black-market Poison for hours after they had left. And always they carried these little vinyl purses jammed with menthol cigarettes and spearmint gum and God knows what else. Out the door and Harlan would kneel on the sofa and pull the polyester sheers aside to watch them leave with a mixture of envy and scorn, aware of their own drastic, wildcat need for escape.

And when they were gone, to a tavern somewhere, or a pool hall or a bowling alley, he'd eat a dozen doughnuts. The small cheap ones with the sharp baking soda tang all covered in sweet white powder. They came twelve to a box and you could find them almost anywhere, in the basements of department stores, pharmacies even. He'd eat them until the sting in his mouth and the ache in his gut was a mild distraction to the desolation he felt. Sometimes he'd slip eight doughnuts on the fingers of both hands and make them beg for mercy before he ate them.

One evening, Harlan's mother surprised him by joining him on the sofa to watch the girls leave the building. Jodie had cut the neck out of her t-shirt and by the time she reached the curb, it had slipped down off her shoulder. Harlan's mother had said, If there's anything a whore can't resist, it's her nature. *Whore* was his mother's favourite word. It denoted the two things that were missing in her life – sex and money.

But Jodie had looked good that night, he recalled now, in her Santana jeans, Nike high-tops, and peacock-feather earrings. He wished he had told her so. And if that was her nature, so be it, for who can resist their nature anyway?

Harlan was stopped at a red light, sitting at an empty intersection waiting for the light to turn green. The streetlights giving the outdoors an indoor appearance. Not a car or another human being in sight. The pavement light grey. The intersection tidy and the roads straight. Despite his mother's best attempts to keep him down and close at hand, the first thing he did when he graduated from high school was join the army. He wanted to hear the constant and merciless barrage of commands exhorting him towards his own excellence, bellowed out through the loudspeakers morning, noon and night. He did not improve, he excelled. And quickly acquired the nickname Overkill, for how much time he spent polishing his boots.

He kept to himself and nobody could say of him that he wasn't a good kid. He seemed to have things pretty well sorted out. His marks were okay. He had a couple of friends. He didn't binge-drink like the guys in his barracks, though he did like a good all-you-can-eat buffet on the weekends. He spent three years in the military and didn't think anything was missing until the day he met a girl who took him to a Leighton Ford crusade, where he'd first felt the powerful love of God. How certain he'd been of God's love for him at the moment of his conversion. He'd been nineteen years old. He was overcome. He found himself on all fours, on a grey meadow of industrial carpet, in an auditorium full of folding chairs, under harsh fluorescent lighting, weeping like a baby. The service was over and most of the congregants had stood up and were collecting their songbooks and Bibles and quietly, peacefully, making their way home. While others, like himself, were being prayed for in small groups.

Dear Father in Heaven, shower this man with your love, we beg you. Let him feel the power of your Holy Spirit move within him. Let him feel the breath of your Holy Spirit like a flame on his tongue, that he should be set free in your mercy, to go forth and witness to the glory of your word, in the name of your son, Jesus Christ. Amen.

He remembered a young Indian man who sat down cross-legged in front of him and opened his Bible. The pages made a wet sound. He put his hand on the back of Harlan's neck and leaned forward until their foreheads were touching. He said in a heartfelt voice, And his father, when he saw him coming, ran to meet him. Such was his happiness.

And such *was* his happiness, he thought. It had lasted well into his early thirties and seen him through two university degrees, his marriage to Connie, and the birth of his three children, so how had he lost it? How had he forfeited the purity of a life surrendered in humility? All he knew was that it had been a long time since he'd felt the reassurance of his faith, and God seemed so remote these days. He needed the communion wine, he wanted the blood of the lamb smeared across his face. Something to wallow in. To match the intensity of his self-loathing. Here I am, Harlan thought, three blocks from home, turning left when I should be turning right. A father unable to turn the wheels of his vehicle towards his family.

His head was reeling and he counted up his drinks – four beers and the last third of a bottle of rum he'd mixed with

Coke back at the office. Harlan pulled over. A quiet suburban street. Turn the engine off. Crack open another beer. Take a slurp. The lawns were so green in the lamplight, neat as buzz cuts, shaved right down to the curb. Harlan lay his head on the wheel. He could hear the sound of water. Like a rushing river, with its banks burst. He saw his sisters, standing upright and stoic in a miniature full-rigged ship, the size of a rowboat, taking a hairpin turn in a swirl of whitewater. He was watching and waving at them from the balcony of a convention centre. They looked like pilgrims on the *Mayflower*. Then suddenly, in a row, three loud and startling knocks.

Harlan lifted his head and a teenaged girl in a red hoodie quickly backed away from the window. She looked alarmed. Are you okay? her lips said.

Harlan lowered the window. Sure, he said in a breezy manner. Juzz ah, his mouth was numb.

I thought maybe you'd had a heart attack, she said.

No, I'm fine, thanks, Harlan said, swallowing, then yawning vigorously.

The girl turned around. He's fine! she shouted at the house behind her. In a bright doorway, an old woman stood, shaking her head. Something like a crucifix glinted on her chest. The young woman – who was so pretty and fresh-faced and wholesome-looking – shoved her hands in her back pockets and nodded. Well, that's good, she said. Have a good night, and she left.

Harlan felt exposed, embarrassed, as if he'd just been caught in a lewd act. There was something about her, though. What was it? And then he realized. He recognized her. She went to his church. Harlan started the car and drove home.

∃ ∈

Connie heard the bleep of Harlan's car alarm before he walked through the door. It was one-thirty in the morning. Her husband was carrying the soft leather briefcase she'd bought him last year, but she had the funny impression it was empty by the way it folded on the table when he put it down. Where have you been? she said, leaning back against the counter with a mug in her hands. She had her reading glasses on and the lenses went snowy as she blew on her tea.

Harlan came forward and held her by the elbows and looked at her the way a child might – an orphaned child, standing in line, waiting to be adopted. Then he hugged her, aggressively. Connie had to brace her arm against his chest to swing her mug out of the way. She put it down on the counter and Harlan got his arms around her. He was rubbing his hands all over her back, as if he could gather up everything that had gone astray.

You're messing up my –

He held her tight – tight enough to sprocket her glasses at an odd angle off her face. A cold snap on the collar of his gore-tex jacket was nudging her lip up into a snarl. Ya smell good, he said.

I had a shower, Connie said, pushing him away. Aw, Harl, I think you've bent my glasses again.

Thass why I told you titanium.

Connie put them down and opened and tucked and retied her bathrobe.

Harlan snaked an arm around her waist and bent sideways to scoop the hem of her nightgown and slide a hand up her thigh.

Your hands are freezing, she said.

But your skin's so warm.

Let's go to bed, she said, but Harlan ignored her. He was paying attention to the curve of her hip, the temptation of her slim waist. He reached up through the neck of her nightgown and held her jaw, then the back of her neck. He kissed her.

Where've you been, Harl? What's the matter with you? You stink of booze.

Harlan turned his wife around and put his face into her hair.

Come on, sweetheart, she said. It's time for bed.

But instead he pushed her forward, gently but firmly, over the sink. Connie had always loved how entitled her husband behaved when it came to sex – how confident he was. In everything else, Harlan had such doubt, but during sex he had authority. Connie could relax. She had no responsibilities, nothing to do. It was like faith – a kind of thrilling surrender. Only, recently, he'd gotten sloppier, a little morose, a little too needy. A bit of that old, familiar self-pity creeping in and sullying her pleasure. The pot-lights in the ceiling were giving off their ivory glow and the blinds were open. People can see us, Connie said, but Harlan had his ear to her shoulder blade. She reached sideways and flicked the lights off. The outside leapt up to press its nose against the glass. There was moonlight on the spruce needles that carpeted a patch of lawn beside the garage, where Connie could never get the grass to grow despite having hired a landscaper and spread three bags of blended fescue. She could see the back wheels of Harlan's Jeep where they weren't supposed to be.

Where did you park?

Harlan had her robe and nightgown gathered halfway up her back. Harl! she said, and his pants hit the floor.

Quiet, wife, he said, his voice hardening. I'm ride here with you.

Connie's arms were in the sink, her hands splayed on the stainless steel by a drain that needed bleaching. Always elbow-deep in dishwater, she thought, and it wasn't even her own thought — somebody else had said it once — and her husband slid into her from behind.

Connie rose onto the balls of her feet. It was a seesaw of want, don't want. The vanishing in and out between self-consciousness and pleasure. Harlan had her nightclothes dragged over her head and she could feel his hot wet mouth on the back of her neck. It left a cool patch, like opening a tiny window, when he straightened up to come, the compulsion tightening him into an arc, like a metal ruler pulled back at the tip to flick and oh! the exquisite agony of succumbing. He collapsed forward, shuddering in waves, while Connie took his weight on her wrists, wedging her elbows against the edge of the sink. She felt a drop like warm wax on her back, then another, and understood that Harlan was crying.

Harl, she said. Talk to me.

Harlan fell to his knees.

What's the matter with you? Connie said, turning around and straightening her clothes.

I don't want to lose you. His face pressed tight against her thighs.

Connie knew this was his weakness and rarely enjoyed reassuring him, but tonight it seemed more urgent. Why would you lose me? she asked and wanted to know. Harlan's face was grey in the moonlight, a blue sheen around his wet eyes.

I gotta go to bed, he said. I'm so tired.

Connie watched her husband stumble out of the kitchen, holding up his pants. Something frightening about this pathetic vulnerability. A serious foreboding set in. She felt the urge to panic, sound the alarm, but she didn't even know what the matter was. And besides, she had to be strong for the kids. Always everything for the kids. When she got to the bedroom, Harlan was curled up on the bed asleep. She sat beside him and stroked the damp hair at his temple, as she did for her children. Hannah had once told her that a person's smell is most purely itself at the temples, so Connie bent down and smelled him there. A familiar smell, like salt water and corn husks. And then a sudden wave of love and yearning. Oh, Harlan Foster, you better not be up to something unholy.

T he ward had the oppressive tranquility of an evacuated building. Zeus had arrived and gone to his locker and put on his lab coat and old, brown leather clown shoes. He picked up his props and made his way down the hall, lifting his knees high and peeling his long soles off the floor, the fine orange hair on either side of his head undulating like seaweed. A gentle rap at the door. If a child looked interested, he'd walk into their room and begin the soft magic of distraction. But, lately, whatever courage he had ever possessed seemed to be failing him. Fenton hadn't come with him for nearly three weeks, and they'd always worked together. Now he was beginning to understand it was Fenton at his side that had ever made the job bearable. It really *was* like standing at the heart of an abandoned building, uncertain as to its stability. He kept waiting for the hospital to collapse in a white cloud of lethal dust, the whole planet falling to rubble and ruin, coming down in carnage.

Zeus carried a red toolbox and a toy accordion that played the first few bars of 'The Teddy Bear's Picnic.' He stopped outside Sam's room and put his things down. He took a pair of white disposable gloves out of his pocket and wiggled his fingers elaborately into their vinyl sockets. From the same pocket, he removed a hospital mask, raised it into the air, stretched it with his fingers like a cat's cradle, and slipped it over his mouth and nose. He picked up his accordion and gave it a squeeze. He let the music play to the half-closed door of Sam's room, then gently pushed it open with his foot. Hey, champ, want a visitor?

Zeus! The boy in the bed smacked his hands together once and held them there. His joy was like a salve. The children saved him, day after day. They reached him in his solitary orbit and touched his heart. Zeus picked up his toolbox and flippered into Sam's room like a scuba diver.

Sam was seven years old and his head looked small on the big white pillow. He had the thin, semi-translucent skin of a tadpole and a clear oxygen tube belted around his face. Zeus held out his hand. Sam shook it weakly and Zeus flopped up and down like a rag doll. He bent his knees and sank beneath the bed, then shot back into the air as fast as Sam could shake his hand. Sam's eyes shone. He laughed from his belly. His teeth were grey. Zeus loved his playfulness. The attitude that said, I will be happy. I have nothing to lose – except my life.

When Sam had stopped laughing over the handshake, he grew very serious. When's Fenton coming back? he asked.

Fenton's on holiday, Zeus said.

A *long* holiday.

Zeus nodded helplessly.

I love Fenton.

I love him too, Zeus said, and as he did, he was stunned again by how much.

Is Fenton going to die?

One day, Zeus said, but probably not for a while.

Will he die before me?

Well, Zeus said, getting onto the bed beside Sam, careful not to snag or dislodge any of his tubes, when exactly are you planning to leave us? He pulled a small pad and pen out of his breast pocket and got ready to write it down.

Before I grow up.

Not if you decide what you want to be when you grow up, then you'll have to grow up first. Do you know what you want to be when you grow up?

I want to be an annie-*theezeegist*, Sam said. So I can put my doctors to sleep.

Zeus had to swallow. How do you spell that?

Sam shrugged and Zeus drew a picture of a doctor with a mask asleep on the floor under a squiggle of *zzz*'s beside a hospital bed in which a child sat upright, holding a squirting syringe. He gave the drawing to Sam and Sam studied it.

Zeus crossed his ankles. Sam, Zeus said, do you believe in moments of consciousness?

Moments of *cushy* — what's it called?

Zeus rescued him. They're moments in life when you're really alive, that nobody can take away from you and that never die.

Like when my sister got into a fight with Anne Jansen because she said I was faking being sick so I wouldn't have to go to school? Sam asked, panting a little.

Yeah, Zeus said, like that. He waited until Sam's breathing was restful again. He was so easily exhausted, even talking was an exertion that could wear him out.

They're like the pieces of a puzzle, Zeus said. You know, like if you put them all together, they'd show you a picture of who you are, and what's important to you.

Like my sister.

Because she defended you, Zeus said, and Sam whispered, That's right.

Yep, that's called a moment of *cushiness*, Zeus said and reached down and hauled his toolbox onto his lap. He clattered around until he'd extracted two spaghetti balloons and a small hand pump. He returned the toolbox to the floor and pumped up the first balloon until it shot past the end of the bed. He started to pinch and twist the balloon into a sword. The balloon squeaked like sneakers on a gym floor.

I remember when I was very young, Zeus said, swimming in a big outdoor pool. There was a boy there, and the other kids were teasing him. They were pretending to play catch with him, but always throwing the ball too high, or right at his head. It was just a beach ball, but I'm sure it hurt a bit when he got hit in the face. It must have been embarrassing, but he wasn't letting it get to him. He just kept playing, you know? He really wanted to be included, even though they were making fun of him. God, it made me so sad, and my sadness was like this physical sensation. It was like a crushing in my chest. I remember sinking to the bottom of the pool and watching the legs of all the other swimmers. I remember how peaceful it was down there, being able to watch without being seen. Because it had made me feel strange, you know? Why was I so sad, when all the other kids found it so funny?

Zeus stabbed the air with his balloon sword and said, Ah-ha!

He gave the sword to Sam, then inflated the other balloon and looped it around Sam's wrist to gauge the size he would need to make the handle for a shield. When he slipped it off, Sam let his hand rest on Zeus's leg. It was such a sweet feeling. The emotional terrain here was so perilous, he thought, but if he could force a gentle nonchalance, for the sake of the

68

children, then it made him feel heroic. Because the children in palliative care were on the brink of an incomprehensible kind of vanishing, and Zeus knew a thing or two about vanishing.

His real parents had been so young when they'd had him – young and crazy and way too into drugs. The small adobe house of his childhood had been full of laughter and screaming matches, but always outside the sun was bright and the sky that vivid New Mexican blue and the clouds obliterating in their whiteness. And often there was a car rally, or a festival with a bonfire crackling into the stars, and sometimes he would have to find his own way home because his parents had forgotten about him. Once, he slept on a hillside and woke frozen to the bone and the woman who drove him said, You should come and live with me, but Zeus said no because when he got home, there were enchiladas smothered in green chili and kisses from his mother and the flowery smell of her dark hair. She'd make him rice pudding – then the whole house would smell of cinnamon. And he'd watch his father slide under a car in his grease monkey suit and out again, the muscles in his arms flexing and making his tattoos come to life – making the lion roar and the flaming heart stabbed with a knife look like it was pumping with blood.

Were these details even accurate, or had he invented them? His mother, Frieda Monterey, was only sixteen when she'd had him. High heels, tight jeans, a black t-shirt, and red lace. Skinny as a skeleton was how he remembered her.

And his father, José Gabriel Ortega, who was a small man, like himself, drove a low-rider that he was constantly working on. A 1978 Ford Thunderbird, with an airbrushed panorama of the famous church on one side and a tableau of his life on the other, depicting run-ins with the law, a dead brother, two dead cousins, and a portrait of Zeus and his mother with the words *ámale por siempre* on a banner above their heads.

When Zeus was eight years old, his dad got arrested and sentenced to six years in prison for drug trafficking. Zeus remembered thinking he'd be fourteen when his dad got out. Then his mother's habit got worse, and she was declared unfit by Child Protection Services. Smile now, you can cry later, she'd whispered into his ear as two female police officers came to take him away. He was put in foster care, and sent to a household with five delinquent boys. He was the youngest and he hated it there. He kept running away and trying to find his way back home. Until he met Rose Crowe.

Tell me another story, Sam said.

Well, Zeus said, let me see. He finished off Sam's shield with a final twist of balloon. There was this other time, he said. I went to this summer camp once, somewhere in New Mexico. Must have been for poor Latino kids. Anyways, I was about your age, Sam. You ever been to summer camp?

Sam shook his head.

Well, I loved it. I mean, I loved being out there in nature, but people were always telling us what to do and when to do it. One day, I don't know where everybody was, but I just started running around like a crazy guy. There was this cliff that dropped down to the river with a rope attached for lessons in repelling. That's when you use a rope to climb up and down a cliff. It was only for the older campers, though, and you were supposed to wear a safety harness and a helmet. I'd never done it before, but I knew I could do it. I grabbed the rope and jumped off the edge, and kept leaping, swinging out into the air and landing back against the cliff with my feet. It was amazing. I felt so free and happy, and the world seemed so beautiful.

You didn't fall? Sam said.

No, Zeus said, I was never afraid of that.

Sam stared at the window and the two of them went quiet, Zeus wandering off into the fog of nostalgia. Moments of consciousness, he thought. Why did he remember that moment and not another one? Why couldn't he remember more about his mother? In a fit of anger, at the age of twelve, he'd destroyed the only pictures he had of her, and could no longer really recall what she looked like. There was Rose, the woman who adopted him, but she was like a photograph left out in the sun. She'd cry a lot and then apologize. I'm trying to be better, she'd said a hundred times, and falling short. Then she'd ask for his forgiveness. Well, Zeus got tired of forgiving her. Sometimes he felt that if he opened up her mouth, all he'd see was crumpled paper.

Do you have cancer too? Sam said quietly, pointing to Zeus's bald head.

Cancer? Zeus said and frantically slapped the top of his head. Sam looked so sad that Zeus leaned closer and whispered, Under this rubber dome, I have a full head of hair.

I wish I could have my hair back, Sam said. My head gets cold sometimes.

Zeus felt like ripping his wig off and shaving his own head out of compassion. You like the Chicago Blackhawks?

Sam nodded and seemed to shrink into the mattress, like the air was going out of him. He was depleted now.

We need to get you a toque, Zeus said and got off the bed and reached into his pocket. He had a yellow beak like a little girls' hair clip he could press onto the tip of his index finger. He slipped his hand out and pushed it through his other fist, birthing the magic. With his white glove he made the movement of a bird trying to fly away. With his other hand he pulled it back and held it to his chest and stroked it. He looked at Sam and nodded towards the bird. He wordlessly encouraged him to reach out and pet it. When he did, the bird tried to fly away again, but Zeus caught it and put it on Sam's head. The bird flapped around on his bald scalp.

Zeus pulled the bird back to his chest, looked at the window, then back at Sam. He raised his eyebrows and Sam silently agreed. Zeus took the bird to the window and stood with his back to the boy. He pretended to open the window, and threw his hands out, and he was no longer wearing the white glove because it had turned into a dove. The dove flapped up through the shaft between the north and east wings of the hospital, almost pink against the yellow brick, and into the bright late-afternoon sky, until it was just an iridescent little soap bubble, and then it disappeared.

After Sam fell asleep, Zeus walked down the hall towards Lalia DeLuca's room. He passed the common area, where two exhausted parents sat watching the *Wizard of Oz*. It was a favourite in the ward, this story of three injured characters taking a magical wish list to a mad scientist who lives in a sterile green castle, not unlike a hospital. Zeus stopped to watch it, and the wife of the couple swivelled her head to take in the whole spectacle of his appearance in the doorway, and her expression was one trapped in the singular, sad position of *why?* He gave her a slow and helpless shrug. Zeus didn't have any answers. Things simply got more confusing the more you learned about them.

Why did anybody's life turn out the way it did? It was just a fluke that he met Tim and Rose Crowe. If they hadn't flown down to Chimayó to help out on a project building homes for families in need, his life would have been very different. Zeus used to sell corn chips and cans of pop and a few hand-painted tin hearts out of a wagon he pulled around his neighbourhood, and the house they were working on wasn't far from his own.

The first time he saw Rose, she was wearing a yellow summer dress, with a thin blue belt, and her hair was golden brown and tied back with a white bandana. She was walking somewhere, holding hands with her husband, a well-dressed man with a beard. She didn't look like the kind of woman who'd pass out on the sofa, or need a jug of cold water poured over her head, or her hair held out of the toilet while she gagged. The next time he saw her, she was making sandwiches on a plywood table set up at the edge of the building site. He pulled his wagon over and introduced himself and shook her hand in such a formal way, she laughed and said, You did that so well, you must be a professional hand-shaker.

Every day that Zeus passed the building site, Rose bought another tin heart out of his wagon. He couldn't help thinking that she was some kind of angel. At the end of the week, he told her that his dad was in jail, that he was in foster care, and maybe she should think of adopting him. She seemed so upset, and he could remember how she'd shook her head and said, Oh, sweetheart. He'd wanted her to hug him.

Right before they left, she told him to hang in there, that help was on its way, and a few months later, the woman who ran the foster home told him he was going to Canada, and that he should pack his things. He was going on a plane journey to a place called Toronto, and when they landed on ten centimetres of fresh white snow, Zeus thought the clouds had fallen. His new parents were there to greet him. They'd brought a blanket in case he was cold. He never heard from his real parents again. They had never tried to find him.

Suddenly, he found himself sitting on a hard bench in a church beside the woman *he'd* chosen to be with. He stared up at his new father, preaching in a friendly way from his elevated position in the pulpit, and wondered how he was supposed to behave. The pulpit was like a wooden tattoo, a carved eagle with its wings outstretched, carrying a lectern on its back. The eagle's beak was gaping and in it was the hard wooden curl of a tongue. He concentrated on the tongue, waiting for it to move like one of his dad's tattoos, but it never did.

Over Christmas, he met his new sisters. Hannah was coming to stay with them for a while, and Connie had flown in for the holidays. They were fourteen and fifteen years older than him, and took him to the movies, and to the zoo. Hannah had thick golden-brown hair like her mother, and was relaxed and funny and easy to like. Connie seemed more like an adult to Zeus, and wore high heels and jewellery. He overheard her say to Rose that his presence in the house made her feel shy. But also that she felt sorry for him, how hard it all must be. He hated hearing his name when he wasn't being talked to directly.

At night, his sisters would come into his room and sit on either side of his pillow and read him books about talking animals who lived in the woods and carried picnic baskets. Everything was so new and strange to him. It made him feel like it was all a mistake, like he wasn't supposed to be there. Even now, after all these years, he could still sometimes get the feeling that he was in the wrong place.

Connie sensed her daughter's presence and opened her eyes. Emma was leaning so close, she could feel her breath on her face.

Mom, Emma said, I have a great idea.

Connie yawned and Emma tilted her head sideways and put her hands on her mother's cheeks.

We could have waffles.

Connie was still half asleep. Ahuh?

Emma gave her mom's face a little squeeze. You could make them.

That's a great idea.

Because I'm really really hungry, and I really think I need to eat a waffle, and we could have frozen blackberries and whipped cream and sit down and eat it as a family.

That was a wily tug on Connie's soft spot, mentioning the family like that.

I'll be there in a minute, okay, sweet pea? Just let me wake up here.

Emma crossed her arms and puckered her mouth in a manner that expressed her impatience. Connie made spiders of her fingers and tried to grab her daughter, who squealed and hopped backwards, then ran out of the room.

Connie looked over at Harlan, asleep with his jaw slack and his mouth open, a damp patch on the pillow under his face – this lack of discipline, even in sleep, annoying to her. She shoved the covers off and pushed herself up. She sat on the edge of the bed, her feet dangling. She flexed her ankles, then walked into the bathroom and looked in the mirror. What if her husband was having an affair? Is it possible he'd given into his demons and taken comfort in the arms of someone who would indulge his weaknesses? Who'd had a similar background? He was always referring to his upbringing – the poverty and dysfunction – as something he had to overcome, and Connie could be very vocal about her impatience. She felt justified because she knew the best thing would be for him to let it go and have confidence in his own evolution. But maybe he'd found someone who would let him wallow. Some bimbo in a bar, wearing a tanktop and tight jeans, who'd let him blubber into his glass and want nothing more than the chance to console him and console him, with her perky little yoga body. Connie shook her head and dismissed her own neurotic imagination. She didn't quite believe that such a scenario was even possible.

She dropped her nightgown and walked down the sloping slate tiles and raised her face to the big brass shower head that simulated the effect of rainfall. She let the water stroke her face, run down her body like warm hands. It was nice not to hate yourself, she thought. And then she recalled an episode of *Extreme Makeover* she'd once seen at Mary-Beth's salon. They'd taken this very plain woman from her very normal life in the

Midwest to some gated Beverly Hills estate for six weeks to undergo a complete physical transformation. The woman hated the way she looked. She'd been teased at high school – had even taken steel wool to her face to scrub off the bad skin. They gave her new teeth, a prosthetic nose, a new chin and breasts and buttocks. It was as if she'd committed a crime and was trying to conceal her identity. Your family won't recognize you, the host kept repeating, as if that was a desirable outcome. When they were done, she looked freakish and unnatural. A ridiculous Barbie doll. Connie had felt sorry for the woman's kids. Where did Mom go? When is she coming back? The terrifying irreversibility of it all.

Connie turned off the shower and got a towel from the heated rack. She wiped a porthole in the mirror and began brushing her teeth. But what does anybody know, eh? Who knows what it's like to be called pizza face, a dog. Nobody's walked ten miles in her shoes. Maybe the woman did feel better. Maybe it really was a dream come true, like she kept saying.

What had bothered Mary-Beth most was how excited her husband looked. Boy, did he ever look excited.

What she needs is a new husband, Connie had said.

Extreme Homewrecker, Mary-Beth said. Now there's a show I'd watch. And they had laughed about that.

Connie spat into the sink and thought about the husband. What a rat bag.

And then she whispered, Oh God, and her mind tightened like a contraction around the nugget of her concern for Harlan.

When, finally, Harlan did get out of bed and make his way into the kitchen, it was into the chaos of waffles. All three of his children, still in their pyjamas, blackberry juice bleeding onto

their plates and whipped cream around their mouths. Theo
even had some in his hair. There was waffle batter on the counter and dripping out of the waffle iron, rising with the slow
determination of a weightlifter. Soon the whole house would
be full of it – batter oozing from the windows and the chimney.
Harlan had on his pale blue summer suit even though it was a
cold day and he was carrying his empty briefcase. Simon held
out a pink rubber superball. Here, Dad, he said. Try this. Harlan
had a quasi-scientific thing going on with his son where they
would run a series of improvised tests on a new toy, create a list
of stats, and then rate its toy-ness on a scale of one to ten.

Harlan took the ball and flicked the leather flap of his briefcase over his wrist and dropped it inside. He looked at Connie
across the kitchen. She was standing with a spatula held aloft
about to ask him a question, but all he could do was rob a
blackberry off Emma's plate and hustle out of the house, cutting
off his daughter's indignant cry of Hey! by closing the door.

It was another thirty minutes before Connie got the kids
ready for school and into the Volvo. Si was belting out a new
song of his own invention. Theo was swinging his legs and
kicking the back of the front passenger seat where Emma sat,
primly unbothered, holding her pet newt in a small terrarium
on her lap. Connie set her jaw against the noise and the
demands of merging traffic. They arrived at the school and the
drop-off area was nearly empty. Emma said, We're late *again*,
and her disappointment was sudden and severe. Today, she was
giving a presentation on newts and had been preparing for it
since the day before. Emma loved going to school and was
already so thoroughly independent. Connie could barely get a
kiss from her before she was out of the car and crossing the
parking lot with quick, determined steps, cradling her little
glass globe in her hands.

Connie took the boys inside, and at the door to his class-room, Simon clung to her neck while his teacher, Miss Koop, tried to cajole him away with promises of awesome games and super-fun activities. I'll be back at two-thirty, Connie whispered. Please don't cry, sweetheart. No, don't do that. It's not Miss Koop's fault. She's just trying to help. Thank you, Miss Koop. Here, take the other sleeve. Then finally Connie was chasing Theo down the hall to scoop him up and carry him back out to the car. She buckled him into his car seat and, to her immense relief, he settled immediately, as if struck by an idea of serious complexity dangling in the air outside the car window.

Overnight, an early frost had hardened the loose gravel of the parking lot. The tops of the fir trees were lime green in the sunlight, their bodies dark as seaweed. Connie closed the car door and turned on the heat. She put her hands on the wheel and stole a moment for herself – the first since her shower this morning. She let out a breath and released her shoulders. They always dropped an inch whenever she remembered to do this.

At the edge of the parking lot, an old man in a yellow tracksuit and a black fedora stopped to talk to a boy. He was stooped and using a cane. The boy had a beautiful golden retriever puppy on a leash. The old man reached out and touched its head and the puppy kicked its back legs like a wild pony and bounced on its front paws as if it were trying to break through the ground. The old man waggled the dog's ears and the boy waited patiently. He smiled and said something to the old man. The old man laughed, still stroking the dog, unable to withdraw himself from the pure, lively joy of the puppy. Oh darn it, Connie said and started to cry in small gasps, like a shoe falling down the stairs. She must have made a sound because Theo called to her.

I'm all right, Theo.

And then he, too, was crying.

Oh, give me a break, she said and reached back and squeezed his plump knee. Come on, sweetheart. But he wouldn't stop.

Well, then, I happen to agree with you, Connie said, digging around in her purse for a kleenex. It's not right. It's just plain not right. What do you say we go find your father and ask him what's going on, find out what's with all this strange behaviour. I can't tell you how strangely he's been acting, she said and caught sight of Theo's face in the rear-view mirror. No, of course I can't. You're not my confidante, you're my son. And this last thought occurred with all the solemn veracity of a prayer.

≩ ≩

Harlan was holding his son's superball in the work area of his store. The space was empty except for a taped cardboard box and the *Yellow Pages* on a stool. There were lighter rectangles on the walls where his pictures and bulletin boards had been. The polished cement floor was pale grey, and gradually over the last ten days, the room had taken on the look and feel of an asylum – refuge and madness both.

Harlan threw the superball down with force and cowered, covering his head with his arms. The ball bounced up, hit the ceiling, spronged off a dent in the floor, hit the wall, boinged towards the centre of the room, and petered out. It was the size of a golf ball and bright fuchsia, and Harlan weighed it in his hand. He threw it harder – this time at the wall. He cowered again. The ball triangulated before dribbling to a stop in the same low spot on the floor. Harlan wondered what height a man would have to jump from in order to kill himself on a cement floor.

He heard a car pull up and park outside the store. Home Protection Plus. The name was ridiculous to him now. Harlan looked through the milky glare of his dirty storefront window and saw Connie's Volvo. Two years old. The familiar outline of her hair. His wife got out, walked around the car to the other side, opened the door, hauled Theo's umbrella stroller off the back seat, and kicked it open in mid-air.

Judgment day, Harlan said.

Connie was just coming through the door when Harlan rushed out of the backroom and blurted, Okay, so I lost the business, but it's not like I killed anyone!

What are you talking about? Connie said and leaned sideways to flick the wheel lock on the stroller with her foot. The store was completely empty. In her sudden bewilderment, she took a puzzled look around.

So I messed up, Harlan said as if in mid-conversation.

Connie brushed the front of her jacket.

I've ruined everything, he said.

She squatted in front of Theo to ask him if he wanted to run around. He got out and she could see the parking lot through the dark blue canvas of his stroller, porous in the sunlight. She stood up. The room was so bright, the sun was hammering it into a flat shape, drawing the corners out like empty pockets, her husband's elongated shadow against the wall behind him.

I'm trying to level with you here, Harlan said.

Connie shook her head like she was dismissing a compliment. I think you're being a little annoying, she said. In this empty, illuminated space, in his light blue summer suit, he looked like a candidate for baptism, penitent at the bottom of a white tiled pool, waist-deep in water.

Where is everything? she said, nudging Theo into the vacant space.

That's what I'm trying to tell you, Con.

Connie smacked her hands together and squeezed them hard. If you're trying to surprise me, Harl, I think you could do better than this! So you finally moved to a new location? Where is it? I hope it's bigger than this one. Is it nice? You should have let me see it first. I could have given you some good decorating advice.

I didn't move.

Connie was chewing her cheek, the bottom half of her face twisted to one side.

The store's gone, he said.

What do you mean, it's gone? You own the business.

Not anymore. They came and took everything away.

Who did?

The heavies, the debt collectors — whatever you want to call them. Harlan hung his head.

Anyways, Connie said triumphantly, if that's true, they took a lot of junk with no resale value. Where are the tourist posters we picked up in Greece?

They took those as well, Harlan spoke quietly. They're also in the business of humiliation.

Come on, she said to Theo and lifted him up by the straps of his overalls and dumped him back in the stroller. I'm not listening to anymore of this crap. Connie spun him around and leaned forward to push the door open and jammed the stroller through and left the store.

She walked the length of the short strip mall and stood facing an access road and a dense patch of dark conifers. Forest had the ability to appear so still. In the distance, a glint of ocean. She thumbed Mary-Beth's number on her cell phone and stood there, waiting for her to answer.

On the ground at her feet was a tarnished orange loonie in a grey clot of matted debris that Connie felt she should pick up. Something to do with money. At the back of her mind an old frugality was standing up and brushing itself off. Connie looked over at the highway as an eighteen-wheeler shot through the intersection, some fir trees shook, and she heard a song lyric in her head. *These are the best days of your life.*

There was no answer. She snapped her phone shut and nudged the loonie with her foot, then bent to pick it up. It was an old ginger beer bottle cap. How strange things can appear, and she thought again of the doctor's gloves at Theo's birth. Like red woollen mittens. How the doctor had raised them up and Connie had thought – a Christmas present.

She turned the stroller around and walked back. She saw the sign in the window, LIQUIDATION SALE. How had she missed that before? She opened the door and walked in. Harlan hadn't moved. Once again, Connie took Theo out of his stroller and turned to face her husband. She took a new stab at optimism. So please, tell me again what's going on.

All the sturdiness went out of Harlan's posture. He fell back and without looking put his hands out to catch himself against the counter, as if he'd been dealt a soft blow. The counter was the only furniture left on the display floor, if you could call it furniture. It was just the hollow box of a counter, fastened to the floor. There was that, and a small, dark green, metal garbage can. It frightened her how thoroughly a room can be emptied, and how quickly. She had known this room. But she didn't know it anymore.

Harlan lifted a hand and smoothed his eyebrows with his fingertips. We're totally bankrupt, Connie. I lost the store, the business. All our assets.

And there it was, she could see it in his face, the sweet, immense relief of confession. *How*, Harlan? How could this happen?

I got carried away.

But you're not impulsive. You're reliable. You were going to build bridges, design highways.

And I landed in security.

See what I mean? You think that was an accident? Connie could not yet grasp what her husband was telling her.

Maybe it was an irony.

No, Harl, we all choose our paths in life.

Sometimes things get beyond our control.

That's just an excuse weak people make.

Is that what you really think? Haven't you ever felt overwhelmed?

Theo had walked over to the garbage can and was rocking it back and forth.

Why do you always have to be the victim? Connie said. You always have other things to blame – your parents, your upbringing. When are you going to take responsibility for yourself?

But I am! That's what I'm saying. I made a mistake!

Do you think this is what God had in mind for you?

I don't know what God has in mind.

I mean, don't you think he wanted you to rise above your station and excel?

My *station*?

Connie was saying words she didn't know she was going to say. It was as if her mouth opened and a voice spoke. But she condoned the message. You know, she said, your disadvantaged background? Connie flicked her hair. She kept her eyes down. She stifled a sudden desire to be soft, to cry and lament. Instead, she threw a log on her anger and her judgment. I mean, how does a thing like this happen?

I couldn't resist it, Con. The big jackpot. The stock market.

What are you talking about? A sharpness in her voice made Theo gravitate back from where he had wandered off.

Please, Constance, don't condemn me. Just listen.

You never call me Constance.

Sweetheart, we're broke. I thought I could make – I made some bad investments. They were supposed to, well, I should've stopped, declared bankruptcy, but instead I kept borrowing, and signed liens on everything I could lay my hands on, and now –

How could you fall for that, Harl? The stock market? You've got a master's in engineering, you were supposed to *work* for a living. There's no such thing as free money.

Not unless you come by it honestly at birth, he said.

What's *that* supposed to mean?

You're middle class, Connie. I don't expect you to understand. How was I supposed to give you the life you wanted? Selling burglar alarms and deadbolts?

What about your patent? Couldn't you have tried to come up with another one?

I *did*, Harlan said. I wanted it all too, for you, for the kids. What have you ever been tempted by?

I try really hard, all the time, to do the right thing!

I know you do, Harlan said. And that's all you care about. As far as I know, you've never done a spontaneous thing in your life.

Connie closed her eyes and clenched her fists. Look, Harlan, you're a strong man and I want you to be strong now.

Harlan felt exhausted. He wanted to sweep Connie up in his arms and take the children and fly somewhere far away where they could start again, from scratch, from hard stone and rippling brook and tree bark. He'd done that once, but he'd done it alone. Could he do it again and with a family?

You've never understood me, Connie said, and her heart ached because already her prescient self had walked forward down the long corridor of the future and understood the hardship that lay ahead. What's going to happen to us?

Harlan crouched and held his arms out to his son with such little confidence Theo thought better of it and stayed where he was, attached to his mother's leg. Harlan rose again. I'm going to work as hard as I can to make it up to you, he said.

Connie walked over to a wall and slid down with her back against it and sat on the floor, her elbows resting on her knees. Theo squirmed his way onto her lap. Connie hugged her son. Inhaled the warm fabric smell of his head. Do you know, she said, slightly amused, as if it had just occurred to her, that I thought of killing myself recently?

Oh, Connie, Harlan said, and his voice was beseeching.

Not seriously, she said. Not really. Just out of some malaise, the thought struck me. But then I didn't think I had any reason to be depressed. I mean, I have everything, right? A beautiful house, faithful husband, three healthy kids in five years. Do you know what it's like to be so full of life you squirt breast milk halfway across the room? I thought, I am at the very centre of this family. I mean, I am so necessary to this life we have together, so integral. This big life we have, Emma and Si and Theo, it all literally came out of me, out of my body. And yet I've never felt so invisible either, so unimportant. I'm just a mother. People don't respect that. People don't even open the door for a pregnant woman anymore. I saw a pregnant woman hitchhiking in the rain the other day. Oh my God, I should have picked her up!

Connie stopped talking and the stark emptiness of the store struck her as embarrassingly obvious. Does the whole town know about this?

Harlan shook his head. I don't think so. He was fussing with a loose thread on the outside seam of his blue pants. A dark hourglass shape walked past the window from left to right. Fingerprints and smudges glowed on the glass. The sun was too harsh, it was peeling everything back.

Stop that! Connie said. Stop that goddamn fiddling! Can't you control yourself?

Don't swear at me! Harlan yelled back and grabbed at his hair.

No, Mama! Theo said and raised his hand and smacked Connie on the nose.

Ow! Connie shouted and shoved her son onto the floor and stood up and watched him roll onto his stomach and kick the floor in a parody of outrage. I'm sorry, sweetie, she said, crouching down again and rubbing his back. I didn't mean to do that.

Harlan took a step forward, towards this unhappy, fragile unit of his family, but Connie threw him a look that was feral.

Don't, Connie said. Get the fuck away from me!

Stop *swearing*! Harlan bellowed, and an instinct so deep and primordial Connie didn't even know she had was alerted. She picked Theo up and slung him into the crook of her elbow and kicked the stroller around. Harlan bent and picked up the small dark green garbage can and launched it into the air. It soared over her head and detonated the front window. The glass exploded, a waterfall of diamonds pouring over the edge of some place they had never gone before. The noise came after and lasted longer, petering out until it was the delicate tinkling of icicles. It was as if they had been forewarned, had had time to stand and turn and face the solid window to pre-pare, for a second, before the spectacle of its shattering. Theo was quiet. Connie held him tight, then her arms shot forward and he hung suspended in the air and flapping as she spun him right, then left. No blood. No cuts. Thank God. She pulled him towards her again and propped him on her hip and rattled the stroller viciously with one hand until it started to close and fold down against the floor.

Harlan stared at the now-clear view through the jagged frame of his storefront window at the parking lot where Connie had pulled up, eleven years ago, with her doorbell in a box, and her soft brown hair, and an air of wholesome promise. He shuddered and clamped down on a deep necessity to cry.

Several seconds later voices began to accumulate outside and Harlan's neighbours started gathering from the other businesses along the short strip mall.

Connie was trembling so violently it was hard to navigate the wreckage. She made a crunching path through the glass. She didn't use the door but stepped over the spiky mountain range of the lower sill. She excused herself past a woman from the bakery, who was still holding a plate with a slice of carrot cake, and opened the back door of the Volvo and sat her bawling son in his car seat. It took both hands to steady the buckle enough to slide it into the lock. She heard a man say, What the hell, Harlan? What the H Christ is going on here?

She winced at the man's crudeness. It held the frightening potential of a crass new life she had just stepped into where people lost their tempers, lost control, where they swore and fought and threw garbage cans through windows.

W hen the alarm went off at four-thirty in the morning, all Hannah could see was the shape of the window soaked in dark purple light and four stars in the sky. They got up and had flashlights and a kerosene lamp to dress by, and Norm made a fry-up of greasy eggs on thick slices of bread, and there was bacon, which they didn't eat but made sandwiches with. Norm flicked on the high beams and they drove to a dirt road off the highway an old man at a gas station had told them about yesterday – a popular caribou crossing between the barrens. The road was pitted and they drove slowly. This is why you should never buy a used rental, Norm said, bottoming out again. They're cars nobody cares about.

They turned off their high beams and the trees tilted back into the darkness. Down the road, two demon eyes of red. There was a pickup truck parked ahead of them and they realized they'd reached the spot on the map. They drove up alongside the truck and rolled down the window. A woman was sitting behind the wheel, holding a 35 mm camera to her chin. See anything?

A man in a green quilted shell came around the back of the truck. Saw two moose about a half-hour ago, he said.

So you're after moose, Norm said.

There was a sound of nylon being scratched and the alder bushes parted and another man walked out, wearing a trucker's cap and carrying a rifle on his shoulder. His eyes were wide and he was breathing hard. Jeeze, boy, I almost got him. Would have had the two of them if we'd been here sooner. If you sees 'em, shoot one of 'em for me, will ya?

The guys got into their truck and slammed the doors and drove off down the road. The brake lights came on again after a couple hundred yards, and they got out and rustled back into the bushes.

Man oh man, Norm said.

What?

All that noise.

They walked into the woods where it was darker and they got lost for a little while, cracking their way through a web of spruce boughs, over moss-covered logs, holding the compass ahead of them. There were creaking noises in the velvety darkness and Hannah felt a little afraid. A city girl deep in the woods. This was not one of those moments when you could belt out a happy song either, because they were trying to be as quiet as possible. They checked the map by flashlight. Things looked the same in all directions – receding pillars of black and blue. There was a green sky growing lighter overhead, and finally a tinge of orange above the treetops. They came across a patch of flattened grass in a small arbour. That's where they slept, Norm whispered.

The forest brightened and ended abruptly and they found their way out onto the open marsh. The ground was soggy and made a soft suction against Hannah's rubber boots. Then it changed and became rocky, dry, crunchy with lichen. The sky was now a light grey and a breeze sighed over the land, making the shadows move. Hannah felt as if she was breathing with her eyes. There, one of them would say and then, No. They walked slowly and stopped often to raise the rifle and scan the treeline through the scope.

The day before, after a late start, hungover and shaky, they'd driven out of St. John's and installed themselves at a friend's cabin. They set off into the woods half-heartedly, and after several hours of cautious advances, long, searching intervals, they saw a magnificent stag. It was Hannah's first sighting, and the animal looked magical, something out of Norse mythology or a child's arctic fairytale. He had a rack of antlers like a huge inverted wishbone and a yoke of white fur. His back must have been five feet off the ground. He pranced out of the woods and sniffed the air, then turned and went back into the trees before walking out again, leading four does and two calves. The herd started to graze, but the stag was skittish. He knew something was up.

Hannah had been trying to find him through the rifle. Norm was whispering, You have to get closer. They were downwind and had crawled and managed to get within a hundred and fifty yards of the caribou.

Kneeling, Hannah held the rifle and caught him in her scope. That stag walked right across it, but all she could do was admire him, so she lost the shot. What would it require to shoot such a beautiful animal? Could she do it? He turned away and never gave her another chance. He must have caught a whiff of them then, because he raised his head and froze. The rest of the herd sprang to attention, and the stag led them at a trot back into the woods — except for one adolescent calf who lingered, who kept looking in Hannah's direction, curious and rebellious, defying his patient father at the edge of the forest, waiting.

A few minutes later, there was splashing as the animals crossed a shallow pond out of sight.

You have to be quick, Norm had said, you can't hesitate, you've got a fraction of a second when the caribou is yours. You want it side on. Then aim right behind the front shoulder, through the lungs and heart.

Hannah realized that she had to stop thinking about the consequences and the beauty of the animal. All she could think about was that spot behind the shoulder and the trigger of her gun and matching those two things.

Today they'd been sprawled on the ground, hiding in the scoop of a little hollow for about an hour when a good-sized female appeared about two hundred yards away. Norm and Hannah bent forward at the waist and lifted their feet high and rushed forward as quietly as they could in their plastic rain pants. But the caribou moved soundlessly and without effort, and they couldn't gain on her.

They're so fast, Norm said, breathing hard from the exertion. Let's try those barrens over there.

No, let's have lunch, Hannah said, and on their way back to the car, Norm spotted some fluorescent pink tape hanging from a branch on the far side of the marsh. They walked the quarter-mile to have a look. The tape marked the end of a trail that led back to the road, not far from where they'd parked. If they could get a caribou near this trail, it would make the job of lugging it out so much easier. There were caribou tracks all over the marsh where the trail led out.

It's Caribou Highway, Norm said. If we come back here, just before dusk, and sit quietly and wait long enough, a caribou will pass.

They returned to the car and sat inside and ate their sandwiches. Who knew cold bacon could taste so good? Hannah said, and they each drank a thermos cup of lukewarm tea and this, too, was very good.

They had a blanket in the trunk and Hannah lay across the back seat, unable to sleep, while Norm slept soundly under his coat, reclined in the passenger seat. The sky was so white through the windows – the car's interior sharply grey and metallic as yesterday's hangover. Hannah was thinking about how it was going to work out, this *living with Norm* business. She had recently moved all her stuff into his apartment. Would she be inclined to defer to his tastes and opinions, or would she find the strength to assert herself in this relationship? She found herself wanting so badly to please him, she may not even have noticed how badly because she hadn't yet begun to question the impulse. Her stomach rumbled. She was still hungry. The exertion of being outdoors and the adrenalin of seeing the caribou had carved out an appetite, but the sandwiches were all gone.

Norman gave a chuckle and Hannah thought he was laughing at her, then she realized he was still asleep. She'd heard a couple of people laugh in their sleep and always liked it. It was a reassuring sign of a person's essential character, like someone who was affable when drunk. Then Hannah remembered something that had happened to her mother once. Rose had woken up in the middle of the night because the bed was shaking. Her first thought was, Lord, if you take Tim, take me too! Don't leave me here alone! Rose thought it was an earthquake, but it was just her husband, sitting up in bed, laughing in his sleep, so hard that tears were streaming down his face. He'd been dreaming about his father, but couldn't remember the next day, what.

And I thought the house was falling down, Rose had said. She'd told this story over dinner in Toronto years ago. They'd all been there – her parents, Connie, even Zeus. What a pretty boy he'd been, with dark hair and dark lashes. Nothing like the rest of the family – prepubescent and funny and excitable.

If I have it my way, her father had said then, I won't live a long life. I don't want to get too old. I'm looking forward to meeting my maker.

Her mother had agreed. This life, she said, is so full of pain and suffering.

Hannah had looked at her sister, wondering what she thought. Connie seemed to be appreciating what they were saying, but Hannah had been depressed by the conversation – this maudlin desire for death, the expectation of a better life to come, and the certainty of their reward. It struck her as ungrateful. Heaven was too easy a scapegoat for the challenge of finding contentment. Okay, she'd said to her parents, so let's say God *did* create the world and gave us this life, don't you think we should be happy with it? I mean, it's what he saw fit to give us. So shouldn't we love it too? And she'd fixed on her sister for confirmation, but Connie just rolled her eyes, like she was being predictably antagonistic. Zeus was leaning forward, though, giving her a dark, soulful gaze. *Because*, Hannah had said to him, if you don't enjoy this life, who's to say you'll enjoy the next?

When Norm and Hannah got back out on the barrens, the clouds were plum-coloured and it had started to rain. They settled in under some low scrub and waited. Hannah listened to the hypnotic tap of raindrops on her waterproof jacket, felt the hard ground underneath, and the slow leaching of body heat. She fought off the urge to sleep, she had to keep herself awake. The wind was northerly, and they were downwind from where Norm thought the caribou would appear. And so they waited, like soldiers in the trenches, feeling the cold rain.

Twenty more minutes, Norm said, checking his watch.

Hannah hugged her knees and tucked her head down. She wondered if Norm would ever change his mind about having a baby. Couldn't he see they were already so clearly a team? They could handle a baby. They would excel at it, even. That's what she thought. It made her whole body ache with longing. Suddenly, she felt miserable, impatient. She was tired of waiting. She wanted to go home. And then Norm whispered, There he is!

Hannah was on her knees.

Take the shot, he said quietly. Take the fucking shot.

The caribou wasn't far. About fifty yards. A noble stag, in profile, brown and grey and white. Maybe three years old, a crown of antlers, nose high, princely. But Hannah wasn't thinking about that. She was thinking – behind the shoulder. Squeeze the trigger. Don't pull it.

Norm hissed, Take the shot!

Her left foot forward, knee up, elbow on knee, gun to shoulder, fur through scope. Hannah squeezed. That shocking noise, and the animal went down. First his hind legs buckled, then his head whipped back and the front of him went down like a slap. All she could see were his antlers above the bushes.

You got him, baby, you got him!

The stag was pulling his head around in a circular motion, trying to create some momentum to stand up. It was awful to see. Hannah put the rifle down and burst into tears. She wept with an intensity that was both alarming and cathartic. Her hands were on her face and she kept repeating, Oh my God, I'm so sorry, you're so beautiful. I'm so sorry, you're so beautiful.

She had shot something that was alive. The caribou had a soul. Hannah saw it in the way he had carried himself a minute earlier. And now that soul was thrashing around inside his broken body. We have to kill him, Hannah said.

Norm crawled over. He hugged her. Hannah could see that he was proud and excited. No, just leave him alone now. He'll die better on his own. That's the best thing we can do for him.

But she saw the neck tugging around. Please, she begged. I can't bear to see him like this. It didn't look like he was dying. There was too much effort in his struggle. Please!

They walked quickly and cautiously over to the caribou. Hannah crouched, still crying, about twelve feet away. Norm reloaded the gun and approached. The caribou was pulling himself in a circle to get away from him. Norm had to follow him around to get a good shot at the head, then held the rifle low to his hip and fired into the caribou's ear. All its limbs dropped, and the empty stillness of the foggy, late-afternoon countryside rushed back in from where it had been forgotten and engulfed them. Hannah noticed the rain again, and the vast, lonely spaciousness of the landscape. She felt grateful for the privacy, like the discrete quietude of a church.

Norm got the hunting knife with the six-inch blade from the army surplus bag and, straddling its neck, lifted the stag's head by the antlers and bent forward and pierced the white fur at its throat. The knife went in with such shocking ease.

You want to sever both jugulars, he said and joggled the knife around forcefully. The blade made a hollow sloshing noise inside the stag's neck. Steam rose into the air and then the fur was drenched in blood. Norm stretched the throat so the blood would drain out easily, and Hannah willed herself to touch the stag's body and her fear dissolved. She stroked it and admired the softness of its hide, the warmth of it, and knelt to touch its velvet muzzle. For an instant before shooting, she had wanted to say a prayer, something formal and ceremonial. But nothing came to mind.

Norm spat on the whetstone and sharpened the blade. Hannah had decided, before they came, to help with the evisceration. If she wasn't able to do this, or shoot the animal, she would have to give up eating meat. Norm handed her the knife and gave instructions. Careful, he said, it's sharp. There was the breastbone to cut through, like the side of a plastic bucket, and the windpipe, like a clean white dryer hose, to hook a finger through and pull down towards the belly. They rocked out the pale blue-green stomach and bladders and intestines, encased in their white but semi-transparent and veined sacs, which spilled out like loose water balloons onto the ground. Aggressive whiskeyjacks flew in from nowhere to begin their five-day feast. Which is all it will take, Norm said, for this mass of offal to disappear.

The vaulted rib cage, emptied now of the organs it once protected, stood like the inside of a small red cathedral. Hannah sliced an inch-wide strip of hide off the back bone. So when you saw through the spine, Norm said, the fur doesn't get into the meat. Then she removed the head with a handsaw and carved out the antlers, the saw blade slicing through just above the eyes, making the ears wiggle. This was the hardest part. The face so undeniably a face.

When she was done, Hannah squatted back on her haunches and surveyed the bright red blocks of meat. She had never felt so intimately connected to the food chain. Or as able, or as fertile. Not guilty, as she might have expected, but full of a ripeness, a connectivity. Nor was she prepared for the feeling of what can only be called *love* that she had for the body.

Norm took the heart and put it in a plastic bag and they started to carry the quarters out, one at a time, over a shoulder. The quarters weighed roughly eighty pounds each. Norm heaved one onto his shoulder and hooked his wrist over the hoof to use as a counter-lever. It looked easy enough, but Hannah could only walk about a hundred paces before she felt pinched by the weight. Norm would throw his quarter to the ground, then hoist hers off and drop it, hide down, onto a pillow of tiny wet dark green leaves. They would go back and make the same trip again with the other two quarters, then a separate trip for the rifle, gear, antlers, and heart, moving forward like this in increments.

Shouldering a quarter was like carrying a dog or an injured lamb to safety. This is a paradox, Hannah thought, or a delusion. But she felt a fierce affection for the still-warm density of fur and muscle and bone, nestled against the back of her neck. It felt like an act of love. There was no shame. Because I know I'm going to eat this animal, Hannah thought. And there is no greater intimacy. It's what we do to our gods, our lovers. *Take, eat, this is my body which is broken for you.*

F enton had called him at the nurses' station and asked him to go pick up a rental truck. Fenton had never driven around in a truck before and today that's what he wanted to do. He gave him an address and his credit card number. Zeus was tired, he just wanted to go home, but it was the first time in weeks that Fenton had expressed an interest in doing anything. So he offered to get a pizza on the way, and Fenton wanted ham and pineapple, an extra dough ball, and a ginger beer.

Zeus changed his clothes and shoes, wiped off his makeup, left the hospital, and took a taxi to the rental place. It was down an alley behind the bus station. He paid the driver and walked into the drafty station. A pigeon escorted him inside and out the other end. He found the office door sandwiched between two dumpsters, and made arrangements with a handsome young man who was wearing a really nice pair of jeans. He asked him for the name of the brand and didn't quite catch it, but it was something ridiculous, something like *the milk of human kindness*. Then he had to walk another two blocks to where the rentals were kept. A white Ford Ranger. For some reason, it looked whiter than any other vehicle he'd ever seen. Maybe it was the black bumpers. A white puppy with black lips. He ran his hand along the smooth side of the truck and gave it a stroke.

Finally, Zeus was sitting inside the high cab, inhaling the masculine smell of a brand-new vehicle. He backed out of the lot and drove to Rossi's. While the pizza cooked, he watched a large woman in a hair net fill an aluminum tray with dough balls, squeezing the dough out the side of her hand and twisting it off with a powdery pop. A sleight of hand, Zeus thought, not unlike the dove trick. Hot little oven-warm dove buns.

Fenton had said only that he wanted to go see the lake. When he came out of the apartment building, he was wearing a dirty silver parka he'd bought at a secondhand store last winter. He was carrying a plaid wool blanket, which he spread over his lap like an old man when he got into the truck. He looked pale and sweaty. He coughed a wet and crashing cough, then closed his eyes and raised a hand to prevent Zeus from asking any questions. Zeus drove north to where the city felt less crowded at their backs. At a red light, Zeus found himself staring at a bungalow on the corner, with small, corrugated fibreglass awnings above the windows. On the front lawn, fenced in by a ring of filigreed wrought iron, a plaster stallion reared up on its hind legs, its two front hooves cracked off.

He parked the truck facing Lake Michigan and opened the pizza box. The water stretched out calm, milky, copper green. The sky to the west was a very pale blue. Large cement blocks, like giant dice, tossed and rolled to the edge of the water. Bordering the cement blocks, a muddy strip of grass covered in bird shit. Three geese stood in a row and watched as a fourth one paraded by.

Canada geese, Fenton said – his voice sudden and startling in the silence – are the black squirrels of the duck world. He was wheezing slightly with every intake of breath. Wherever they make their nests, they take over and drive all the other ducks away. Like the black squirrels, who drive out the grey squirrels, who in turn drive out the red. The red squirrels are the prettiest, but they're the weakest.

Zeus was watching him. Fenton grimaced into his pizza crust. He had only taken a few small bites, while Zeus was on his fourth piece. The cab smelled of grease and cheese.

I'm dying, Fenton said.

You'll be all right, Zeus said.

No, I'm *dying*, Fenton said, and his green eyes flared gold beneath the halo of his dark red hair. I got all my test results about a month ago.

What do you mean, tests?

I've got liver cancer.

No, you don't.

From my chronic hepatitis.

I thought you had that under control.

It's all through my body. The doctors wanted me to do chemo and surgery, but I decided against it. I don't want to put myself through all of that if I'm going to die anyway.

You are *not* going to die.

I haven't even told my parents. Those pills I'm taking, they're morphine, but I'm not in that much pain, weirdly.

What are you talking about!

I'm sorry, Zeus, I couldn't tell you. I felt like telling you would've made it feel real. And I didn't want you to suffer – any more than I know you're already going to. He touched

Zeus's arm, but Zeus didn't move. I don't want to leave you, and I guess that's why – I don't know, Zeus. I just don't know how to handle this.

Zeus stared out the window and wiped his mouth on his sleeve. He offered the pizza box for Fenton to drop his slice on, then closed it. He nudged the door open and the handle shot out of his greasy fingers. Yanking on it impatiently, he felt the plastic crack a little and shoved the door open with his shoulder. He almost fell out of the cab. The pizza box slid sideways and he scooped it up and it started to flip and he wrestled it in the air. The box swung open and Zeus screamed, Fuckin' shit-fuck, you just gonna stand there like that, or what? And flung it at the geese as they scattered.

Zeus drove while Fenton slept. Fenton had wanted to see more of the countryside, so they'd headed further north. It was dark and they were alone in the landscape, following the elongated funnel of their headlights. Zeus would not accept that Fenton was going to die. Why hadn't he come to him sooner and asked him how they were going to fight this thing? How could he just resign himself, as if the date was set in stone and he was expected to be there on time, at death's door, in his white satin jumpsuit and battered old suitcase, smouldering like he'd just been pulled out of a fire.

Fenton stirred and coughed and half woke up. Isn't it interesting, he said, as if he was picking up from where he'd just left off in a dream, how everything seems to go back to the father?

Our fathers are always there, Zeus said. Even when they're not there.

When I was eighteen, my dad insisted I spend a year in the Israeli Army. It's your Jewish duty, my boy, Fenton said in a gruff

voice, then rattled up another mucousy cough. He pulled himself up in the seat. What did *I* know? I'd only been to Israel
once before, on a high school exchange, to this kibbutz in the
middle of nowhere. Fenton shrunk back down inside the
padded shell of his parka and leaned back against the door. I was
a fifteen-year-old goatherd from Chicago, he said in a tone of
amazement. So I turn eighteen and head back to Israel at my
father's behest. This time as a soldier. I can barely do ten push-
ups, but I learn how to assemble an AK-47.

It was unusual for Fenton to go on about himself, and
Zeus wanted to hear more. I can't imagine you holding a gun,
he said and Fenton didn't answer him. After a while, he started
to snore, like he used to when he was drunk. Damn you, Fenton,
I can't imagine a lot of things, Zeus thought. You know?

When they first met, Fenton had been wild and restless,
full of anger at the world, and rebellious. I care about nothing
and no one, he announced one evening at a bar and tossed a
little bag of cocaine onto the table. He was thirty-seven. Zeus
couldn't believe how old he was when Fenton had first told
him. In fact, he had trouble fitting Fenton into a description of
any age. He'd had a few jobs – gallery assistant, overnight security guard in a museum – and had saved up some money, so
Zeus never had to worry about paying for drinks, although
they did share most of the bills when he finally moved into
Fenton's sweet, third-floor walkup. They used to go from his
apartment to the bars and back again, for days on end, cruising
the city like sharks, reeking of aftershave. Fenton would gorge
on pork souvlakis and bacon sandwiches, and Zeus used to
punch him in the arm and say, You know, for a Jew, you can be
a real *ham* – which always cracked him up.

Fenton was never one to give into pressure, or hide his
opinions, but the one thing he couldn't do was stand up to

his father. One day, he told Zeus that his father had been a member of the Zionist movement in the 1970s. He said it like it was a terrible secret.

How in the world, Fenton said, can anyone condone military violence against innocent civilians in the name of protecting the so-called Jewish homeland!

Zeus had wanted to sympathize, but he was too distracted by how amazing Fenton looked, his eyes glowing with outrage. Fenton was always so well dressed, in his secondhand retro suits and narrow ties. So different from himself, in his jeans and motorcycle t-shirts, the higher the trucker's cap the better. A child of New Mexico.

Fenton had got so worked up that a faint sheen appeared on his upper lip. It made Zeus stare at his mouth while he kept up his rant. He watched his lips move and fantasized about kissing him. Apparently, his dad had a gun in his office. Had he ever used it in the movement? It was some kind of Russian World War II thing. Would it incriminate them one day? And what about his mother? What if she got arrested? Did he ever think about *that*? This kind of speculation used to drive Fenton crazy, but he would never know what the story was because he couldn't bring himself to talk to his father about the past. His dad's own parents had died in the camps, and Fenton wasn't going to be the one to stir that up. Suddenly, Fenton broke down and cried. It was the first time Zeus had ever seen him this way, and it left him feeling churned up and sorry.

Families, Zeus thought. The things you can't talk about. He'd always wanted, for instance, to ask Tim Crowe if he ever felt bad about what he'd done to him. He might still be in contact with the Crowes if Tim hadn't caught him in the garage that day, half-naked and on his knees in front of a boy from school. Zeus could still feel the shameful, emptying-out dread of it. Tim had announced to Rose that it was a problem he would handle with prayer and the Spirit, and took him straight to church, where he painstakingly lectured Zeus on the perils of homosexuality. Tim was a rational man, not prone to hysterics, but adamant about living life in a righteous way, as he knew the word to be defined. Tim's own view of the situation was that homosexuality was like an illness, unwittingly caught as if by contamination and cured through prayer, forgiveness, and celibacy. A prayer team was quickly gathered and asked to pray for his adopted son.

So Zeus found himself kneeling again, this time uncomfortably on the oak floor of Tim's office, surrounded by a small coterie of his spiritual advisers. They circled him like protective fencing, and had a casual way of joking that was a preamble to a great seriousness. They laid their hands on his head and his shoulders, and he thought about pigeons landing on a park statue – the repeated phrases, imploring God to make eminently clear the correct, high, bright, and admirable path his life should take. He felt dizzy and claustrophobic. The women wore too much perfume, the men too much cologne – and yet it still couldn't mask the locker-room smell of the warm crotches that pressed in around his head. It was a smell he would always associate with a sickening feeling of disappointment.

That night he'd dreamt he was sailing past the shores of heaven in a slave ship with all the other heathens and non-believers. He knew there must be other people out there who were like him. A tribe he could belong to. That's how he'd felt with Fenton, as soon as he met him, like everything was going to be okay because he wasn't alone in the world anymore.

Drunkenly, they had tumbled into the gay nightclubs of the city, and took ecstasy and danced, drenched in sweat, until the sun came up. They fell in love and were proud and self-serving until Fenton walked through a park and saw that film of Yuri Nikulin that had made him stop and change his life. One day, he came rushing into the kitchen with his big Toshiba laptop. He'd found the very same footage on the internet. He forced Zeus to stop what he was doing and watch it with him. They must have watched it twenty times, each time more hilarious and poignant than the last. The film became a standard for their own clowning – it actually made them want to be better than they were. It was like a challenge, and Fenton gave it everything he had. Except for this, now. This death thing. He was bowing down in front of it, as if it was something sanctified.

Zeus really needed Fenton to get over this cancer and get better, come back to work. Salvage your fighting spirit, he begged out loud in the humming cab of the Ford Ranger as Fenton slept beside him like an astronaut in his puffy silver parka.

Harlan did not come home the night after their big blowout. Connie invented a story to tell the kids but thought Emma could sense something was up. Emma threw a tantrum and took a pair of scissors to her favourite pink wool blanket, then was inconsolable over the loss. After dinner, Simon stabbed Theo above the knee with a pencil. Connie couldn't squeeze the lead out. When she finally got to bed, she was exhausted but wide awake. A car turned into the drive and the headlights through the curtains projected a bright pattern of lace onto the wall. The pattern slid sideways, bent in the corner, and scurried like a colony of ants over a lampshade. The car reversed and pulled it all back, leaving a thickness in its absence that made her aware of her own breathing.

Harl did not come home the next day either, and it was the first time he'd ever left her like this. The phone rang and she rushed for it. It was a call from a collection agency. She told them they'd have to speak to her husband and hung up. Harlan was probably at Jodie's. She was the only one of his sisters he was close to, but when Connie had called her place earlier, there'd been no answer. She was furious. Then her mother called.

Am I disturbing you, you sound funny?

No, Connie said and felt as if she was being tackled by a big, soft, rubber balloon.

You're not in the middle of lunch, are you? I'm not interrupting some delicious meal you're in the process of whipping up?

No.

How are the kids?

Good. Fine.

And how's Harlan? Did he get that spotlight fixed?

It's fixed, Connie said. She wasn't anywhere near ready to tell her mom what was happening at home.

Dad just bought a bunch of automatic timers for the lights here, for when we go away. So they'll go on and off inside the house when we're not here. All you do is plug whatever lamp you want into this little timer.

Ah-huh.

Have you ever seen one of these things before?

I don't know, Mom.

They're really a very good little invention.

I'm sure Harl knows all about them.

I could pick some up for you.

Can we talk about this later? Connie said, more impatiently than she would have liked. Too often her mother's phone calls were like the sudden appearance of an unnamed request that left her guessing at what she'd failed to provide. A gravy boat full of love. What? it made Connie want to scream. What what what what what?

Well, I don't really have anything to say, Rose said, and her tone meant she was injured by what Connie had said but wasn't going to mention it. Her mother's ability to dissemble was champion. She did it in the name of love – of a thoughtfulness that was so emphatic it formed a barrier to that love. I just called to say hello, she said. So, hi there, my dear!

Hi, Mom, she said.

Rose gave a nervous laugh into the phone. She didn't like empty spaces – even her walls were covered in pictures.

Is everything okay, Con?

I'm fine. I'm just a little stressed out, that's all.

Can we do anything for you?

Not really, but thanks.

Well, just so you know, my dear, I'm really proud of who you are as a woman. I really delight in the woman you've become.

Connie wondered how much praise it would take before her mother felt she had made up for a lack of ever complimenting her daughters when they were growing up. And then her heart broke out of remorse. She could be so hard. Look, Mom, Connie said, thanks for calling, but I've got to go.

Okay, Rose said. Well, love you!

I love you too. And they both hung up.

Connie took a deep breath. The kitchen was fragrant with steam. She had pinto beans on the stove, cooking in a chicken broth, with saffron and onions. She stirred the pot and the smell was deeply satisfying. On the surface, things seemed so normal in the house. Emma was in the den on the piano, plunking away at a Mozart waltz and singing along in a crazy operatic falsetto. Connie thought she could hear Simon and Theo dropping bombs downstairs, fighter jets flying across the room, smashing into army bases, screams of agony. For a moment, she felt a deep, exhilarating pleasure in domestic life, then there was a knock at the side door and Mary-Beth standing in the rain with a tote bag and a bouquet of flowers, as if someone had died.

I bought you some pink gerberas, she said and gave them to Connie. Mary-Beth put her bag on the floor and reached back out the door to close and bring in her wet umbrella. Look, she said, I have to make up two dozen gift bags for a promo tomorrow morning. I have my sewing machine in the car. I'll set it up in the dining room and we can finish them off together.

Mary-Beth had come over yesterday when they'd finally connected by phone and Connie told her what was going on, and now here she was again, with the purpose of distracting her. Connie marvelled at her care and generosity. She submitted herself willingly, and felt grateful for the friendship.

Your TV's not on, Mary-Beth said.

It's not always on around here, you know. Connie threw her hands up. I haven't exactly been thinking about the election. Aren't you sick of it yet?

I'll tell you what I'm sick of. I'm sick of waiting to find out who the new president is going to be, Mary-Beth said. The suspense is awful. She turned on the small TV in the kitchen and angled it towards the dining room.

They sat across from each other and Connie lost herself in the sorting and assembling of small pink and gold sachets of hair serum and conditioner. Mary-Beth's hands were lit up under the bright arch of her sewing machine. The rain fell outside and the sliding glass doors to the patio were slightly open to let the saffron steam out. CNN churned out the news while Mary-Beth kept up a spirited commentary. The sound of her children's voices in the house, the chug-chug-chug of the machine, it reminded Connie of when she was a child. The rumble of her mother's sewing machine, the gorgeous smell of freshly baked bread. That time her sister ran down the hall and sunk her bare foot into a huge metal bowl full of bread dough, which had been sitting on the floor over a hot air vent, with a tea towel to cover it. Hannah had laughed so hard. Sometimes all three of them would laugh until the tears streamed down their faces. Her mother was so beautiful when she was happy. A string of dark beads against a soft wool sweater. A silver watch band. A brooch she used to wear that Connie had always loved, with a three-dimensional cream-coloured Bakelite rose, fastened to a smooth, dark brown, wooden oval.

Connie looked at Mary-Beth and said, as if there was no shame in the thought, I wonder what it means to feel so peaceful here on my own, without Harlan, wherever he is. She didn't feel like chasing him down, it was up to him now. He was the one who would have to make the next move.

In the morning, Connie dutifully carried out her usual pre-church routine with the kids. She sat in the kitchen with Emma between her legs, pulling her daughter's hair into a tight French braid. The night before, Emma had asked again where her father was. Connie had said, Daddy's tired. He's just taking a little break. He's sleeping in a fancy hotel, on a big soft cloud-bed, with a blue silk eye-mask on his face. And fuzzy slippers.

Emma said she didn't know about those hotels.

Connie nodded. I'll take you there one day. Now Emma rested her hands on her mother's knees and patiently let her finish her hair. Simon was dressing Theo. They came and stood at attention like a small outfit of recently recruited militia. They were pleased with themselves. They looked as if they'd been dressed and then shaken. Excellent, Connie said, snapping the final loop on Emma's hair elastic and twirling her around. You all look fabulous.

Connie stood up and loosened her shoulder, then bent forward like a baseball pitcher, with one hand behind her back, and squinted. Spit in your eye, she said and ground her foot into the floor.

Why are you doing that? Simon asked.

Connie shrugged. I don't know, I just felt like it. And she did it again, her children glancing at each other for confirmation, then permitting themselves to laugh. Connie hugged them all at once, closing her eyes briefly against their hair to mask the anxiety she felt. She bundled them out of the house and saw her husband step out of his Jeep and into the daylight, still in his light blue summer suit. He didn't look like he'd been gone for three nights. He looked ready for church. Connie was so relieved at not having to go there on her own and make her explanations, she almost forgave him everything. The consequences of his actions were still so theoretical and vague, perhaps nothing had changed. Harlan waved from the driveway and motioned for them to get in.

Daddy! Emma yelled and ran to meet him in her black patent-leather shoes.

The family all piled into the Grand Cherokee and Harlan reached back to give Simon his pink superball. Attached to it by an elastic band was a small piece of paper folded many times. Si snapped off the elastic and opened the paper and reached across Theo to give it to Emma so she could it read out loud. Bounce – 96% (awesome). Colour – 75% (too pink). Smell – 33% (nasty). Texture – 85% (very nice). Overall rating – 72.25%. Theo tried to grab the paper from Emma and she shouted, Stop that! Simon said, Give it to me, and Theo got a hold of one corner and ripped it, and then all three of them were screaming. Harlan produced two more superballs from his suit pocket and gave one to Theo and the other to Emma, and then it was Simon's turn to sulk. Harlan pulled a pen out of his other pocket, one with a scuba diver kicking back and forth in a vial of water, and gave it to him. Here, Si, how's that?

Things are going to be fine, Connie said, touching Harlan's thigh. What could be so wrong? Then she noticed the sweat on his upper lip. She'd never seen him sweat like that before. She looked up at the dark green spears of the trees against the bright blue sky and a vicious fear dug its claws into her chest. How helplessly I sit, she thought, in the middle of a crisis.

They arrived at church and the kids bolted, ran to meet friends and head down into the basement for Sunday school. Connie and Harlan joined the informal procession through the open doors, immersing themselves in the warm, muted buzz of conversation that a demure crowd will generate, organ music in the background, and took a seat in their usual pew. The sun was pouring through the stained-glass windows at the front of the church. The shiny pine of the altar was honey-coloured. The organist struck an extended, portentous note and the congregation all rose for the processional hymn.

At some point in the middle of Reverend Finch's sermon, one of the older kids brought Theo back upstairs and he slid along the pew until he was sitting next to his father. Harlan stroked his son's hair and, after a while, Theo fell asleep with his head on his dad's lap.

Because his name is *Wonderful*, the reverend was saying. Counsellor, Mighty God, Prince of Peace. Because it's in the *name* of Jesus that we are healed. For his name is *holy*. You can't separate Jesus from his name. Blessed be his holy name.

My name, Connie thought, used to be Constance Cybil Crowe, an embodiment of constancy and flight, at the centre of which, a prophetic voice. But I don't know a single thing anymore. Maybe I never did. I have no clarity, she whispered into Harlan's ear. I've been praying for a sign. I want God to show me a sign. Because I'm stuck here in the darkness, Harl, and I want something for myself now. I'm going to give him an ultimatum.

Don't do that, Harlan said. Don't bargain with him, Con. Trust me.

How can I trust you?

Don't punish yourself, sweetheart. You haven't done anything wrong.

Connie felt such an oppressive inhibition, as if she was lacquered in a veneer of propriety. She wanted to crack through appearances – stand up and lift her hands to heaven. Shout, Oh Jehovah! Run down the aisle to the front of the church and fall on her knees. And why not? This congregation was supposed to be her spiritual family, her community in God. Feed and nurture her spiritual hunger. But all she saw around her were people whose souls were crying out, but trapped beneath a prim reticence. Where was God in that reticence? In this tight, formal house of worship. Connie had never fully expressed herself. She was living in a prison, guarded by the threat of embarrassment. She couldn't break down in front of anyone. She feared their judgment. But then, while she was having these very thoughts, she found herself standing up where she was and raising her hands into the air. She shouted, Lord, we praise you! Why don't you show yourself to us? She woke Theo up.

The reverend froze in mid-sentence, his mouth an O-shaped hole, his hand about to come down and curl around the edge of the pulpit. He was leaning forward with the full thrust of his argument, and it took a moment for him to reverse his momentum and settle back on his heels. Harlan was hauling Theo onto his lap, as if to protect him, while an overweight woman two pews ahead swivelled around like a tractor, in several laborious stages, to gawp in amazement and admiration. Connie's eyes darted around the congregation. She lowered her face, nodding, closed her eyes, and gave an apologetic wave and sat down again. She was blind and deaf with mortification. The reverend, in his own awkward but heartfelt way, prayed quickly and moved on to the offertory hymn.

In the parking lot after the service, Connie was dismayed by how automatically her face clicked into an expression of false cheer. She could sense that people were giving her looks and assessing her as they hadn't before. She was desperate for something wilder than what she knew right here in this parking lot. It feels very lonely to pretend when you're about to rip the pearls off your neck and smear your chest with gravel. But Connie just tilted her head like all the other mothers and made sympathetic small talk. Her shiny brown hair was up in a loose bun, and she was wearing her fitted wool skirt, pink cashmere sweater, expensive high heels. She was the picture of wealthy respectability. It should have been someone like odd Mrs. Sachton, she thought, standing there in her blue tuque, running shoes, and thick tan-coloured nylons, who had shouted out during the service.

Connie saw the school principal's daughter come out of the church in a red hoodie and wave sheepishly at someone in the parking lot. Then Connie watched Harlan saunter over to talk to her. The girl twisted her foot on the ground, in a coy and bashful way, and for the second time that day, Connie heard the words *spit in your eye*, only this time they took on a different tone.

Then Mary-Beth came out of the church, pushing her son down the handicap ramp in his wheelchair. Connie waved and called out, Hi, Jay!

The boy swung his head around as if it was connected by a loose spring and spoke out the side of his mouth, Hi, Connie. Looking good!

Thanks, Jay. You too.

I'll call you later, Mary-Beth mouthed while holding her hand to her head like a phone.

Come on, Connie said to Simon and turned to locate Emma, who was pulling Theo around by his collar. Emma! she called out. Over here! It's time to go home!

They got into the car and Harlan was already waiting for them behind the wheel. He drove without speaking. What was that all about? Connie said.

What was *what* all about?

Shell Lunetta, the principal's daughter?

Who?

That girl you were talking to.

I didn't know her father was the principal.

Well, how do you know her then?

She goes to our church, doesn't she? How do *you* know her?

Connie just shook her head. When they reached home, Emma and Si got out. She extracted Theo from his car seat and held him on her hip. Harlan hadn't moved. Aren't you coming in the house?

No.

Why not?

Because I've banished myself.

Oh, snap out of it, Connie said, for Pete's sake.

But Harlan wouldn't budge.

Don't you think, Connie said, before you banish yourself, that there might be a few things you should come into the house and sort out? Or can't you get past punishing yourself enough to think about the effect this might be having on the people around you?

I need to be selfish right now, Harlan said.

Oh, I hate you right now, Connie said and slammed the door. She watched his Jeep reverse out the drive, and then she wanted him back. I'm sorry, she whispered into Theo's neck. Please come back, Harlan, please. I don't care about the money. I forgive you. Just don't leave me here alone. Not with the kids. I can't do this on my own.

Zeus stood near his open locker, disinfecting his props. He was thinking about what he could do for Fenton. They needed to get a juicer. They should go on a raw food diet. He'd go to the Thai place and bring home some spicy noodle soup. Or maybe the spices wouldn't be good for his liver. He'd ask one of the nurses. Then he caught sight of the little country house on wheels, sitting patiently in the corner, unused. He laid his forehead against the cool metal of the locker and relaxed his face.

Zeus had a rubber stethoscope that played 'You Are My Sunshine' and this is what he resorted to now. For Lalia, Zeus had to wipe down his toolbox and all his props with isopropyl swabs and, in addition to his face mask and gloves, wear a pale blue surgical gown and cap. It was because of her immune system, which was weak, though her spirit was so strong.

Standing outside her room, he put the stethoscope into his ears and pretended to listen to his own heart. He could hear people talking on the other side of the door and wondered whether he should come back later. He knocked and Mrs. Deluca answered and immediately broke out, with frantic delight, Oh look, Lalia, it's *Signore Zeus!*

Lalia loved Zeus so much. It almost shocked him how firm she could be in her demands for him. Today, she didn't want him to leave. Even as the doctors talked to her parents in hushed tones, she insisted that he stay. Zeus pulled a joke syringe out of his gown and squirted a murderous red ribbon at the doctor, for Lalia's sake, and she had giggled right through his speech, while her parents wept quietly into their hands. Zeus caught her father's eye and it was like the eye of an animal in the jaws of a trap — fearful, uncomprehending. It was at moments like this that Fenton's father would appear to him, smacking the foot of the hospital bed the way he'd pound the dinner table, and bellow his rousing encouragement, A gag is a gag is a gag! Don't fuck with the joke, Zeus! Sometimes it's all you've got!

The previous time he saw her, Lalia had patted him gently on the back of the hand, in a maternal way, as if she knew he needed reassurance. The kids could always tell. They know everything, a nurse had told him once. Astonishing in their wisdom and thoughtfulness, giving encouragement when *they* were the ones who were suffering.

More tests were required and Lalia was transferred to a gurney with a clear plastic tent. Before she was wheeled out of her room, Zeus took out his pocket watch with the terrycloth dog and wound it up and snapped it open and read in her eyes hope, heartbreaking courage, and a little plea to save her. He waved goodbye and one of the wheels on her gurney spun wildly as they pushed her down the hall.

He went to Sam's room, but Sam wasn't there, so he flapped over to the nurse's station in his big shoes and was told the boy had been taken to ICU the night before.

Zeus laid his hands on the counter to steady himself. He

considered taking off his costume and laying it neatly at the nurse's station. He could walk out of the hospital in his underwear and never come back. He went into the staff lounge and lay down on a cold vinyl cot.

He must have fallen asleep because it was nearly midnight when he woke up with a start. He took off his surgical gown, put on his morning jacket, and flippered conspicuously out of the ward. In a faint-hearted attempt at dignity, he took off his long, flat brown shoes and tucked them under his arm like two folded newspapers.

The suspended glass walkway that joined the upper levels of the north and south sections of the hospital was one of his favourite places. He liked how it hissed with the unseen circulation of air, as if it had lungs in a perpetual state of exhalation. The walkway was a bright glass vein of bluish light. The glass itself glowed, who knows where the fluorescence was hidden. Zeus padded silently into the tunnel, eleven floors of thin air beneath his feet, and stopped at the halfway point. Between his socks, cars nosed along the street below – and one tiny pedestrian, who seemed engaged in conversation with a mailbox. He looked out over the cityscape. Office towers shining like stainless steel appliances in the moonlight. The moon was so full and bright it seemed to surpass the potential of mere reflection. Zeus raised his thumb like a painter and covered it. The moon was the size of his thumbnail.

It wasn't hard to make a thing disappear. And when it was gone, you sometimes wondered whether or not it had ever existed. Would it be that way with Fenton? The thought made him feel as if he was coming apart, like aspirin in water.

Hey, Zeus! This was from a young doctor rushing through the glass corridor, lab coat open, holding a can of Diet Coke. You've got to have your shoes on, it's regulation.

Zeus waited until the alarming disruption of her sudden appearance had subsided, then he bent forward to place his shoes soundlessly on the floor and slip them back on.

At the ICU they weren't allowing visitors, but he went and stood outside the room Sam was in. Behind the door, he could hear a woman's voice, elevated, urgent. She began to shout, This is completely unacceptable! Where's the goddamn doctor! I want my son moved to another department – *now!* Her voice sounded disembodied, unnatural, like the voice of someone being electrocuted, or possessed. There was a low murmur, in a man's voice. Quiet male anguish. Zeus wanted to burst in and do a silly routine, make Sam laugh. That's what he should've done, to hell with the rules. Make him laugh again when, all around him, people were choking on their grief. But he couldn't do it. Zeus no longer had the heart, or the stomach, for this kind of thing anymore. Not for *anything* anymore. He took a few steps down the hall, then went back to the room. He pried off his feathery orange wig. He hung it from the door handle – a ritual of defeat – and walked away.

In the morning, Fenton was having trouble breathing. Zeus was crying and Fenton said, I think it's time to go. Zeus packed him a bag and accompanied him to the hospital, where a doctor they'd both met before was on duty. She did a quick assessment and told them Fenton had pneumonia. He was admitted and given a bed in a shared room. He looked so thin and sickly, Zeus wondered how he'd failed to notice the extent of it. It was only now, against the white sheets, that he realized how yellow Fenton's skin had become. His hair was dark and matted against his forehead. He had an oxygen tube taped under his nose and an IV inserted into the back of his hand. Even his hands, on top of the sheets, looked strange, like they didn't belong to him. Zeus touched one of them. It was surprisingly hot and dry. Oh Fenton, he said. I don't know what to say.

What's there to say? Everything's obvious now. And what isn't, no longer matters. Fenton coughed and put a great effort into adjusting himself and sank back into the same position.

You're my best friend, Zeus said and pulled the curtain around the bed and carefully got in beside him. What am I going to do without you?

Fenton rolled over slowly and did what they'd done for many years — he spooned Zeus. It made Zeus feel protected, cared for. It gave his body such a warm deep pleasure, almost childlike, to be cradled this way. He realized how tired he was. He didn't want to go anywhere ever again. He could feel himself falling asleep.

Remember when we were in the truck, Fenton whispered, and I told you I was in the army? His voice was so close to Zeus's ear, it woke him up.

There's more to it, he said. Something I never really got over but didn't understand until a year ago. I think it's why I got sick.

What do you mean? Zeus said.

We were sent to Lebanon, Fenton said. There'd been these massacres in the refugee camps there. The Israelis were blamed, but it was the Lebanese Christians fighting the Lebanese Muslims. Fenton's lungs began to whistle and he rolled onto his back and gave a sudden, ripping cough.

Zeus got a glass of water from the bedside table and lifted Fenton's head so he could take a sip through a white straw bent sideways at its accordion hinge. He lowered him back onto the pillow and lay down beside him again. Zeus told him maybe it was better he didn't talk so much, but Fenton said he needed to tell him.

We got there at the end of the war, Fenton said, but it was still awful. We saw a lot of bodies. I remember there was this baby on the ground. She wasn't crying. Just lying there with these huge, wide eyes. Right where she'd been dropped. Tiny hands trembling in the air from shock. Nobody was picking her up.

For a moment, Fenton stopped talking and the room filled up with all the familiar hospital noises – a blowing air vent, a beeping monitor.

There was a boy there too, he said. Somehow he became my responsibility. He was bawling his guts out, just hysterical, and I couldn't stand it. I couldn't get him to stop. He was six or seven years old. We carried chocolate bars for the kids. I mean, they were given to us by the army, to win them over, pacify them. I gave him a chocolate bar so he'd stop crying. I must've given him about ten of them because I didn't want to hear him cry again. Your parents have been murdered. Here, kid, have another Hershey's bar. What the hell else was I supposed to do?

But you were just a kid yourself, Zeus said.

So there I am, a year ago, Fenton said. I'm sitting in this cab and the driver says, I know you. I say, no you don't. He says, yes I do. You were in Lebanon. No, I wasn't. It was such a long time ago. I hadn't thought about it in years. I'd put it out of my mind. You gave me chocolate when my family was killed, he said. Nobody knows I was there. How could this guy know? I didn't know what to say. I started to cry, right there in the cab. I apologized – he said it was okay. When we got to my door, he wouldn't take my money. I thought, why is this guy being so nice? What had his life been like? He's a cab driver now in Chicago, and I'm a clown, working with kids, still trying to pacify them with little gifts of sweetness, right in the face of death.

Fenton made a gasping noise, like he couldn't get enough air. His lungs were an abandoned barn, something cavernous, with rafters. Zeus could hear pigeons in there, flapping their wings in the dust. But that story's a good sign, he said. It's *optimistic*. It shows how things we give away can sometimes come back to us, that the things we do, whether we know it or not, can have a good effect.

You don't understand, Fenton said. I was in the army. I was trained to kill people. I was involved in that killing, and it was after meeting that man again that my body started to break down. I thought, why? Why did I meet him? Was it to take me back to that moment in Lebanon? Or to a moment just before that, when my father sent me to the army in the first place and I didn't refuse? Because what enemies did I have? Talk about Jewish duty. It was my duty to refuse. It's *everybody's* duty.

Fenton had to stop and rest.

That's what I'm guilty of, he said, in the smallest voice. That's why I'm dying. It's why we'll all die.

No, it's not, Zeus said.

I wanted to do the baby swap with you, Fenton said. I wanted to see Lalia and Sam. How can God live with himself? Why does he always take the best children?

Norm flicked back and forth between election coverage and the baseball game – one moment a CNN anchor talking to a holographic image of a correspondent in Dallas, and the next, Cheeter making a dive for the ball and hanging for a second parallel to the ground before catching, in his tan glove, that little white snowball with such quick and unnatural precision it was as if a plug had been pulled in the earth and the first two things to get sucked down were Cheeter and that baseball.

Norm pressed a wrong number on the remote control and found himself staring at the Weather Channel. A jazzy instrumental version of a U2 song was playing. A map of the world spun and threw up the temperatures in London, Stockholm, Cairo, Marrakesh. There was something about the jaunty blind optimism of the music and the authority over the planet and knowing what the weather was in some faraway city that made him feel lonely here in this small apartment, full of melancholy and something to do with brotherly love.

He turned off the TV and went outside onto the balcony and rummaged through a shelf made of milk crates until he'd gathered up a small plastic pot, some newspaper, and what remained of a bag of soil. He took these things into the kitchen and laid them on the table. In a shotglass of water, an avocado pit hung suspended from the lip of the glass by three sewing pins. When they got home the day before, Norm had noticed that the pit had sprouted while they were away, a small white tongue was pushing its way out of a crack in the stiff brown shell.

When the phone rang, his hands were furred with soil. He picked it up delicately, so as not to get it dirty. It was Hannah's sister.

So you're finally back, Connie said. I've been calling for days. I wasn't sure when you were coming home.

We didn't get any messages, Norm said.

Well, you know me, she said. I hate talking to a machine. And I guess you could say it's been pretty bad over here. Things are kind of rocky at the moment. I mean, who ever said life was going to be easy, right? And her laugh rang hollow, a desperate jackal, waiting on the outskirts of camp. I honestly don't know how things are going to turn out, she said. I suppose only time will tell.

They had only met a few times and Norm had found Connie distant and hard to talk to, but something was pouring out of her now that he needed to catch. He wanted to feel solid for her. He nodded and then matched his gesture with words. Time's a healer, he said and could think of nothing else to say. All he had for her was sympathy, though she wasn't making it clear exactly what had happened. There was no judgment.

It's just that everything's such a mess right now, she said. Maybe Harlan needs to go see a counsellor. I mean, we could all use a bit of counselling after this. And again there was that forced jovial laugh.

Norm understood there was embarrassment and there was shame. He knew from Hannah that her sister was the kind of person who had a strong idea of the shape an admirable life should take. How different the sisters were from each other, it seemed. As Connie spoke, Norm was holding the phone with his shoulder and rinsing his hands. He dried them on a dish towel and looked at a picture of Hannah's niece and nephews taped to the fridge. Their faces were so beautiful. How are your kids?

Well, you know. I mean, how do you talk to a child about something like this? Connie said and stopped abruptly.

Kids are resilient, Norm said.

Yeah, but that shouldn't be an excuse.

It's not an excuse, he said. It's a good thing.

Connie went quiet.

How easy it would be to fail as a parent, he thought. It had occurred to him that it might be selfish cowardice to avoid that risk in life, but he wasn't swayed by romanticism. He didn't feel the need to improve himself. Sacrifice was not an urge in Norman Peach. He had very little, if any, superstition. You had to embrace what you loved in this life. There was no consequence or reward beyond the grave, and unhappiness was all the proof he needed that he wasn't living his life well.

Will you please get Hannah to call me as soon as she can? There was a new tightness in Connie's voice that felt like an accusation.

Of course, Norm said. She'll be home soon. I know she'll want to talk to you right away. Is there anything we can do for you?

I just really want to speak to my sister.

They hung up and Norm gazed out the kitchen window at a view of a brick wall so close you could touch it. So close you could throw a wineglass out the window and it would smash and fall into a triangle of dead space below, full of accumulated junk – paint cans, rusty aluminum table legs, an old-fashioned telephone on top of a filing cabinet that every winter expanded to cartoon proportions under the snow. Hannah had done that once, like a drunk pitcher. One knee up, she had hurled a glass across the kitchen. It was summer and the window was open, but only partially. She'd been so impressed with her aim. Why did you do that? he'd yelled at her. It had frightened him. I don't know, she said, full of smug delight. Hannah was a glass breaker. She had gypsy blood. Get loaded, smash something. That moment when you feel so full, you just have to throw something away.

Norm was happy with Hannah. He knew he could be happy with her for a long time. It was easy to be with her. She was funny, she made him laugh. And she came with her own checks and balances. She could be moody and selfish and insecure, but when these things made her lash out she would catch herself and apologize. She was self-aware, she didn't flinch. He'd never known anyone to duck so quickly out of an argument. Sometimes it was so sudden she'd be laughing seconds after accusing him of unforgiveable neglect. Then she'd look sheepish and probably do a little dance to mask her embarrassment. Bury her face in his armpit. And all of this made him want to please her. He would give her anything but what he knew she truly wanted – a baby. That was his limit and it made him feel churlish.

∃ ∈

It was early evening when Hannah started walking home from the Y. In the fluorescent glow outside a dry cleaners, a midget

128

sat on a stool, playing the balalaika. His fingers had the deft, pudgy articulation of a child's. He was playing the theme from *Doctor Zhivago*. Suddenly, Hannah was Lara in the ice castle. She doubled back and dropped a toonie into his case and whispered into her collar, *Nostrovia,* in her most melodramatic tone. Just to feel the language on her tongue, so redolent of ice and fur.

She pulled her collar up higher against the cold air. The convenience stores on the way back home had barrels of pumpkins out front, in anticipation of Halloween. At the corner of their building, Hannah noticed how fast the clouds were moving. They were like mauve peonies, the sky velvety and a dark mushroom grey. She could hear honking, and headed through the narrow brick passageway that divided their building from the one next door, so narrow it was hard not to graze the skin off your knuckles when pushing a bike through, reared up on its hind wheel. Norm called it the gauntlet.

When she came around the back, she saw a woman in the alley, standing by the open door of an idling SUV. She was leaning on the horn now. Another car was parked in front of her, blocking her way out. The woman was wearing high heels and a long ginger-coloured sheepskin coat. She swung herself inside, revved the engine, then got out again. She shouted, Goddamnit! and stomped her foot like a child. A window opened in the wall above her and a young man with tattoos leaned out.

Asshole! the woman yelled.

Shut the fuck up, lady. You're disturbing the whole goddamn neighbourhood.

The woman shouted, I don't give a shit because you and your stupid friends kept me up 'til five o'clock last night with your stupid fucking music!

That was true. Hannah had heard it too.

Parties are good for people, he said, but SUVs are killing the planet. He pulled his head back inside and Hannah walked up the clanging metal staircase to their apartment. If Norm heard her coming up the stairs, he'd go to the door and open it before she had a chance to put her key in the lock. She looked back over her shoulder for a moment.

What the fuck are you looking at? the woman said. This is none of your goddamn business!

You know, Hannah said, you're making an awful lot of noise yourself.

This asshole has me blocked in, she said, pointing up at the window the tattooed man had leaned out of.

I don't think that's his car.

Shut up, the woman said. I don't have to listen to you. You'll be gone in a couple of months. You people never stay for more than six months anyway. I used to own that building. I used to own the whole fucking block! But now the place is a dump and y'all live in these filthy apartments.

Well, at least I don't have a filthy mouth! Hannah shouted and turned towards the door and there was Norm. Crazy bitch, she told him, and Norm looked curious and amused. Oh, how she loved the face on him. She held it between her hands and Norm said, Get in here. He closed the door and slid his hands up under her shirt.

Hannah ran her fingers through his thick black hair. You're my little black rabbit, she said and soon they were in bed again. What a luxury liner this love was – high and solid and unsinkable, though Hannah drowned all the time. It was a willing submission, but it wasn't subservient. It was increments of liberation. She was slowly uncovering Norm's abundant permission to be more herself. She trusted that Norm really loved her. It was that simple, and that revolutionary.

You need to call your sister, Norm said, stroking her face. It's important. She was pretty upset.

Really?

Yeah, something's going on over there.

Are you being serious?

Why? Why are you so incredulous all the time? It's your sister. She called. It's not bewildering. If I had to guess I'd say that she and Harlan were having some marital problems.

Is that what she said?

Not in so many words.

What else did she say?

Norm threw his hands up in surrender.

Hannah pulled a face and got out of bed. She was naked and could feel Norm watching her. What are you lookin' at, eh?

You, he said. The soft, pliable mechanics of your body.

Hannah looked pleased and did a little undulating dance. A moment later, she walked back in with the phone. Why is the phone covered in dirt? Hannah watched Norm cross his ankles and put his hands under his head in a posture of contentment.

She dialled her sister's number and went into the kitchen and noticed the fresh pot of soil on the table. Norm had a green thumb. He could coax anything to life. Except a baby, she thought and tried to banish the idea. She opened the fridge, taking out last night's chicken and the dill pickles. She started opening a bag of bread, got Connie's answering machine, and left a message. Norm came in just as she was hanging up the phone. Here, give me that, he said, taking the bread. I'll do that. Norm was also, she thought, the Sandwich King.

It was nearly midnight. Norm was slouched low on the sofa, one leg flung over its arm. He was reading Marcus Aurelius, Hannah a book by Paula Fox. There was a stillness between them that was comfortable. Hannah looked up from her book and found the mere shape of Norm's leg in his blue jeans miraculously attractive.

If we ever got married, Hannah said, do you think we'd be the kind of couple that wraps a few sandwiches in wax paper, rinses out the thermos, throws the sheepskin coats on the back seat of the car, and drives to the country while reading *Out of Africa* out loud to each other?

Sure, Norm said after thinking about it. I hope so.

Oh, Hannah said. She sounded disappointed.

What's wrong with that?

It's so bourgeois.

Well, how would you have it?

I'd have Captain Beefheart on the stereo, Hannah said. And a king can of Molson X in my hand.

Norm looked at her then, as if he was seeing her again for the first time. The things you say, he said, they surprise me sometimes.

I'm glad they do.

Hannah crawled across the floor and up between his legs, resting her head in his lap. She looked up at his face and it seemed she'd known this face for a very long time. I've been looking for a face like this, Hannah said, all my life. You've got a big face, Norman Peach. A face like a tree.

A few weeks ago, on their way back from a bar where they'd met up with some friends, including a woman Norm had dated for a while, Norm had said, What if I made out with another woman? What if I find another woman attractive? Do you want to hear about that?

Not really, she said. She was that happy. She was feeling that strong. I mean, I know you'll have feelings for other women. That goes without saying. I just don't want you to indulge those feelings under the pretext of being honest. So no, Hannah said, I don't want to hear the whole truth about how you feel. I want to hear what I deserve to hear.

It was this big love that was making her wise. She was opening the gate and letting her maturity wander out onto sunny pastures. Norm took her back to bed. He turned her over. She was lying on her stomach and Norm was on top of her. He fit the contours of her body like a hand on a breast. His breath was warm on her cheek. His cock was like a torch filling her with light.

Tell me something, he said.

I want to have a baby with you, baby.

I know you do. Now tell me something I don't already know, he said. Tell me what this feels like.

Norm's request made her feel self-conscious. Hannah's mind went blank and she felt dull, uninteresting, like she was letting him down. She wanted to say something smart, something beautiful, to capture the moment. She didn't answer Norm right away, and then she forgot to answer him at all. She gave into the gentle, absent-minded rhythm of their bodies. She hardly even noticed when, after a while, she said, Your skin's so warm, babe. I can hardly feel it against my own. I feel like there's no one here but me.

The next morning, Hannah went up behind Norm, who was doing the dishes, and rested her cheek between his shoulder blades. She'd never known a body to give off so much literal good feeling. His body made hers buzz, made it feel urgent. He was the only man she'd ever wanted to have a baby with – she'd waited so long and been so careful about this, not getting pregnant. And now her whole body was singing, it's time. Singing it like a holy-roller gospel choir. They'd joked so often about having a child. Norm called him Lefty. If they burnt a piece of meat, Norm would say, Lefty'll eat it. So Hannah suspected him of wanting a baby too, beneath the obvious resistance. Whenever she brought up the topic in a serious fashion, he'd ask her to stop pressuring him, but she needed him to make a decision soon. She was thirty-six years old. Last night, she'd had another dream about having a baby. It was theirs – plump, about seven years old at birth, with an old man's face and the small busy hands of a squirrel. Hannah closed her eyes and said, So, Norm, are we ever going to have a little chomper or what?

Why do you always make it sound like an accusation? he said.

Do you know how ruthlessly I've been trying to be patient here?

But you mention it all the time.

Babe, I'm carrying around a very painful hope.

Hope, Norm said, can make even a kind person disregard all manner of cruelty.

Hannah stood back. And how quickly hope, once spurned, can grow barbed and attack the tender spot where it's been harboured. You can be a pompous ass sometimes, she said, you know that? What's cruel about wanting to have a baby?

Norm sighed at the cupboards. Hannah knew he was longing for more physical space, some sort of escape.

I seem incapable of wanting a child, he said. And I would rather be alone than unhappy.

You're not happy with me? Hannah said. Her skin was prickling.

No, I'm *happy* with you, he said. All I'm saying is, maybe I'm destined to be alone. Because, while the thought of it makes me very sad, it's not at odds with my constitution.

Hannah felt disoriented.

I can't do it, Norm said. I don't think I want to have a baby right now.

But you might at some point?

I can't say. I don't know.

You don't *know*?

Norm shrugged, and the fact that it seemed so willful – like a decision, not an incapacity – as if he was *feigning* helplessness – infuriated her. His refusal struck her as close-minded, a stubborn lack of effort. She felt betrayed. But we've had a running joke, she said. The whole time we've been together. You've laughed every time I've asked you.

Because you ask me in your baby voice.

I use that voice, she said, to express my most – there's nothing lighthearted about it!

Norm curled his hands over the edge of the sink. He looked down at the last grey bubbles on the surface of the dirty dishwater.

I want you to *think* about this, Hannah said.

I *have* thought about it, he said. I can't do it.

This was new. Norm's certainty seemed to be coming out of nowhere and it seemed to her it couldn't be influenced. It seemed to have no real source or discernible cause. Nothing to attack or criticize. It made Hannah panic. Her hope had given her such confidence, and to feel that she'd been so far off the mark. She wanted to hit him.

The way Norm looked at her made her wonder if her face had turned ugly at that moment. Why are you asking me to prove my love in such a predictable way, he said, when neither of us aspires to be conventional?

Is your life so precious, she said, you can't afford to?

Actually, money *is* an issue, Norm said. Neither of us has any of it, unless one of us produces a bestseller. I have the teaching, but it's not a full-time career. I know what it feels like to be miserable, Hannah, and I'm happy right now. I don't want to jeopardize that.

Maybe a baby would make you even happier.

Maybe, Norm said, cupping his hands as if they held the answer. But I suspect the opposite. Why can't you just accept that this is my decision?

Because I don't think this is inevitable! I think the opposite is inevitable.

Norm closed his eyes and exhaled. I don't want to force you to make a decision you don't want to make either. You could have kids with somebody else.

Somebody *else*?

The room shrunk, then restored itself. A passing streetcar made the apartment tremble. I've come through everything in my life to arrive at *this*? Hannah thought. I've always wanted to have kids, she said carefully. I took it for granted that I would. But I wasn't reckless. It was never the right time. Not until now. But now, suddenly, I'm not allowed? It's the last thing I expected. To be denied when I had finally arrived at what I thought was the right place. You've broken my heart, Norm.

Hannah stood there for a while longer. When she understood that Norm wasn't going to say anything, she felt an awful pressure, like lead being packed behind her eyes. She left the kitchen and fell onto the futon.

She was still crying when he brought her a cup of coffee with steamed milk and two pieces of toast, cut on the diagonal and fanned out on a plate with a royal blue napkin wrapped around a silver knife, and a little jar of jam she'd saved from a hotel and left in the door of the fridge, to be forgotten until now. She was sitting so limply on the edge of the bed, it was as if she sat there only by coincidence of her vertebrae being stacked. She felt drained and exhausted. This was a new kind of grief he was causing her, and he must have known it, because he looked so sorry. The plate was a peace offering. A delicate, artful arrangement of remorse.

Hannah pushed her hair back and wiped her face. Norm sat down beside her and she leaned her head on him as she ate, feeling her jaw push into his shoulder as she chewed. She understood some things were over now, and that her life would take a new direction. She didn't know where or how, but she was toying with the newness and the adventure of it, instead of dwelling on what she was about to lose. She was in a dream state. It wasn't that bad, but it wasn't real either. She could be civil and magnanimous because it was all melodrama anyways. It was a play, for the meantime. A piece of toast. How nice.

When she was finished, Norm got up and said he was hungry. He was teasing her now. *You* ate, but I didn't.

That's because I was crying, Hannah said, poised and haughty as a child. And the crybaby gets the loaf.

F enton's parents came to the hospital every day, and stayed for long hours, camping out at a hotel room nearby. Any number of a dozen relatives also came and went, people Zeus had never met before but with whom he might share a colourless meal on an orange tray in the cafeteria downstairs. Fenton's sister, Becca, came with her new son, Max, but found it too hard to spend time in palliative with a newborn. She stayed for an hour, then Fenton told her to take Max home. This is no place for a baby, he said, and Rebecca started to cry. Max looked so much like his uncle, but no one dared remark on it. Only Fenton had, once, into the waxy flower-bud of Max's ear, whispered, Are you my reincarnation?

No one questioned Zeus's presence at Fenton's bedside except for one elderly aunt who insisted on expressing her objection. Did we not give him everything a boy could want? she shouted, out in the hall. Fenton could have been a Supreme Court judge! But no, he had to go join the circus. You think this is funny? Do you have any idea what kind of people join the circus? Who is this man anyway? Why is everybody calling him Zeus? And why does he keep holding my nephew's hand?

For the most part, Fenton's family spoke in the gentle, hushed tones of people who realize the end is near and refuse to let anything petty mar the tender atmosphere. There were gifts of muffins and hot coffee, and somebody replaced the empty kleenex box with a fresh one, and somebody else took care of the flowers, pulling out the wilted lilies and leaving the hardy ginger.

Fenton's condition got worse faster than anyone could have predicted. The pneumonia was deep in his lungs and he was too weak to fight it. If only he'd come in sooner, the doctors said. He died just days after arriving in hospital. Zeus stood next to his bed and watched the flame that animated his lover's body sputter and go out. Fenton's parents were there. His mother raised her face to the ceiling. Her mouth opened but no sound came out. His father let out a terrible choked sob and lurched towards the bed, coming in between Zeus and Fenton's body. At some point, a nurse touched Zeus lightly on the waist to move him aside. She removed Fenton's IV and turned off some machines. She looked at Ronald Murch to get the okay, then closed his son's eyes forever.

Zeus left alone and walked home, feeling his way along the street with his skin, like some blind, transparent fish plucked from a deep, frozen pool in a dark cave. Trembling uncontrollably, he spotted Fenton four times. Each time in error. Each time feeling his heart leap into his throat with a longing that was so painful it forced him to clutch his chest and sink down onto the pavement, where people rushed past him, thinking he must be drunk.

~

Without Fenton, the apartment took on an eerie menace – the wigs, the Vaudevillian posters, Fenton's little black slippers. Zeus felt things had to shift immediately. He needed to open the windows, let the air in. He started to strip the bed. He threw off the duvet and yanked the bottom fitted sheet. It ripped in the corner, near where Fenton's head used to rest. Zeus picked Fenton's pillow up off the floor and sat down on the waterbed and held it for a while, bobbing gently. He smoothed the old stained pillow across his lap, then laid his hand in the hollow that Fenton's head had made.

Reaching to unhook the torn corner of the bedsheet, Zeus felt something tucked into the space his weight had pried opened between the wooden frame and the mattress. He pulled it out. A small envelope, yellow with age and creased. There was Fenton's name, in a hand he didn't recognize. Zeus opened it and pulled out a card with Hebrew writing on one side, framed by scrolls and doves and harps. The other side was written in English. *There is a time-honoured Jewish tradition associated with childbirth, for the mother to have with her a Shir LaMa'alot card during labour and delivery. After birth, the card is placed in the baby's bassinet in the hospital and later, in the baby's crib at home. I will lift mine eyes unto the hills, from whence cometh my help.*

Zeus looked up and heard his own sorrowful breathing. His body rocked slightly, with each beat of his heart, his stubborn blood pushing through him rhythmically.

The sun shall not smite thee by day, nor the moon by night. The Lord shall preserve thy going out and thy coming in.

Fenton had kept this card all his life, Zeus thought. He should have had it with him at the hospital. I should give it to his mother.

Zeus started to cry. His *going out* and his *coming in*. Somebody had been watching over Fenton all his life. All Zeus seemed to know was newness and change, and loss. He didn't want to give the card back to Ruth. He wanted to keep it for himself. He wanted to pretend it was his own, that he'd had it since birth. That his own mother had given it to him. Where was she now? Where was Rose? She waited in hope, Zeus knew, for him to call her. That's what she always said. Call me anytime, okay? She loved hearing from him. The door is always open, she'd say. That was something – a kindness she'd always shown him. Rose had wanted to rescue him and perhaps she had, from something worse than what he'd had to endure in Toronto. Perhaps she was all he had now, as good as he could do. Suddenly, he wanted to hear her voice. He wanted to say hi, and sob into the phone that his one true love was dead, that his best and only love was gone.

People gathered for the funeral. Zeus stood at the back of the synagogue and greeted old friends from clown school, nurses who worked at the hospital, and couples whose children he and Fenton had known and had also passed away. It was a big crowd to handle. Zeus accepted their condolences with a dullness that nobody held against him. Just before the service, a Buddhist monk showed up like a giant tiger lily in his orange robes. He stood near the door with a garland of pink and yellow flowers and caused a flurry of people to turn their heads. Zeus walked over and the monk asked if he could speak to Fenton's father. Zeus got Ronald and together they listened to what the monk had to say.

I am honoured to be here in your house of worship, he said in a gentle voice, to remember a dear friend. We were very fond of Fenton at our temple, where he was a devotee for over three years. His humour and humility was an inspiration to us whose great aim in life is to end all suffering through enlightenment and achieve nirvana, or the deliverance of the mind.

The rabbi came over and stood with them, and the monk continued.

But the Buddha also emphasizes the importance of the present life. In Buddhism, we find all social, economic, ethical, and intellectual aspects. How similar to Judaism, I thought, with its numerous directives on how to lead a spiritual life.

The monk passed his garland of flowers to the rabbi. But the Buddha speaks not *only* of the present life, he said. There were lives before birth and there will be lives after death. This is what we call re-becoming. We do not use the word *reincarnation*. When one attains nirvana, there is no more rebirth. We saw in Fenton many qualities of the Buddha. May he reach nirvana! Or failing that, find a good home for re-becoming.

The rabbi thanked him and the monk bowed slightly, then left. Zeus watched as the door opened and the monk was subsumed into the maw of daylight, then closed again, gathering in its oak-panelled arms all the respectable darkness of the synagogue. The rabbi walked over to the bima, where he laid his wreath of fragrant flowers. Zeus suddenly wanted to talk to the monk, but when he reached the door and looked out, he was already halfway down the street. Zeus took a few steps out into the cold air, bent forward with his hands on his knees, and tried not to hyperventilate.

They buried Fenton in an oak casket and Zeus couldn't look at the final resting place so definitively in the ground. He didn't want the memory of it, or the knowledge that Fenton was buried dressed in clothes chosen by his father. Brand new. Probably uncomfortable. He should have been laid to rest in a costume made of swan feathers.

At a distance from the grave, he leaned up against a grey stone angel pitted and flecked with orange lichen and raised his eyes to the sky. It was natural to think that's where Fenton was. Up there, somewhere, because it was infinite space. It was the unknown. It wasn't heaven. It's just that, where else are you supposed to look?

Oh Fenton, he thought, how am I going to survive without you? Where do I go now?

Two men from the funeral came over and lifted him back onto his feet. Had he fallen over? Don't touch me, Zeus said. He felt panicked. I'm sorry, please leave me alone, he begged them, backing away and then stumbling over another grave. Something was happening to him. It made him feel sick. He was somewhere with a huge crowd and loud music and people everywhere, laughing and crying. He was just a boy, he was only fifteen. Of course he didn't understand what was going on. He was confessing to a small group of people that he was worthless. He really felt it, like there was nothing good in him at all. He was sitting on a chair, and people kept putting their hands on him. He remembered that on the floor nearby a woman was lying on her back, shaking like an epileptic. Suddenly, her head and limbs rose off the floor and she cried out as if something was being extracted, a long tapeworm dragged out of her mouth.

War Lord! someone shouted and he didn't understand why. Tim had told him they were going to a special religious service, and had taken him to a conference centre somewhere in the suburbs. Zeus felt like he was losing himself, and it was terrifying, but there was pleasure in it too. He was caught up in the emotional swell, feeling the satisfaction of his father's approval. There was a note of triumph in the voices as they prayed for him. It was so loud, he couldn't think.

Do you accept Jesus Christ as your Lord and Saviour, and renounce the devil and all his works?

I do, he'd said, and someone clapped him on the back. More Lord! someone shouted, and he realized it wasn't *war* Lord, it was *more* Lord.

At some point, Tim knelt down in front of him, his face softer with love and approval than Zeus had ever seen it. Son, your life's in God's hands now, he'd said, and you can't go astray. Zeus had tried to get up, but two big men pinned him to the chair, as if they were supporting him, but the next day there were bruises on his arms.

Several hours later, Zeus was standing next to the red-brick fireplace in the Murches' crowded living room, eating a toasted white-bread triangle, spread with chicken liver pâté. He was stroking the edge of the shag carpet with his toes when Ronald Murch came over and handed him a large padded envelope with his name on it, in Fenton's unmistakable hand. Fenton had touched this envelope! Written his name on it! It was like a small resurrection. A white shock of electricity.

Fenton asked me to give this to you.

Zeus stretched his bottom lip into a shield against the physical urge to cry. Ronald held out his hand and they shook, and Zeus knew they would never see each other again.

He moved into the hallway and stood beside the stairs. He stared at the envelope and slowly flipped it twice, got his thumb under the flap and tore it open. Inside was a manila folder and two neat packets of hundred-dollar bills. How much money was that? Zeus removed the folder and opened it and took out the first thing. Attached with a paperclip to a handwritten letter was the colour photocopy of a picture of two people at an outdoor party or a barbecue, drinking beer, a man and a woman in their late thirties, early forties. Zeus was transfixed, felt his legs go weak. Was it a picture of his parents? He could recognize his own features in their faces. They looked happy, a little drunk, laughing and toasting the photographer. His father looked tough but good-humoured, his mother softer, her hair long, still beautiful. Where did Fenton get it? All this time. He'd gone so long without seeing their faces. Zeus sank to his knees at the bottom of the stairs and let the envelope slide onto the floor. He leaned forward on his hands and for the second time that day tried not to hyperventilate.

Ruth Murch rushed past him on the way to the kitchen. She reappeared with a paper bag and, with the top folded over her hand like the petals of a flower, held it to his mouth.

Breathe deeply, she said, and the bag started to shrink and expand with the sound of small breaking twigs. Dark vertical streaks appeared on either side of the bag. His breathing calmed, and Zeus sat back on his feet.

What does the letter say? she said in a soft voice. Is it from Fenton?

He slipped the photograph out from its paperclip and read the letter beneath.

> *My dear Zeus, saviour of my days, companion of my heart, hammiest partner to a Jewish clown like me.*
>
> *I did a little research and came up with this. Your dad, José Gabriel Ortega, got out of prison seven years ago. He and your mother, Frieda Esqualier Monterey, still live in Chimayó. It's a famous Catholic pilgrimage site — of course. Some of its magic must have rubbed off on you, Jésus Gabriel Ortega. You don't know how magic you are. Hey, Zeus. How often have I called you by your proper name without realizing it?*

*I know there's an incomplete equation in you.
Take a break from the hospital. It's not abandonment.
It won't be construed as such. It's time for you to go
home. You need to go find your people. I did some
research on the internet and found your birth records,
and your parents'. I made copies of all the information
I could find. And I made you a map to their house.
That's in the folder as well. So when you go back to
your parents' place I'll be right there with you, in your
hand. I found the picture on google images. I don't
think there's any mistaking they're your mom and dad.
I hope you don't mind that I took this liberty, but I
wanted to leave you with something – something to
head towards after I'm gone.*

*And take the money. It's all I have. Twenty
thousand smackers. When did I stash that away, huh?
Trust a Jew to have a secret pie fund. It's all I have. But
then, so were you.*

*If ever you should wonder, they didn't bury my
heart in a casket, Zeus, because I already gave it to you.
You made a sad clown very happy.*

I love you.
Always and forever,
Fenton Murch.

I t was mid-morning. Connie was standing in the kitchen, her hands resting on a cold bag of milk that was on the counter. She was just about to lift it by the corner and drop it into its tight jug when the doorbell rang. She went to answer it, checking her watch on the way. She needed to pick Theo up from his play date in an hour and a half. Passing the hallway mirror, she noticed how unbrushed her hair was. Her eyes looked puffy. She was wearing sweatpants and a t-shirt. Did I look this shabby when I drove the kids to school this morning? Whatever happens, Connie, she scolded herself, don't you dare let yourself go.

The doorbell rang a second time.

Coming, she said and opened the door. An enormous man in work boots and jeans stood there with a clipboard. In the drive behind him, a long white moving truck. She put her hand to her chest, sucked in a short, quick breath, and took a step backwards. She knew something was unravelling and didn't know how to find the source, to tug it back and keep the rest of her life from coming undone as well.

I've got a court order here to repossess the house, he said and turned the clipboard around and pointed it at her stomach. Sign there. He held out a pen. He wore a name tag that said, *Jim*. She took the pen and signed. How could she not? And then Jim walked past her and four more men came around the door and walked inside.

They wore sandy-coloured work boots and loose jeans, and two had open, long-sleeved checkered shirts over t-shirts. Two of them wore leather weightlifting belts. One had a t-shirt that said, *I offered my honour, she honoured my offer. All night long, I was honour and offer.*

Jim was delegating. You and Stacy start at the top and work your way down. Jackson, you start in the basement. We got five hours and I wanna be outta here on time today. Excuse me, ma'am, but you might wanna get dressed and out of the way if I was you.

Connie hadn't moved.

You don't know what's going on, he said, do you.

Connie shook her head.

Jim made a sucking noise in his mouth. Scumbag, he said. Fucking love this job. Okay, ma'am, so we're here to take all your furnishings and appliances, he said slowly and loudly, as if talking to a deaf person. It's called a repossession. I take it your husband didn't warn you? Which means you didn't get much of a chance to stash anything away, but I'm afraid we can't make any exceptions. Not once we get started. The best thing you can do, little lady, is stay out of our way and let us do our job, okay? That's all it is. At the end of the day, it's just a job. Jim nodded a few times and, satisfied he'd made himself clear, headed down the hall.

From the den, Connie heard him yell, Hey, we got a baby grand in here! Shithouse, go get the hoisters!

Jim came into the kitchen a few minutes later. Connie was standing next to the counter, holding that bag of milk at the end of her arm, unable to move.

Look, lady, Jim said, coming up behind her. He put his hand on her shoulder and Connie spun around and gave him a backhanded slap across the face with that cold, damp bag of milk. In her mind she'd killed him. Smacked everything she'd ever known out of her life. There was no one left to trust.

Jim gave an abrupt laugh, loud and aggressive. Well, fuck me, he said. If you'd'a told me this morning. And then a dark menace passed over his features. You better get dressed, lady, and get the hell outta my way. This house doesn't belong to you anymore.

Rose had offered to come pick up Connie and the kids, over at Mary-Beth's. There wasn't any time for discussion. Mary-Beth held Connie by the shoulders and said, Things have a way of working out.

Connie couldn't pause enough in the moment to feel the reassurance of her friend's faith. All she could do was plead with her eyes and then hug her. Mary-Beth stood in her doorway and waved goodbye.

Her mother was being overly cheerful and she smelled of perfume and her bracelets jangled and she was intent on distraction. She played a CD of children's songs on the car stereo, and they sang 'Skimmery Rinky Dinky Do' over the Malahat while Connie stared at the passing trees, feeling haggard and destroyed. When they arrived at her parents' place, her mother stopped the car and flashed her a look as if everything was *of course* going to be okay. She patted her leg in a way that made

Connie flinch, then bundled the children out of the car and into the house and set about getting dinner ready and making up extra beds.

After dinner, the kids went upstairs to watch a movie in their grandparents' bedroom. In the kitchen, Rose needled Connie with statements about how she must be feeling this or must be feeling that. Connie hated how her mother's attempts at empathy always sounded instead like a projection of her own emotions. While Rose made tea, Connie leaned forward with her elbows on the counter and held her head. How at once selfless and narcissistic a mother's love can be. There was so much about each other that she and her mother didn't know. Will I be the same with my own children? Connie wondered. She wished, with an intensity she could feel in her body, to be better than that.

Her dad came home and they sat in the living room and Connie told her parents about the man with the clipboard and the moving truck, how they'd taken things right off the walls, emptied drawers onto the floor, stripped the beds and taken the mattresses. Rose started to cry, and Tim pinched the bridge of his nose and kept his eyes closed while he said, They couldn't have taken everything. When are you allowed to go back and get the rest of your stuff?

I've got forty-eight hours to rent a U-Haul trailer, Connie said.

Okay, Tim said. We'll help you with that in the morning.

And then, defeated, Connie lay down on the couch and fell asleep for forty-five minutes and woke abruptly.

It was dark outside. Across the living room, her mother was knitting a child's sweater. Rose lifted the strand of wool and pulled another length out of a plastic bag at her feet. Feel better? she asked.

Not really, Connie said.

The furnace kicked in and the forced air blew, warm and dry, into the house. Her father came down the stairs. They're all asleep, he said. I told them a bedtime story about a boy on a flying ship who made his own wind by eating cans of beans and sailed all over the world. Tim chuckled and went into the kitchen to make a cup of tea. Connie realized that her father was getting old. He was drifting towards jolly distractedness, and she wanted to catch him before he got there and say, I love you.

Have I ever told you, Rose said, how I started a Bible study with a bunch of women in the neighbourhood when you and Hannah were very young and we were living in Tsawwassen?

Connie nodded. She always found these artificial gambits of her mother's slightly annoying. Rose had something to tell her and this is how she'd start it.

I didn't think I could do it, Rose said. I mean, who was I? What did I know about the Bible? I wasn't an expert. But I said, God, if you want me to do this, I will. If there's any interest at all, then I'll go ahead with it. So I started spreading the word, and within two weeks there were eight women coming to the house, once a week, with their kids in tow, and sandwiches, and their New Testament Bibles.

Dad must have loved that, Connie said.

Well, he was doing his theological degree, so he was away a lot of the time.

Little did he know, his wife was getting her own degree at home.

Six out of the eight women converted, Con.

That's great, Mom, she said, letting her head fall back on the sofa.

The point is, Rose said. There was this one woman, Sheryl.

The one with six Doberman pinchers.

Yes, that's right. Well, one night her house got ransacked by evil spirits. The whole house turned upside down – furniture knocked over, things tossed everywhere – but those dogs of hers never woke up. Sheryl got up in the morning and found her house like that and came shrieking over to our place. So we prayed. But how do you pray for a woman whose house has just been ransacked by evil spirits?

Connie marvelled at her mother's usual lack of sensitivity. I'm sure there's a manual somewhere, she said.

And then a week later, Joanne, this other woman, she came racing over to tell me that her house was shaking with demons too. So we ran over there with salt and bread and a cross and my Bible, only to find that her washing machine was off balance and making an almighty clatter in the basement! Oh, how we laughed! We just collapsed in fits of giggles right there on her front lawn.

That's pretty funny, Connie said and felt a sudden hard clang of sadness for having loosened up for a moment and let her defences down. If she'd felt safe enough, she would have cried in front of her mother endlessly, but instead she needed to be hard. Her hardness is what was keeping everything together.

Tim came out of the kitchen and gave Rose a kiss, then Connie. Goodnight, daughter, he said. God bless. And he went upstairs to bed. Connie knew that he was concerned about her situation, maybe even deeply, but wished, just this once, that he'd express it. His composure sometimes felt like a deliberate blindness, and it hurt her now.

Rose tugged more wool out of the bag and resumed her knitting. All I'm saying is, it was a very high time for me *spiritually*. I loved being in the thick of it, out on the front line like that – and it came after the worst time in my life, Connie. The lowest I've ever been. I was so depressed in the months after I had you.

I know, I know.

Rose looked up again and rested her hands on her lap. It was terrible. I thought I'd have to check myself into a hospital, it was that bad. And I remember praying to God to show me his love or else I don't know what I would have done. Then I got pregnant with Hannah and I thought, this is it. I've just about had it. I think I wanted to die.

Rose tilted her head and smiled with the uncomfortable exposure of such a confession. So I was praying like stink, she said, just praying and begging God to send me a sign. And he *did*. I remember it so clearly. I felt so certain of his love for me. I don't know how else to describe it. And then that certainty kind of faded. And I never really felt it again until five years ago when I went, with a delegation from our church, to the Kingdom of Salvation Center in Wichita.

I *know* that, Mom, Connie said. And you've been talking about it ever since. I *know* how good it was for you. Why are you telling me all of this right now?

It's just that I felt the most powerful manifestations of the Spirit there, Con. The Lord was really present to me, and I think he'd be present to you too. They have a prophetic ministry service there, and God has been speaking for a long time, directly through their prayer counsellors, sending out some really transformative stuff. It might just help you deal with what's going on right now. You could take Hannah with you. She's living off a grant this year. She's got no kids. Her schedule is completely flexible. When was the last time you two girls spent any quality time together?

Is this all you're ever going to say when something goes wrong? Go to the Salvation Center?

I just think you might really benefit from going, Rose said earnestly. I've been thinking about this for so long, and now –

Benefit? Connie said. Because I could stand to do with a few improvements? You think this is *my* fault? Why is your advice always so loaded with criticism? Why do you have to be so controlling?

I'm not trying to control you, Rose said.

No, you just want me to go to this crazy mega-church and have the exact same experience you did, so – what? So you can take the credit for my spiritual recuperation?

It's not about taking credit, Rose said. I'm just trying to help.

You don't even know *how* to help.

Well then, *show* me. I feel so helpless sometimes. It's so hard to know what you need.

What about *listening* for a change?

I'm listening all the time! I got a call from Zeus today. The defensiveness had suddenly dropped out of her voice.

Zeus?

I haven't heard from him in ages. Rose looked so hopeful and excited.

Well, what do you expect? Connie said. When you guys found out he was gay, all you did was make him feel sinful.

That's not true!

Well, you didn't exactly *embrace* it. It obviously became impossible for him to stay, because who leaves home at the age of fifteen?

I'm not the same woman I used to be! Rose shouted and started to cry. All I've ever wanted is for my children to be happy.

But Zeus was your child too. You *adopted* him.

I know I failed him, Rose said. You don't think I know that?

Rose cried often, and her face immediately showed all the signs. It was almost flagrant how puffy her eyes got, how pink her nostrils looked. She put a hand on her chest and started to wheeze. Stress of any kind always triggered her asthma. She stood up stiffly and went into the bathroom. Connie heard the mirror open and the puff of her Ventolin, followed by the deep inhalation.

After a while, her mother came back into the living room. She looked unreachable, like someone travelling across an empty landscape. Connie didn't enjoy hurting her mother. It made her feel awful, but she couldn't banish her own cruelty and impatience. Why are you always trying to *fix* everyone? she said. Why can't you just support me without shoving your opinions in my face?

I'm not trying to fix anyone, Con, that's not what I'm saying. Rose looked so injured. This is just something I thought would be really good for you. Something I wanted us to share.

Connie pulled her hair back away from her face.

You don't have to go – Rose took another quick suck on the little snorkel of her inhaler – it was just a suggestion.

Sure, let me just take a thousand dollars out of my non-existent bank account, leave my three children, and fly off to Wichita.

I was thinking *I'd* pay for the trip. You know I've saved up a little, and nothing would make me happier. Think of it as a favour you'd be doing me, Rose said and gave Connie a weak grin.

A favour? Connie said. You want me to do *you* a favour at a time like this? This is *my* crisis, Mom. It's not yours. See what I mean?

There was silence for a long time. One of the children upstairs cried out in their sleep.

Let's just talk about it in the morning, Rose said, and Connie immediately felt a profound need to sleep.

The next morning, she came down for breakfast, headachey and nauseated from lack of sleep. On the table were three bowls with the remains of cereal, half-drunk glasses of milk. Rose was just cleaning up. She stopped when Connie entered the kitchen and wiped her hands with a dish towel. She watched Connie take a seat.

Zeus wants to go see his birth parents, Rose said. And he asked me what I thought, and I hesitated to encourage him. But I think I was wrong. Of course it's what every child needs – to know their parents. I've been thinking about this all night and I want you to think about it too.

Think about what? Connie said. She was distracted by the noise of the TV in the background. The volume was on way too high. What about his boyfriend? she said. Doesn't he have a boyfriend?

He just died.

Really? Oh no, poor thing.

Rose passed her half a grapefruit in a bowl.

We've never been much good to him as sisters.

Well, now's your chance, Rose said.

What can *we* do?

I don't know, Rose said. But I was thinking if the three of you drove together to Wichita, it would be a chance to re-connect with him, and then you'd at least be taking him part of the way to New Mexico. You could fly to Toronto, get Hannah, drive to Chicago, pick up Zeus, and head down to Kansas.

Connie stared at her mother in disbelief.

I'll pay for it, Rose said. Your ticket, the rental, and money for gas, the lot of it.

Whoa, whoa, whoa, Connie said. I can't really see this happening. Honestly, Mom.

Hannah would agree if you asked her to do it for you. She loves road trips. Besides, she's always had a soft spot for Zeus, you know? She's more loyal than you give her credit for. Rose turned and resumed washing the dishes.

You and Hannah were so different growing up, she said, looking out the window. Hannah always so lost in her imagination. There was never anything quite as compelling as the stories she conjured up for herself. You, on the other hand, Rose said, turning back to Connie and drying her hands. You've always been so grounded. You didn't like to be caught off guard. You hated surprises. I remember thinking, Con will never be impulsive, but she'll always be prepared.

I've never been prepared for anything in my life, Connie said.

That's not true. You're a great planner, and things have pretty much turned out the way you wanted them to.

Connie leaned forward and stared into the glistening intricacy of her half-eaten grapefruit. I never planned to go bankrupt, she said, then straightened up. Why am I even thinking about this? Have you forgotten what just happened to me? Where am I going to live? How am I going to pay the bills? Where's Harlan? I don't even know where my husband is!

Rose passed Connie a mug of coffee. You're just going to have to be patient for a little while about a lot of things.

Connie looked at her mother and clenched her jaw. What about the kids?

We'll take care of them, Rose said. She was gaining ground, and she knew it.

And you think Zeus is just going to buy into this sudden family convoy?

There's only one way to find out.

Don't you think, Connie said, that what I need right now is to stay and try to work things out with Harl? Shouldn't I be out looking for him?

You won't find him if he's not ready to be found.

What if he needs me right now?

He needs to hit rock bottom is what he needs. And then he needs to pick himself up again.

It was true, the last thing she really wanted to do, right now, was talk to Harl. Let him rot over there for a while at his sister's place, if that's where he was, in that sour and smoky living room, drinking a Kokanee, with the TV on full blast.

Rose stood behind her daughter and put her hands on her shoulders. This will be something good for you, for all three of you, whether you know it or not. Rose was massaging her shoulders.

Emma called her from the living room, but Connie didn't want to move. Emma and Theo came into the kitchen, both talking at the same time about what cartoons they wanted to watch and who was allowed to use the remote control. They stood very close and Connie stroked their soft faces and said, in a gentle voice, that she'd be there in a minute. When they were gone, she asked her mother, And what if I decide not to go?

Nothing changes if you don't give it a chance to change, Rose said and kissed the top of her daughter's head.

2

H annah and Connie carried their luggage through Chinatown. They were waiting at the corner of an intersection for the light to change. Beside them was a pet store. In the window sat a fat brown bunny, its nose twitching rhythmically. Connie was tired from her flight the night before, and the time change, and perhaps that was why she found it so impossibly sad to see this flaccid bunny on sale, first thing in the morning, with a price tag for twelve dollars. Today was Halloween, and above the rabbit, the cardboard cutout of a witch on her broom hung from the ceiling by a string, rotating in the circulating air.

I don't know how I can persist in loving Norm as much as I do, Hannah blurted, when he's causing me so much grief.

Well, at least you know you *love* him, Connie said wearily. The light turned green and somewhere behind her a man whistled and it made Connie stiffen. Then she realized it was the crossing signal for the blind.

I just can't reconcile how really life-affirming this relationship has been for me, Hannah went on, with his refusal to have a child. It's like a death ship at the centre of something really beautiful.

Death ship? Connie asked. Her sister could be so melodramatic. Don't you realize, she said, that everybody's just trying to reconcile all the time the good aspects of their lives with what they hate about it too?

Connie didn't sound very sympathetic, Hannah thought, but then she understood she was probably thinking about her own situation. She'd noticed how sad Connie looked when they left the apartment. Norm had made a big show of saying goodbye to her in front of her sister, and it made her feel sorry for Connie.

It had taken them only five days to plan the trip, from the moment Connie called her until now. She liked the idea of being there for her sister, who rarely, if ever, appealed to her for help. She hadn't seen Connie in a long time and was amazed by what was happening to her. To have your house repossessed, and all the things you thought you owned? It was unbelievable. She'd never had the luxury of having any money to lose. It had always been a struggle.

Besides, now was as good a time as any for a getaway. She wanted Norm to stew over the baby thing – and she really liked the idea of seeing Zeus again. Connie had asked her to call him, and she'd agreed. Then she and Connie had talked about how Hannah should introduce herself after so long and what to say to him. When they'd come up with a plan, she made the call and found Zeus easy to talk to and open to their offer of getting him at least part of the way to New Mexico. The last time she saw him, he was fourteen and still living with her parents in Toronto. She'd been visiting from London and had taken him to her favourite bakery on Queen Street, where they sat by the window and ordered mint tea and ginger muffins with lemon curd. It was an incredibly sunny day and she remembered how the yellow curd had gleamed like amber. Zeus had hung on her every word – aloof and yet with a smouldering intensity that signalled he was in need of attention himself.

He'd carefully smoothed the lacquered curd across the open face of his muffin, then offered to roll a joint.

My God, Zeus, she said, how old are you?

I'm fourteen, he said.

I guess that's about as old as we ever get.

Look at me, he said, shrugging helplessly. I live in a rectory. I don't have many friends.

When they got up, Hannah had hugged him, exuberantly, then felt silly because she hardly knew him. They left the bakery and she said, Come on, and took him to the roof of an old warehouse downtown, where they sat looking out over the skyline and got high. It started to get dark and a fog came in off the lake in a milky haze, blurring the bright billboards and neon ads. They could just make out the name of the Sutton Place Hotel. The letters seemed to hover in the air, attached to nothing, like the lurid dreamscape of a futuristic city. They rechristened it Mutton Face, then the Lamb Chop Hotel. They spoke in cat and dog noises. They talked about staging an opera consisting entirely of barks and meows and police sirens. Hannah da-da-dee'd the finale to *Turandot* while Zeus swung one-handed from the fire escape. They both froze and stared when his trucker's cap came off and floated down to rest on a flat expanse of pebbled roof twenty feet below.

How could Hannah have forgotten about a boy like that? What monkey selfishness was she carrying around on her back that she hadn't considered his need for a phone call once in a while? She hadn't bothered, not once, to go see him. She was pulling these memories out like the soft ear of some forgotten pocket of her past and feeling remorse for not having taken her role as a big sister more seriously. She would go with him and her sister to Kansas. She would make amends. She would think about calling Caiden Brock. He and Julia live in Wichita now, Connie had said. Apparently, they had three boys, that's what Mom had told Connie.

Caiden's parents were friends of the family, and whenever they'd come over to visit, Caiden would pull her aside when no one was looking and feel her up. He had his foot in her crotch at Christmas dinner one year, the whole time under the table. It turned her on so much. But she was so young – just thirteen, fourteen – and he was nine years older. Hannah didn't know what to do. He'd come by the house and take her for a ride on his motorcycle, then drop her off and leave. It drove her wild with helplessness. She wasn't sure he was interested in talking to her at all. She just wanted him to keep doing those things to her body. She used to like going to his parents' place, even when he wasn't there, because his mother would always pamper her. She'd order Chinese food. They never had food like that at home. Mrs. Brock was the only person she'd ever heard speak in tongues. It happened in her living room. Hannah hadn't wanted to be rude, so she pretended to be moved.

There was another time she faked it, at Anglican summer camp. Caiden was there as a camp counsellor. They sat together at the big final worship service, where all these urban kids from non-religious families were getting up and approaching the rustic communion rail to be saved and converted. Hannah wanted to show him how spiritually deep she was so pretended to be having a religious experience. She even stood up and lifted her hands into the air and pretended to cry a little.

Nothing like this was going to happen at that church on the outskirts of Wichita because she had no intention of actually going inside, but something about the trip excited her. Something about a bland life having no taste. Like the white of an egg, she thought, noticing a box full of quail's eggs that an old man was selling. He was sitting on a red bucket, the eggs on an up-ended wooden crate. Beside him, a woman selling tiny bird's-eye chili peppers out of a styrofoam take-out container.

I need to go to the bank, Connie said, and exchange some money. Are you taking any cash?

Hannah shook her head. I booked us a rental and got CAA maps, so don't go faulting me, as usual, for doing nothing.

Let's try not to fault each other for anything on this trip, okay?

Hannah said she was fine with that, and soon they were crossing a nearly empty lot towards a car rental office. This is the place you chose? Connie said. It looked dilapidated.

Hannah said she'd reserved a Prius, but they couldn't see a Prius anywhere. The only two vehicles in the lot were a Cadillac and a small, brand-new, white pickup truck. They got a really cheap deal on the truck, a Ford Ranger, and this is what they took.

Connie was too tired to drive and complained of having to do so much of it at home, so Hannah drove, aggressively and with the lock-jawed concentration of someone who rarely drives. They lurched and bolted their way out of the city. Traffic thinned past the suburbs, and after an hour or so, they started to come across open farmland. Properties divided by a single line of trees, their trunks grey and black, like fences made of tarnished cutlery. Here and there, marooned in the fields, small islands of green conifers. In the shelter of a long escarpment, the trees still dark red and orange.

Connie was leaning against the door, her cheek resting against the cold glass. Her body gave a sudden jolt. In a fraction of a second she'd imagined it – sucked out onto the shoulder, the rip and claw of gravel as she hit the ditch. I thought the door was swinging open, she said. Once again, she double-checked the power locks by pressing the switch four times.

That's the third time you've done that since we got in, Hannah said.

Is it? Connie said distractedly. Her thoughts were elsewhere. She was missing her children, their ripe pear-scented breath. And then she conceded. I don't know why I'm so nervous, she said.

It comes from trying to conceal a desperation, Hannah said. You know, the loss of all your worldly possessions? Maybe you just need to let it go and grieve.

What, and make the tragic spectacle of my life even more public?

I'm not public, Hannah said.

Look, I can only behave the way I know how to behave, Connie said. And at the moment, I'd rather keep my feelings to myself.

Sorry, Hannah said.

Connie didn't want to open up to her sister but found she couldn't help herself. I don't want to care about the house, she confessed, but it's crushing me.

Maybe it's good not to get so attached to that kind of thing, Hannah said.

Well, of course I was attached! I know that's hard for you bohemian types to understand, but I was very attached to the way things were. My house, and my family in it. It took me years to collect all that stuff, my artwork, my furniture, my rugs. I don't care if it seems shallow and unenlightened, but it really hurts to lose it all now. I used to look around the house and think, oh yeah, this is who I am. This is what I've built with my life.

So do you think people who haven't amassed all that stuff haven't built anything with their lives?

No, all I'm saying is that, for me, it was reassuring.

Hannah had, on more than one occasion, rolled her eyes at her sister's big house and fancy cars and closet full of expensive clothes. She'd once stood in Connie's closet and stroked one of her folded cashmere sweaters and heard the muted crinkle of tissue paper beneath the exquisite wool. The price tag was still on. Connie's lifestyle was excessive, and Hannah felt her sister wasn't even aware of this. And it seemed odd, especially in light of her Christian faith. But, in fact, Hannah *was* sympathetic to the material – the need for embellishment, to make things beautiful – and often found the most heartbreaking vulnerability to be expressed through the material, especially when money was scarce. In the acquisition of a thing that had no intrinsic value but could cause such joy. Her mother had once made a special trip to IKEA to buy some pretty paper napkins that were on sale for half-price. It was a trivial gesture pinned to the hope of something small and sweet, to be available at some future opportunity for hospitality. This was the kind of thing that made Hannah want to weep. I mean, Hannah said. And then she didn't know what to say.

Connie felt unfairly criticized and had retreated into angry silence. Why did her sister insist on challenging her, and at such a low point? Her anger kept ricocheting between what she knew to be Harlan's failure and what she perceived to be her own. She was angry that the man she had chosen to marry had screwed up so badly, but what did it say about her own judgment? She had tried to avoid weakness, but that's exactly what she'd married into. And she was at a loss now to explain how she could have been so wrong about the quality that lay barely beneath the surface of her own life. Look, Connie said, I just want to meditate quietly on the landscape, if that's okay with you.

I never said it wasn't, Hannah said and wondered why she couldn't be soft.

I'm trying to get the colours right, Connie said, and it took all her concentration not to cry. The late October sky was like milk with a drop of blue paint in it. The ground scrubby, the fields shaved and corrugated. Buzzed rows of mustard-coloured stalks. Last night's rain had left ribbons of bright water in the furrows, like incisions revealing another sky that lay beneath the earth.

They drove on broodingly, past some crows yelling at each other in a field. I made a road trip CD, Hannah said and reached for her bag. Can you get it for me?

Nick Cave sang a woeful, gritty ballad.

Hannah took a quick look at her sister. She was tolerating the music. I had a dream last night, Hannah said, about Emma.

Connie closed her eyes.

I dreamt she was having a baby.

Do I want to hear this?

No, Hannah said, probably not. And it was true, the dream had been lurid. There were some body parts in a bag, a T-bone steak, which was part of the new baby. Emma was giving birth and her little right leg was deflated like the finger of an empty rubber glove. She was holding her hands above her head and trying to squeeze the baby out. The dream had made Hannah feel dirty, for having such thoughts about her niece, with their implication of sex and adult behaviour, but then she'd realized what it was all about. Of course the dream had nothing to do with Emma, Hannah said. It's about my own thwarted desire to have a baby, that's all.

Connie was silent, then said, I can't be casual about my children, okay? I just can't be. And I would like you to exercise some restraint about the things you tell me on this trip. I want you, just a little, if it's possible, to take my feelings into account. I mean, my situation – is that going to be too hard for you?

No, Hannah said. I just keep forgetting, okay? Her sister could be so severe. You know, Harlan doesn't need to be damned, she said. He's not a bad man.

I'm not even thinking about him, Connie said, and again she felt the painful vulnerability of talking about her intimate life, and yet she was compelled. It had something to do with a desire to be known. *To be known.* Now that would compensate a little for this feeling of fear. It's just that being a mother is so terrifying at times, she said, and as soon as she did, she was flooded with the reassuring confidence of love. That's what being a mother was like too, she thought, overruled constantly by love. Emma's getting really independent, she said. She's so headstrong. I overheard her talking to some of her little friends recently about how she crosses the street with her eyes closed and that she's never been hit by a car. This totally freaked me out, of course, but it also made me think how for some people the prospect of opening their eyes is more terrifying than keeping them shut.

Sometimes I think we all live by faith when we're children, Hannah said, and then spend the rest of our adult lives trying to regain that trust.

The sun had punched through the clouds and the sisters drove through a pulsing corridor of tall dark trees and came out along some more shorn fields. Long, straight alleys of bright yellow stalks slid and stretched, then flashed by, one after another. They stopped for tea at Tim Hortons and Connie wandered out alone behind the squat, brown-brick building. The back half was made of grey cinder blocks. Beyond it, an empty trailer park, the grass wet and shiny like fish scales. A little mirrored pond where the ground had been flooded, yellow leaves in the clear water, still as fossils. Her best audience wasn't there to witness this and somehow that's what made things real, was sharing them with Harlan and the kids. Without them the world felt insubstantial, made of theatrical sets and facades. Like this building, the best bricks reserved for the front, the rest just cinder blocks. Cinder blocks! They might as well have been selling doughnuts out of a bunker. She looked up and the landscape looked stripped and abandoned. Would she ever get her family back together again?

They got back into the truck and the sun was dazzling overhead. Silver flashed off the chrome parts of the cars on the highway. The woods looked purple and rust-coloured, the grasses brown and ochre. The zinc dome of an old silo flared like a lighthouse in the distance, marking the end of the fields. The sisters were coming into a suburb. They got off the 401 and took Highway 3. After a while, Connie noticed a sign for the American border at Ambassador Bridge.

They drove past the duty-free shop, then Hannah slowed the truck to get in line. She reached for her bag. Connie, too, was getting her passport out. They pulled up to a booth and a border guard stepped out. Where y'all headed?

Chicago, Hannah said.

What's in Chicago?

Our brother, she said and it felt strange. She wasn't in the habit of mentioning a brother.

The border guard requested their passports and handed

them to another officer sitting in the booth behind him. He put his hand on the roof of the truck and stooped to look into the cab at Connie. She wasn't looking at him. She was looking across the pavement at a young couple with a child. They were standing next to an old, dark green Volvo while four officers pulled the seats out of their car.

The border guard straightened up. He was broad in the middle, and around his waist he wore a black belt with pouches, nightstick, and gun. He strolled down the length of the truck and back again. You carrying any firearms?

Hannah shook her head.

What's in the storage box?

Nothing, as far as I know.

Is it locked?

Hannah pulled the keys out of the ignition and handed them over. It's that one, I think. There was a small key for a padlock on the ring. When they'd rented the truck, they'd put their bags behind the front seats and neither of them had checked the storage box.

The border guard stayed where he was, leaning up against the truck. He sucked on his teeth, then sauntered to the back, pulled down the tailgate, and got up onto the bed. The truck dipped and bounced. He unlocked the storage box and lifted the lid. The sisters sat still and sullen, as if they were strangers to each other. The border guard got down and the truck rocked like a small sailboat. He took his time talking, with his back turned, to the other officer in the booth.

Okay, he said, handing the keys and their passports through the window. You're good to go.

There was exhilaration and relief as they drove into the States, and towards their imminent reunion with Zeus, but immediately there were roadworks, so Hannah took a marked detour around Detroit — following a long, sweeping curve of orange pylons — and slipped under a railroad overpass made of iron panels, rusted a solid reddish brown and covered in graffiti.

Why did you say Chicago? Connie asked her sister. And not Wichita?

I thought the Global Kingdom of Salvation Center would be harder to explain than going to visit our brother, if it came up, she said and followed the arrows onto Warren Street and soon they found themselves driving through a residential neighbourhood. It was cloudy again now, grey and cold.

It was weird hearing you say our brother, Connie said.

It was weird *saying* it.

I still can't believe we're doing this.

I know, Hannah said. I'm surprised Zeus agreed to be picked up at all.

Zeus, Connie said. What a name to have.

We gave it to him, don't you remember?

No.

When he first arrived at Mom and Dad's, that first Christmas he was in Toronto. We told him he had to change his name or else the kids at school were going to call him *cheeses.* Hey, cheeses! But he kept insisting, do you remember this? My name's Jésus! And he'd pronounce it the way you say it in Spanish. And that's when I said to him, Zeus! That's what you've got to call yourself. Then it'll be like, hey, Zeus, in the schoolyard, and the kids would be pronouncing his name properly, and they wouldn't even know it.

Connie gave a huff of recognition. Oh yeah, now I remember.

They were still following the detour, and the houses along the street were old, red brick. Large houses with gabled windows and gingerbread trim and wide, flat overgrown lawns.

Some of the houses were boarded up, others had broken windows, caved-in porches, mossy roofs. It would have been a well-to-do neighbourhood once, but it was derelict now. It went on for miles.

What if he's chickened out, Connie said, and he's not there when we get to his place? What if he lives in a neighbourhood like this – look.

Connie pointed to a house. One side of it was charred and the sky was visible through an upstairs window, but the house still looked inhabited. A stained mattress hung over the porch railing. A small carved pumpkin on the front steps. At the next red light, they watched a grey-haired black man, in blue sweatpants and a mustard-coloured trench coat, push a rusty lawnmower across an empty lot. Where the engine would normally be was what looked like the white perforated tub from a washing machine. Through the pattern of holes, the orange flames of a small fire flickered on and off. It was a portable campfire and the man was wheeling it somewhere as it burned.

Connie hugged herself, feeling a chill. Hannah turned the heat up. Two women on the sidewalk trying to carry a broken-down sofa. A young man with a skinny dog walking slowly, as if he had no place to be. All this poverty, Connie said.

They passed the side of a building that had a weathered mural of a Latino-looking Jesus.

Remember what it was like when Dad decided to move us all to Montreal? Hannah said. I sort of fell in love with it the moment I saw it, which is kind of weird. I mean, for a kid to fall in love with a city?

It's a decadent and historical place, Connie said. Of course you loved it.

It was a new kind of vibe for us, wasn't it? Suddenly, we were hanging out with kids whose parents drank and smoked, and ate hotdogs that got delivered to their door in little white paper bags. And their fathers probably went to those strip clubs Mom and Dad objected to so strongly. Didn't they organize a protest through the church once?

The signs were too graphic, Connie said. That's what they were trying to get changed.

I remember sleeping over at this friend's house, and in the morning her mom made me a baloney sandwich on white bread to take to school and when I ate it, it tasted like cigarette smoke.

They got back on the highway and the world appeared unthreatening again. Connie took out her cell phone. I just found all that stuff kind of intimidating, she said, calling their parents' place to speak to her kids. You guys all sorted out with your costumes? Connie said. Well, why don't you ask her that yourself? I love you too, sweetie pie. And remember, no candy until you get home and Nana's checked it for you, okay? Her voice was so tender and affectionate towards her children that it gave Hannah a pang.

After another half-hour or so, they passed a large, unpainted wooden church with a wide, uneven strip of green down its side. One man at the top of a ladder, with a single can of paint. That's a totally ridiculous way of going about painting a building that size, Connie said.

Maybe, Hannah said, he considers it to be an expression of his devotion.

I think *faith* is the best expression of devotion, Connie said.

Of course you do.

What's that supposed to mean?

Well, maybe we're not all equally predisposed to having faith. Maybe it's predetermined by our character.

No, Connie said, it's about choice and free will.

Maybe it's about temperament, Hannah said.

Faith has nothing to do with temperament. Faith *overrides* temperament.

Are you kidding me? Faith is an *outcome* of temperament. You're religious, Connie, because you have a religious temperament, and I'm not because I don't. We've got no choice in the matter. And it drives me crazy how often faith gets disguised as a kind of humility.

Connie threw up her hands and gave a little growl of frustration. It's not your temperament, Hannah, it's your pride. That's what's standing in the way.

In the way of what? Being grateful for having a flawed design. Look, she said, if God created me, then he planted the idea of immortality in my head — he made me at least smart enough to imagine it — but he didn't give me the means of achieving it, unless I confess to being a worthless sinner and *needing* him. What kind of glorious creation does that make me?

Connie was shaking her head. None of that has anything to do with faith.

You shoplift a chocolate bar when you're five years old, Hannah said, and there goes your perfection and immortality right there.

You know, Connie said, combing her hair back with her hands, you can intellectualize until the cows come home, Hannah, but faith is a mystery. That's why it's so impossible to describe, and why it transforms those who have it and baffles those who don't.

Connie was looking at her sister's profile, so foreign and familiar at the same time. It was a face she loved and could provoke such annoyance. Maybe you keep having to walk through doors all your life, she said. Because I feel like I've walked through them before. But then maybe I haven't. Maybe this trip is going to be a chance to do what I've only *thought* I've done in the past. Leave everything behind – my fear and all my security? My *wealth?* Connie said and her voice was pleading. Because I'm right here, aren't I? Out of my depth. Out of my comfort zone. Riding in this ridiculous pickup truck with you, and I'm sitting here and it's hot and stuffy now, and it stinks because I think you just farted, and all you see is some kind of giving over on my part and not the courage I feel this requires.

Hannah lowered her window and felt bad. She didn't want to be cynical, but still she had no compulsion to cross over into her sister's camp. If at any point in her life she'd had any certainty about it, she would've been a Christian in a heartbeat.

On the dashboard, next to the stereo, was a button with the little symbol of a smoking cigarette. Connie pushed it in and when it popped, she said, I didn't think cars still came with these things. She held the orange coil under her palm and felt the warmth of it.

Connie and Hannah drove all day and into the evening, pushing to get to Zeus's place by when they told him they'd be there. From a distance, the glittering mass of Chicago's skyline gradually rose up out of the earth. Connie read the directions to Hannah that they'd printed off the internet. Otherwise, the sisters were quiet, concentrating on their new surroundings, taking in the details. After the darkness of the countryside, the city looked artificially bright. They took the exit for Augusta Boulevard and everything seemed to wind down, unnaturally slow, after the highway. West Town looked a little rough, but there were kids still out trick-or-treating with their parents. They found the right street after two wrong turns and sat idling the truck across from their brother's building. A screaming pack of older kids, in masks and army boots, carrying bows and arrows, tore down the block. One boy wore the American flag as a cape. They were only twenty-five minutes late. Not bad, Hannah said.

A brown metal door at the bottom of a brick tenement. Connie blew out her cheeks and thumbed his number into her cell, leaning forward to look up through the windshield. Before there was an answer, a bald head appeared in a window on the third floor. He waved. Is that him? Connie said, snapping her phone and waving back.

Hannah blurted the truck horn.

I guess we should wait here, Connie said.

A few minutes later, the metal door opened and out he came, carrying a coat and a duffle bag. He was a small man and, at twenty-two, looked younger than his age. He paused in the doorway, and in the light of the entrance, they could see that his head was shaved and he wore pale green cotton pants, like scrubs a surgeon would wear, tucked into red high-top sneakers and a grey sweater with sleeves so long they hung to his fingertips.

He looks like a kid, Connie said.

He's a professional clown, Hannah said and got out of the truck. Maybe he *wants* to look like a kid. She closed the door and walked across the street and stood in front of him.

You look just the same, Zeus said.

Well, I wouldn't have recognized *you*, Hannah said. You've got no *hair*.

Zeus didn't move.

You ready? Hannah said gently.

That truck, he said and put down his bag.

What?

Zeus continued to stare at it. Never mind, he said, it doesn't matter.

Let's go, she said and picked up his duffle bag and crossed the street. It was too bulky to toss behind the seats so she jumped onto the truck bed and unlocked the storage box and put his duffle bag in there. Zeus was still lingering on the doorstep of his building. Connie lowered her window. What gives? she said.

Something to do with the truck, Hannah said. C'mon, Zeus, she called. We should get a move on.

Sorry, he said when he got to the truck. It's just a really weird coincidence, is all.

What is? Connie said.

You're driving the very same truck my boyfriend and I rented. I'll get over it, he said, shaking his head back and forth as if rousing himself from a dream.

Connie got out of the truck, and they shook hands awkwardly. Mom told us about your boyfriend, she said. I'm really sorry.

Zeus looked sideways for a moment, then he smacked his hands together. So I hear we're setting off for some right-wing church in Wichita, is that right?

Yeah, well, Connie said, we'll see how that goes. She turned back to the truck and stared into the cab. We got an excellent deal on this truck in Toronto, she said, but I guess we didn't really think about how small it was going to be with the three of us in it. It's not going to be a very comfy ride, but we'll help you get a little closer to New Mexico.

Great, Zeus said agreeably. Do you want me to sit in the middle?

Would you mind?

He shook his head.

They all got in and Hannah started the truck. Zeus looked straight ahead and held his knees together, trying to make himself even smaller. They drove on and he hardly said a word. Every once in a while, the sisters asked him a question about his life and he would answer politely but succinctly. Two hours south of Chicago, they got off the highway and hit a strip with traffic lights. Cars puffing out ribbons of red exhaust. It was already after eleven, and they settled on a Motel 6 in Bradley.

Does this mean it's like two points worse than a Motel 8? Connie asked as they walked along the second-floor cement balcony to their room. Connie and Hannah had talked earlier about whether or not to get one room or two, and asked Zeus if he'd mind sharing because they were trying to economize. After hesitating for a moment, he said he was fine with it.

When they got to their room, Zeus lay down, fully dressed, silent, and closed his eyes. Connie looked at Hannah, and Hannah shrugged. How uncomfortable this must be for him. How uncomfortable for all of them. Hannah sat beside him on the bed and put her hand on his shoulder and said, We're really sorry about Fenton. He nodded without looking at her. We're sorry, she said, about *everything*. And he rolled over and curled up into a ball. She looked at her sister, and Connie seemed agitated.

I'm going to go for a walk, she said.

I don't think it's a good idea to go alone, Hannah said.

I'll be okay. Just give me half an hour.

Let me come with you.

I'm tougher than you think, Connie said and left quickly.

She started off down the main strip, past the fast-food joints and gas stations. Neon signs blinked out of the darkness, and a string of coloured bunting hung artificially still above a used car lot. A boy outside a Denny's tried to sell her a scooter for five dollars. His face was unnaturally red. Maybe an allergic reaction, she thought and kept on walking. It wasn't until she was on the next block that she thought of the pregnant woman she'd seen hitchhiking in the rain and realized she should have helped the boy. He was just a kid. She hurried back, but he was no longer there. You had a mission field right there in front of you, she thought, and you didn't even know it!

But then Connie started to feel like a mission field herself.

And where were the good samaritans in *her* life? How long had it been since *she'd* been ministered to? She felt like talking to her kids, but it was too late, they'd already be in bed.

On the way back to the motel, she saw a man bundled in a sleeping bag, sitting outside an all-night convenience store with · his dog. He was blowing on a harmonica and there was a hat on the ground in front of him. Connie started to approach him. She took a toonie out of her pocket, then remembered she was in the States. All she had in her wallet was American twenties.

That's a pretty nice coat you got there, he said.

I'm sorry, she said, I don't have anything to give you.

Hey, bitch, he yelled. Don't walk away. I'm talking to you!

Connie ignored him.

You're a real classy lady, ya slut!

Connie looked back over her shoulder briefly as she hurried away. Three guys in leather jackets and chaps over their jeans were coming out of the store. Behind her, she heard them fire up their Harleys and rumble like tanks into the street.

Zeus and Hannah were already in bed by the time she got back to the motel. Don't undress, Hannah said.

Why not?

The beds are kind of gross.

Connie checked the sheets and placed a towel from her suitcase across her pillow. She lay down, fully dressed, and willed her body to unclench itself. She was so tired. Zeus was a silent lump under the covers. Is he okay, do you think? she whispered to her sister.

I don't know, Hannah said and hoped that her sister was okay. Good night, she said and patted Connie on the hip. Hannah would have liked some reassurance herself. Something about a motel like this made her uneasy. The sudden, sharp noise of people passing outside the window. They sounded so close, it made the room feel flimsy, not protected at all. Outside, motorcycles growled incessantly up and down the main strip. She missed Norm. Life was better when he was around. She lay on her back for what felt like an hour, looking up at the dark shapes on the ceiling and trying to get a good memory going. She wanted to set it on play and rewind, luxuriate in it, but an argument on someone's TV was penetrating the thin walls and distracting her. Furious male threats, then female noises of distress. No, it must have been coming up through the floor. It went on and on. Breaking glass. It sounded so real. And then sirens, as if they were outside. A red light flashed along the edge of the curtains. A door slammed, more shouts, angry, male. This fight was real.

Hannah sat up in bed.

What's going on? Connie asked.

Something bad, Zeus said. He was propped up against his pillows like he'd been there for a while.

Hannah got out of bed and went to the window and peered around the curtain. Six police cruisers. Kankakee County Sheriff. Someone was getting arrested. A barefooted man wearing nothing but a pair of sweatpants was being escorted, handcuffed, over to a police cruiser. A blond mullet. An ambulance with its back doors open. Two medics with first-aid kits walked towards the motel and disappeared under the balcony.

Connie was wide awake now, leaning up against her elbow. She'd just had a dream about Harlan. He'd punched an old man in the face, for insulting her, and broken his nose, then come home with an Oscar for best supporting actor. When he took it out of his bag, the statuette was still cold and covered in condensation from being in the hold of the plane. Connie started thinking about her husband. She knew how much worse things got for him when he was withdrawn. He found it hard to forgive himself at the best of times. She couldn't bear that he felt so ashamed, full of self-loathing. Suddenly, she was worried for his safety and wanted to talk to him. But she was beginning to feel like this time apart was crucial, as well, that it was going to be good for both of them.

It's all over, Hannah said and came to bed. You can go back to sleep, she said, and Connie lay down again, her anxious head on the pillow.

I n the morning, things felt better. Even Zeus seemed a little sunnier. Bright, white solid clouds ferried smoothly across the blue sky. They got into the truck and after half an hour stopped at a busy gas station to fill up in a town of white bungalows with immaculate front lawns and flagpoles clanging in the wind. Over everything was a smear of campaign posters. Small red-and-blue flags fluttered on almost every car, railing, and post. Hannah was squeezing the trigger of the gas pump when a distant whine grew into a deafening, eerie drone. Connie turned to look at her through the rear-view window of the cab. What's that noise? she mouthed. Hannah raised his shoulders. It sounded like an air raid siren.

People were filling their tanks as though they couldn't hear it.

Connie got out of the truck and stood holding her elbows. This town's a little *Twilight Zone*, she said.

Is it possible they can't hear it? Hannah said.

On the other side of the pump, a couple was gassing up

their enormous pickup truck together. She held the hose while he leaned against the truck and talked. They were both overweight, the man balding, in jeans and a baseball jacket. His wife had short permed hair and a pink cardigan over a floral blouse.

Zeus jogged nervously back from behind the building, tucking in his shirt. He went straight up to the couple. What's that noise? he asked them.

Oh, it's nothing to worry about, hon. First day of the month they always give the sirens a test, she said, even at this time of year.

Zeus thanked the woman and returned to stand beside his sisters. Maybe there's a mine, he said. Or some kind of power plant.

All three of them stayed together as Hannah went in to pay, and Connie asked the woman behind the cash.

Tornado warnings, she explained.

Oh, Connie said.

An older woman in sunglasses was standing behind them, holding a giant thermos and a stick of pepperoni. They used to come through here all the time, she said. Used to be Tornado Alley.

Is it just me, Connie said as they were leaving, or do the States seem like a particularly dangerous place to be?

They're certainly on the lookout for their own safety, Hannah said.

Zeus had bought a stick of pepperoni as well, and they shared it in the truck. They left the town of Ashkum, and for an hour, the highway slid across the flat countryside like a dull knife blade. A string of farmhouses in the distance like metal charms. Silver silos. Silver barns. A man in a Hummer riding the tailwind of a semi so close it looked like he was being towed. Connie's eyes were following the line of a wire fence rise and fall between its posts in short, sharp waves. She saw a handmade sign in a field next to the road. Black letters on a white background.

CRIMINAL MENACING?

In fifty yards, they passed another one.

WOMAN ALONE?

Then another three.

DETERANCE REQUIRES.

MORE THAN A PHONE.

GUNSSAVELIFE.COM

Did you get that? Connie said.

Hard not to, Zeus said.

They turned west at Champaigne and drove until lunchtime. Just past Decatur, they bought sandwiches to eat in the truck. They talked carefully about Zeus's life in Chicago, and about Hannah's time in England, and Connie's kids. Neither Connie nor Hannah mentioned their parents, and Zeus didn't ask. They passed a field of small oil pumps pecking the ground like oversized chickens. Then a red farmhouse, close to the highway. A boy was stuffing something purple in through a ground-floor window. He swung around as if he knew he'd been spotted and swivelled his head, keeping his eyes on the truck as it passed. What do you think's going on there? Connie said, and Zeus shrugged. Beats me, but there wasn't enough room for him to turn around and look.

I think it's going to rain, Hannah said, and a yellow school bus floated across the sky above them on a turquoise overpass as they sped towards darker clouds overhead.

Past Jacksonville, the Illinois River. The air and light had a pewter quality. First, a high view of the wide, flat brown basin and a tractor in the distance, trailing a streamer of dust, then two bridges flying back up out of the flats. A ship in the distance, with a flag rippling from its tallest mast, turned out to be a mill made up of a cluster of silos connected by conveyer belts and grain elevators. A lot of hawks around New Salem, one perched at the tip of a dead tree like a weather vane, beak into the wind.

Late in the afternoon, they stopped in Hannibal. They parked by the river and stood watching a turtle poke around at the edge of the water. Connie swung her bag over her shoulder and said, So, are we going to see this town or what?

They walked to the intersection of Main and Church. On one corner stood the Mark Twain Hotel, across from an empty lot. Next to the lot, the Main Street Soda Fountain, now closed. Next to that, the Star Movie House, also closed down, the awning fringed with dark holes where the light bulbs used to be.

Zeus went over to the Soda Fountain and held his hands against the glass and peered inside. Everything was chrome and linoleum. There were booths upholstered in brown and blue. A classic American diner, just like one he and Fenton used to go to in Chicago. In the display window, plastic replicas of a plate of fries, a banana split, and a black forest cake on a tin cake stand, all of it covered in dust.

Three boys with jackets flapping over white karate suits and orange belts ran down the street. It was the first sign of life. The sisters followed the boys up Main Street towards the sound of piano music until they came to a ballet school. They stopped on the other side of the street and stared as a gaggle of little girls in jackets and pink tights, thin lycra skirts, swarmed out of the building and ran into minivans that were waiting in the parking lot around the corner. There was a sound like applause, or rain, only syncopated, and they realized there was tap dancing on the second floor. The parking lot emptied out and one small ballerina wandered back to the lobby, unmet by her parents.

Kids have such gorgeous bodies, Connie said. Who knew I'd love their company so much.

A red corvette ripped down the street. Two bleached blondes in the front seat, white flames painted down the sides. They took a corner, tires squealing, then faded into the distance, silence rushing in behind them to fill the empty space like water.

What a strange place, Hannah said.

Zeus came up the street now, walking pensively. When he was within earshot of the tap dancing, he did an understated little shuffle and flap, then went heavy again.

Connie looked like she was on the verge of tears. What's the matter, Con?

Connie clutched her chest. I miss my children!

Let's go get something to eat, Hannah said and put her arm around her sister. You're hungry, is all.

It was nearly dusk when they got back on the highway. Connie let her head fall back against the headrest. She closed her eyes for a moment. They'd eaten hamburgers and fries and the smell still lingered.

It wasn't until Fenton died that I found out he was a Buddhist, Zeus said, quite out of the blue, opening up for the first time about Fenton. I mean, the whole time we were together — I was pretty shocked to find out that something that was so important to him was something I didn't know about. He never even told me how sick he really was. I didn't even know.

Hannah glanced at Zeus, who was digging at a small scar on the back of his hand.

People are complicated, Connie said.

I just thought I knew him, Zeus said.

You probably did, Connie said. As well as anybody can know anybody else.

I don't know. I still feel like I failed somehow, like I didn't pay enough attention when he was alive, all the time we were together.

Well, what was he like? Hannah said. What are your memories of him?

He was a really funny guy, but he could get angry about things he didn't believe in. He took his clowning very seriously. Once, when he was eighteen, he joined an army. It was the biggest mistake he ever made. He told me about it just before he died. We always worked together, until he got sick. Zeus's voice trailed off.

You mean, with the kids? Hannah said, wanting to pull him back.

Yeah, but I'm done with that now. I'm just thinking about my own family now, and where *I* come from.

Of course, Hannah said, you must be. That's, like, a huge deal.

Family is everything, Connie said and checked her cell phone.

I guess I just didn't really know him, Zeus said. Not really.

Look, I thought I knew *my* husband, Connie said. But then one day he told me he'd lost everything we owned. These guys came and cleared out his business, then they came and took our house away from us. I used to live in this big beautiful house in Mill Bay, overlooking the water. But now where am I going to live? Where are my kids going to grow up? I have no idea. There are some really rough neighbourhoods in Victoria. Will I be forced to tell them ridiculous things like how it's okay for people to live on the street and shoot up in alleyways and panhandle for money? How some people have chosen to adopt the habits of birds and make nests for themselves out of newspaper and live outdoors instead of indoors?

You see? If I don't first drive myself insane thinking about the worst-case scenario.

Connie gave a false, almost derisive little laugh, then bent to get her purse off the floor, took out a kleenex, and blew her nose. After a while, she said, You know what the crazy thing is? After all the effort my husband made to leave his welfare childhood behind, he's ended up right back where he started.

There are worse things than being poor, Zeus said.

Fine, I just don't want my kids to have to go to a school covered in graffiti and full of drug dealers and bullies.

But you get all that stuff with the rich kids too, Zeus said. Maybe it's even worse because you can't see it. I mean –

Did I tell you? Connie said, suddenly leaning forward to look over at her sister. This friend of Simon's was on TV playing her violin. She's Si's age. Six years old!

Which one is Simon? Zeus said.

The order is Emma, Simon, and Theo, Connie said and she realized her voice sounded impatient, so she softened it. You know, technically speaking, they're your niece and nephews.

That's right, Zeus said. I guess I'm an uncle.

You'll have to come out and meet them some time, Connie said, and the offer hung in the air, making them all think about how they'd never been as a family.

How did you do it? Hannah ventured. How did you live with our parents by yourself for all those years? You're so different from them.

Zeus stretched his legs as far as the cab would allow and adjusted his position. I was really into hockey at the time, he said. I just got totally obsessed with it and eventually got used to being in Toronto.

Hockey? Hannah said. I'm sorry, but you don't really strike me as the typical hockey player type.

My coach didn't think so either, Zeus said. He actually took me aside one day and said, have you ever thought about figure skating? Figure skating! I was twelve years old. I was trying to be cool, trying to fit in, not get picked on. But at the same time I could see what he meant. I was all wrists out on the ice. I skated with my hips. I was so slippery no one could check me. But I forgot about the puck, that aggressive thing you've got to have for the puck. I was too busy cutting figure eights around my opponents.

The image of Zeus as a twelve-year-old boy, doing curlicues on the ice, was so graceful and evocative in their minds, it mirrored the circuitry of thought and they all glided off towards something nostalgic.

Zeus, I'm really glad you're here with us, Connie said at last.

What about me? Hannah said, and Connie didn't answer her.

What was it about her sister, Connie thought, that she felt left out so much of the time? Hannah was starting to feel aggrieved, and Connie hated that.

They checked into a Days Inn in Mexico, Missouri, ate enchiladas with black beans and guacamole, and each had a cold, wet bottle of Corona at El Vaquero, in the one-storey strip mall across the highway. Zeus spoke to the waitress in Spanish. Her two front teeth were framed in gold and it reminded him of his childhood, the low-riders, a rhinestone cactus he'd once seen on the back of a leather jacket. Zeus offered to pay for the meal, but Connie insisted they all pay their fair share, so they split the cost three ways, as they'd decided to do again with the room.

After dinner, they headed back across the highway and Connie stayed in the lobby while she called her parents on her cell. Her father answered and told her that the kids were being really well behaved, considering they each had a stash of Halloween candy they were quickly making their way through. Has Harlan called? she asked. He didn't even know where she was.

Yes, Tim said, and Connie felt the back of her neck tighten. He's at his sister's, Tim said, and she relaxed slightly with the predictability of that scenario. Did he ask about me?

Well, I was surprised, Tim said, that you hadn't already talked. I just assumed you'd told him about the trip. It was a little awkward. But he's coming around tomorrow to take the kids to a movie or something like that. But I made it clear they were welcome to stay here.

Connie wanted to ask him more, but Tim had already moved on to tell her that Rose was out with them now, feeding the seals in the marina. It was Tim's habit to respect other people's privacy, but it was a habit that suggested a reciprocal desire to be left alone. Couldn't he muster a bit of sympathy for once? Give some intimacy? She wanted her father to know her, with its implication of acceptance and approval.

Tim asked after Hannah, and that's where they transferred their unsettled feelings – onto the troublesome, unreligious, younger sibling. I wonder, he said, if she's ever going to marry that man? Connie said she didn't think so. She says she loves Norm too much to marry him, and they shared a chuckle. They both appreciated Hannah's sense of humour, it took the edge off what at times felt sordid. It's nice to see Zeus again, Connie said, and there was silence at the other end. Connie felt drained by the effort it took to be cheerful. I know, she said, it's a little weird. She was looking through the glass entrance at the parking lot outside. There was no debris on the ground. It had a vacuumed look. She couldn't see anything green or alive.

The hotel lobby smelled of disinfectant and it made the world outside seem like a sterilized extension of the indoors.

Before they hung up, Tim offered to pray for her. *May the blessing of God Almighty, the Father, the Son, and the Holy Ghost, be with you and remain with you always.*

Thanks, Dad. Talk to you later.

When Connie walked through the door of their hotel room, Hannah was standing between the beds with one hand on her hip, saying to Zeus, He wants me to ride his death ship!

What death ship? Zeus said.

Pirate flag flying from the main mast? Hannah said. Skull and cross bones? A hook where a hand used to be? Coat hanger for a womb? Just stuff my mouth full of dry twigs, why don't you. Just make a *husk* of me and call me a woman.

Zeus was shaking his head in disbelief. Why do you want to have a baby so badly? Don't you think there are enough people on the planet already?

I've never been pregnant before, Hannah said, sitting down on the edge of the bed and flopping backwards. I don't even know if I *can*.

He's afraid, Connie said, taking her coat off. You have to help him find the courage.

How? Hannah said and then she stood up resolutely. She shouted, I refuse to be anybody's nurse! Zeus and Connie stared at her blankly. I'm going to have a shower, she said and went into the bathroom and locked the door.

She just had some kind of an argument with her boyfriend over the phone, Zeus said.

Connie nodded sympathetically. That's too bad, she said and flung the covers down on the bed she would share with her sister tonight, inspecting the sheets for bed bugs. The shower started to grumble through the wall. Zeus was sitting at a table by the window in front of what looked like a folded white silk flag. A pair of flattened black slippers lay on top. What have you got there? Connie asked.

This is Fenton's old clown suit, Zeus said, patting it with his hands. I don't know what to do with it. I'd like to do something symbolic. A funeral pyre maybe, he said, giving a short puff through his nose. But that's not the easiest thing to bring about.

We could make that happen.

I'm not sure I'm ready. Zeus gathered up the suit and slippers and placed them back inside the duffle bag at his feet. He took a small bottle of lavender oil out of a black leather shaving kit and put it on the table. He undressed down to his underwear, the ones that were pale pink, he noted, from a laundromat mishap with a red sock.

Connie busied herself with her suitcase.

Zeus sat down at the table again and stared out the window, his fingers resting on the small brown bottle. After a while, he unscrewed the cap. Would you do me a favour and massage a bit of this into my scalp? It gets itchy as the new hair grows in.

Can't you do it yourself? The idea made Connie feel squeamish.

It's not as effective.

She thought about it for a moment, then took the bottle from Zeus and poured a gold coin of oil onto her palm. She rubbed her hands together, inhaling lavender, and placed them on his head. It felt warm and the skin moved with the suppleness of suede, as if his scalp was a soft, suede cap that fit loosely over his skull. She laughed self-consciously, I feel like I'm massaging a knee cap. I've never felt a shaved head before. Why do you shave your head, Zeus? You're not going bald.

It's for a boy called Sam, Zeus said. He was going through chemo and had lost all his hair. Suddenly, it felt sort of greedy to have so much of it. But then he died. And then Fenton died as well, and that's when I finally did it, and I'm going to keep doing it for a while. It's like burning a candle, or something. A kind of memorial.

Connie was tugging softly at the edges of Zeus's ears. She squeezed his earlobes and Zeus suddenly bent forward and covered his face with his hands. Sorry, Connie said, did that hurt?

I'm travelling with the clothes of a dead clown!

Connie rested her hands on Zeus's shoulders.

I miss him so much, he said. I loved him so much. He used to make me laugh all the time. I think I could have been happy living with him for the rest of my life. Do you think it's possible to be really happy with someone and not know it?

Well, you can be really *unhappy* with someone and not know it, Connie said. So I don't see why it can't happen the other way around.

I don't think I ever really let myself trust that things are going to work out. My real parents, they just let me go. So why wouldn't everybody else do it too? Fenton always thought it would be good for me to find them. He thought it would resolve some things for me. It was the last thing he ever told me.

I'm sure your parents loved you, Connie said. But love isn't a guarantee of anything. Parenting is a skill. It should be taught in schools. And not everyone has the knack for it. No matter how much they love their kids. I remember my mother telling me, when I was about thirteen, we were in the garage, standing over the deep freeze. She said she'd been terrified of having girls. She'd wanted sons. When she was young, she prayed to God not to give her girls because she knew she wouldn't be able to teach them how to love themselves.

Rose told you that? Zeus swivelled to look at Connie, to see the vulnerable child in her.

It shocked Connie for a moment to realize that, of course, Zeus knew her mother.

God, what *is* it with parents? Zeus said.

Connie was holding her oily hands up like a surgeon. It's not easy being a parent, you know? You may have the best intentions in the world, but you're still going to mess up somehow. We all need forgiveness.

Connie dropped down onto the edge of the bed and sat there for a moment. Zeus came over and sat beside her. He put his arm around her shoulder and she leaned into him and let herself go and just sobbed. He had the faint smell of a barn-warm animal and hay. Then it occurred to her that she was being consoled by her brother, a young bald man in pink underpants. She started to laugh, and Zeus joined in. It grew into a hysterical, purging kind of laughter. She used a corner of the bedspread to wipe the tears off her cheeks.

Zeus was sitting so close to her their bodies were touching. The door to the bathroom opened and Hannah came out in a tiny threadbare towel. They looked to Hannah thick as thieves, like the best of friends, guilty of some secret mischief. She felt a little jealous. Nice to see you're getting acquainted, she said and they both raised their flushed, depleted faces to look at her helplessly, recovering from a moment of hilarity too ephemeral to explain.

Hannah woke in the morning to find Connie sitting up in bed, writing in her journal. Hannah was the writer in the family but had never been able to keep a journal like her sister could. I just had a dream about Caiden Brock, she said.

Connie put her pen down and looked curious, amused. Did you and Caiden ever sleep together? It was as if Connie had been waiting a long time to ask her this. It felt scornful, hostile somehow.

No, Hannah said, don't be ridiculous. She got dressed and went to inquire about the free breakfast. The fact was, she was excited and nervous to see him. How on earth had he ended up in Wichita, Kansas? She hadn't thought about him in years, not until her sister brought him up.

She used to fantasize about him all the time. He was so spoiled and cocky and handsome, full of arrogant bravado. And the secret of their little affair had been so thrilling. It was a warm, flat stone she hugged to her belly underneath her shirt at a time when she'd felt so lonely. Sometimes she took refuge at his parents' place. Effusive, generous Mrs. Brock, with all her children grown and gone, loved having her around the house. Hannah slept on the pullout sofa in the basement. Occasionally, by coincidence, Caiden would be at home too, even though by then he was living on campus. This was Hannah's strongest wish – that he should be there. She didn't realize at first that, when he was, it was because he'd come to see her. It was his mother who would alert him – for she had fantasies about the two of them, as well, that one day maybe they would marry. Hannah would lie in the basement and throb with expectation. After his parents had gone to bed, Caiden would sneak downstairs. One night, he asked her to go for a midnight swim in the backyard pool.

Hannah felt his warm breath against her ear, and a delirious feeling like a hive of bees started buzzing between her legs. It was one of those warm summer nights when the air is thick and the distance blurred in a sultry haze and there isn't a breath of wind and everything is as motionless as a dream. Hannah dove into the turquoise pool, the underwater lights warm to the touch and yellow against her skin. She was sure pilots flying overhead could see their shiny rectangle from the air, their insect bodies in the water. There was the brightness and being exposed and almost naked and wet. The water spinning its silver threads of mercury across the surface. Hannah hung under the diving board and watched Caiden swim towards her through the oily blue water, his chest whiter than his arms, his brown hair puffing out like a jellyfish as his body caught up before the next breaststroke propelled him forward again. He crossed the pool in one breath, surfacing indecently close to her, and hung off the diving board too. Wrap your legs around my waist, he said and Hannah did. Then he slipped a finger inside her bathing suit.

You're like a swollen butterfly, he said, and Hannah didn't really know what the protocol was, so she just hung there from the diving board, passive as the air, feeling the ecstatic currents coursing through her body.

Around midday, they passed a chaingang of inmates, in grey overalls and orange vests, picking garbage off the roadside with silver claws at the end of steel rods. It was Connie's first time driving the truck. Just past Kansas City, a billboard with white and yellow sunrays bursting out from behind the word JESUS printed in bright green capital letters, with *For President* graffitied underneath it.

Someone must have told them I was coming, Zeus said, dead-pan.

Do your parents know you're coming? Hannah asked. Have you even spoken to them yet?

Zeus was shaking his head.

So you don't have any concrete plans about how this is all going to pan out?

I'm thinking I'll arrive by bus, he said. That's about as concrete as it gets. Zeus lifted his legs and hugged his knees, then stretched his feet out on top of the dashboard with the toes of his shoes bent back against the windshield.

You must be nervous, Connie said and took her eyes off the road for a moment to look at him sideways.

Nervous isn't even close to what I'm feeling, Zeus said, dropping his feet to the floor and sitting up again. I mean, what am I supposed to say to them? What if they don't like how it makes them feel, to see me face to face?

I guess there's no way of knowing, Connie said.

Well, if it's any consolation, I'm nervous about coming face to face with the Global Kingdom of Salvation Center,

Hannah said. I don't want to get smothered by people with good intentions.

But misled hearts? Connie said. It's not one of those crazy right-wing places, Zeus. At least, I don't *think* it is.

Look, I'm not against Christians, Hannah said. I've got too many in my life that I love, right? And sometimes they do good works. A lot of poor people get fed by Christians every year.

And orphans adopted, Zeus said.

Thank you, Zeus. Another *excellent* example of Christian charity, Hannah said. It's just that I don't like spiritual pushiness. Or too much earnestness, or reverence. Too much reverence always makes me feel like causing trouble.

You don't have to get involved, you know? Nobody's *forcing* you, Connie said. I didn't even think you were planning on going inside.

How about showing a little respect for *my* religious feelings here?

I didn't think you *had* religious feelings.

Why does everything have to be so spelled out for you before you'll even acknowledge it?

Because it's hard to know what you're dealing with when things are so, what's the word for it – nebulous?

Hannah laughed. As if God, himself, isn't nebulous.

Can you just be genuine for, like, one moment?

I thought I *was* being genuine.

Connie rolled her eyes. So what about you, Zeus? We're not that far away now. What are you going to do when we get there?

I'm going to have the pancake special, he said and pointed at a sign advertising breakfast specials at a restaurant just off the highway at the next exit.

The sisters both glanced at him with something like appreciation. It was turning out to be so good having him there, sitting in the middle, with his own disarming perspective.

Okay, Zeus, Connie said, go have your stack o'pancakes, and she signalled for the exit. It was Friday, mid-morning, the parking lot wide open. Connie drove diagonally across the white lines and stopped outside the restaurant. A sloped red roof. In the window, a poster for their Halloween specials.

When they got out of the truck, the sun was warm and the air so gentle for the first of November that they lingered outside. Hannah leaned against the truck and Connie sat down on the curb outside the restaurant. Zeus joined her and together they raised their faces to the sun and closed their eyes until a car pulled up and parked nearby. A woman got out and opened the back door for a little girl who was bawling. The woman said, Come on, Britney, I've had enough now. Do you want your flapjacks or not?

The girl nodded, still crying in the back seat. The woman left her there and walked into the restaurant. The girl threw herself down on the seat and disappeared from view. Her crying petered out now that her audience had left. She got out of the car and kicked the door shut. She was wearing a pink tracksuit and white runners and her hair was pulled into a ponytail, the size of a banana, on one side of her head. To Connie, she looked about the same age as Emma. She started heading towards the restaurant with all the lamentation of a funeral march, stooped forward and dragging her feet, arms heavy at her side. She walked past them and Connie said, tenderly, What's the matter, sweetheart?

The girl looked indignant – that her sad pageant should be interrupted at all! I lost my fucking tooth, she said. And now she was all sass, one hand resting on her cocked hip.

Zeus leaned back and lifted his shirt. He was doing something with his muscles that made his stomach fold in on itself so that his bellybutton disappeared. And *I* lost my fucking bellybutton! he shouted.

The girl took a second to decide, then slapped her leg and threw her head back and laughed. Without looking back, she skipped into the restaurant, still laughing out loud. They followed her inside.

Apart from the girl and her mother, the place was empty. A stop sign immediately inside, asking them to PLEASE WAIT TO BE SEATED. A waitress waved them to a booth, two over from the mother and her daughter, and came back to take their order. She was wearing earrings made of a dangling cluster of red, white, and blue stars. A coffee for Hannah and an orange juice for Connie. Zeus ordered tea.

Sweetened or unsweetened? the waitress asked in a southern drawl.

With sugar, please, Zeus said, and she brought him an enormous glass of iced tea.

Oh, he said, when she put it down in front of him.

You wanted hot tea?

That's all right, he said, clenching his buttocks to get high enough to close his mouth around the open throat of the tall white straw.

He moved the glass with both hands, like a child, Hannah thought. That glass makes you look small, she said and suddenly felt the soulless, desolate fact of a place like this. She ordered French toast, Connie had a waffle, and Zeus took the special.

They were all looking out at the parking lot when a guy on a big Harley pulled up beside the truck, black-and-white markings on the gas tank like a baby killer whale. The driver seemed to have stopped to admire their truck. He was wearing black leather boots with shiny buckles, a voluminous hip-length fur coat, the colour of butterscotch, fur mittens to match, and a skull-cap helmet. He was sitting on a plastic garment bag, laid over his gas tank, with the tip of the hanger hooked around the gas cap.

Look at that idiot, Connie said.

I think he looks great, Hannah said. I think he looks really cool.

The mittens are a nice touch, Zeus said.

Connie tsked. That kind of extravagant vanity out there, she said, is a slippery slope.

I'm sorry, Hannah said, but who on this trip's got the fancy clothes and the expensive European cosmetics?

Those are transient luxuries, Connie said pompously, pushing a finger through the syrup on her plate. Gone the way as all the rest of my worldly belongings. Nope, as for me now, I'm looking forward to the rewards of heaven.

You know, Hannah said, Mom said the very same thing once. In a restaurant, in Toronto. In fact, we were all there. Even you, Zeus, although you were just a kid. She said, if Dad ever died, she'd want to die too, or very soon there afterwards. In fact, they were both kind of looking forward to, you know, shacking up in the afterlife, so to speak.

Speaking of morbid, Connie said. Remember that time Mom told you about that vision a friend of hers had? How you appeared to her in a vision? You were surrounded by people in long, hooded robes and you were naked.

Yeah, yeah, yeah, Hannah said, and I was inserting a phallic object into my vagina.

Je-sus, Zeus said, shooting backwards in the booth.

Nice, eh? Connie said.

Why was she even talking to a friend about you like that in the first place? Zeus said.

It was when she was doing exorcisms in the attic of that house in Toronto, Hannah said. Before they moved out west. Did you even know that was going on? It was happening when you were living with them. Mom was casting demons out of middle-class professionals. That was her job.

Yeah, I'd get home from school and someone would be screaming at the top of the house.

Really? Hannah said.

Connie let out a cheerless breath and rested her forehead against her fingertips.

Don't you have to have a licence or something to perform an exorcism? Zeus asked.

Connie raised her head again. How am I supposed to know? she said. I'd already left home by then. All I know is, Mom had a degree in counselling psychology and was running a Christian practice, so I guess she was attracting clients with certain kinds of problems. I don't think she woke up one day and said, hmm, today I think I'm going to specialize in exorcisms.

In the end, what she was doing wasn't all that different from Freudian psychoanalysis, Hannah said. Only, if you happen to be a Christian, like our mom, then you turn it into a religious phenomenon. If it's evil, it must have something to do with the devil and demons.

Apparently, Zeus said, where they live now, it's got the highest ratio of Satan worshippers per capita in all of North America.

What, in Victoria? Connie said.

Zeus nodded. It's a statistic. I read it somewhere on the internet. A lot of cats go missing there just before Halloween.

Hannah shook her head at this.

Connie looked nonplussed. So you don't believe any of that stuff is real?

I didn't know *what* to believe. The point is, Zeus said, at the time, no one was explaining anything to me.

It's called the confidentiality agreement, Hannah said.

But she *did* encounter demons, Connie said.

Her experiences were very compelling, Hannah said, but I'm not sure I'd be as quick to interpret the scratches on somebody's back as the work of a demon.

But what if those scratches were made in a way that would've been impossible to inflict on yourself? I don't doubt Mom's stories, Connie said loyally.

They could still have been self-inflicted, Hannah said. There are more reasonable explanations than demons.

Connie made an exasperated noise as the woman with the young girl pulled her daughter past their table, making their way out of the restaurant.

Look, all I'm saying is –

The fact is you're trying to discredit her!

She's my mom! Hannah said. I'm trying not to be totally freaked out about what it is she used to do.

For what it's worth, I think it used to freak her out too, Zeus said. She used to say she didn't really know what she was doing.

Connie was spinning the salt shaker on the table. For a moment, it was the only noise in the restaurant. Remember those home movies? she said to Hannah.

Yeah, Hannah said. We have about twenty minutes of Super 8 family footage, she told Zeus. But I'm not in any of it. They must have run out of film by the time I was born.

Our mom is like a colt, or something, in those films, Connie said. She's in her early twenties. Sort of awkward and long-limbed but full of energy and mischief. There's a lightness there.

She was really beautiful, Hannah said.

Thing is, she keeps hiding from the camera.

I *know*! Hannah said.

I want her to just stop being so insecure, for just one moment, so I can have a good look at her. For *myself*. To know who I come from.

There must be a connection, Hannah said, between that kind of insecurity and her need to help other people. She's dedicated her whole life to it.

It sounds like she's made it her business to be a rescuer, Zeus said, because she's always been at risk of getting lost herself. Remember that Bible verse she had in a frame on her desk? I read it so many times I still know it by heart. *And if you spend yourselves in behalf of the hungry, and satisfy the needs of the oppressed, then your light will rise in the darkness, and your night will become like the noonday.*

The waitress came over, cleared their plates and returned with the bill, and none of them had made a move or said anything. Above the restaurant, a flock of geese was flying south for the winter, their honking audible from inside.

You know, Hannah said, putting her hand on Zeus's arm. I know we haven't been in touch over the years, but I used to wonder how you were doing. I don't know why we never tried to contact you, not properly, and I'm really sorry about that. You were our brother and we really kind of failed you, and there was this weird, I don't know, silence in the family. Hannah made eye contact with Connie.

It's like we couldn't talk about it, Connie said.

But we never found out what happened, Hannah said. We never really understood why you left home so quickly.

Zeus looked down at the table and chewed his lip for a moment. He lifted his shoulders. What do you expect me to do? Cry about how your parents reacted to finding out I was gay? I mean, sometimes I do. Tim put me through some pretty heavy stuff for a fifteen-year-old. He wanted me to be different than I am. He thought I needed to be cured.

And Mom? Connie said.

Zeus sighed and looked out the window. She did her best, I guess.

A fly landed on the table, then hit the window, buzzing back and forth against the glass. They all sat there in silence, not knowing what to say.

Hannah knew she could never reconcile herself to the way her parents were, but she wasn't sure how to help her brother. For some reason, she was thinking about the time her mother cured her of an infected mosquito bite with a bread-and-onion poultice. *That* was the kind of thing she loved about her mother, all her homespun traditional wisdom. There was another time too, when Hannah was six years old. Rose got bit by a Great Dane, right through her duffle coat. They'd been walking home from the laundromat – Rose, Connie, and herself – with a basket full of clean clothes, past a neighbour's front yard with a six-foot fence. They'd heard barking, then a huge dog hit her mother's back and knocked her to the ground. Rose had left the laundry sprawled where it had fallen and picked the girls up and run home.

When they got inside, she took off her coat and her shirt was soaked with blood, but all she'd cared about was getting her daughters home safely. She'd always had that in her, that instinct to protect her children. Maybe she hadn't always done the right thing, Hannah thought, but that instinct was in her as strong as anything else. Hannah wanted that same kind of instinct in herself right now. It would guide her, she thought, in knowing how to help him. Con, what's wrong?

I don't want to talk about Mom and Dad anymore, she said. Excuse me. And she got up quickly and left the restaurant.

B ack at the truck, Connie held the keys out to Zeus and said, You got a driver's licence? He nodded. Why don't you take us the rest of the way? And he took the keys and got into the driver's seat. Hannah got in the middle and gave Connie the seat by the window.

When they were on the highway, Hannah found a classical music station on the radio, and they drove quietly across the grasslands of Kansas. After a couple of hours, Zeus steered the Ranger off the highway and followed directions Connie had got off the Global Kingdom's website, through a grid of streets on the outskirts of Wichita, where a few resilient fields flexed their shrunken boundaries against the encroachment of the suburbs. They entered an industrial neighbourhood, with grey-and-white one-storey warehouses, storage units, manufacturing outlets. The area was so still and empty for three o'clock on a Friday afternoon, and there was something eerie, Hannah thought, but also joyous that only the trees were moving.

They passed an intersection, then located the church, and slowed down as the map indicated a low brick building to the left with a small parking lot out front. On the other side of the street was an enormous windowless building, two storeys high, covered in aluminum siding, with two vast empty parking lots on either side. Across the front was a huge sign that read, THE GLOBAL KINGDOM OF SALVATION CENTER. Zeus swung left into the small parking lot and pulled up behind a row of cars. There were three picnics tables out front, and a simple entrance with a large yellow door, and above it a more discrete sign with the church's name.

Well, here we are, Connie said.

Zeus got out of the truck, walked over to a bench by some planters, and sat down. He spread his arms across the backrest, dropped his head back, and closed his eyes.

The sisters sat where they were, taking it all in. A bumper sticker on a nearby car asked, GOT JESUS? She noticed another one, orange flames rising up to consume the warning, IF YOU'RE LIVING LIFE LIKE THERE IS NO GOD, YOU BETTER BE RIGHT. It's going to be okay, Connie thought to herself. You're here for Jesus, not the people.

Does everybody in this state, Hannah said, have to have a Support Our Troops sticker on their truck or what?

Keep your hat on, Connie said. Things are different in the States.

Let's call home, Hannah said. Let Mom know that we've arrived at this friggin' place we've been hearing about for years. I mean, it feels kind of monumental, don't you think?

Here, Connie said, getting her cell phone out of her bag and handing it to her sister. You do it. I'm not in the mood.

Hannah dialled her parents' number. The phone rang and

her dad picked up. Well, we got here, Hannah said, in one piece. We thought Mom would want to know.

Tim admitted, somewhat reluctantly, that he'd taken her to the airport that morning, and that now she was in the air. She was going on and on about how great it would be to be out there with the three of you, Tim said, at the Salvation Center, that I suggested she buy a last-minute ticket and fly herself out.

What? Hannah said, and Connie turned to her sister. Hannah lowered her face and rubbed her forehead with her free hand.

You still there? Tim said.

Yes, I'm still here.

She thought it was a bit risky, but I encouraged her to go.

That's great, Dad, Hannah said. We'll talk again soon, okay? Everything's fine here. We're all good. You don't have to worry about us.

I hope so, Tim said. I hope the trip brings healing.

Hannah let her eyes go out of focus for a second. Thanks, Dad, she said. Bye for now. And she closed the phone while new emotions exploded inside her like silent fireworks. Zeus was walking back to the truck.

What's going on? Connie said.

You won't believe this, Hannah said, but Mom's on her way out here.

What are you talking about?

Zeus got back in the truck.

Dad dropped her off at the airport this morning, Hannah said, and she's flying out to be with us.

Rose is coming *here*? Zeus asked.

Without even speaking to us first? Connie said.

You know what she can be like, Hannah said.

What about my kids? Connie said. Is Dad going to look after them all by himself?

I'm sure he'll manage, Hannah said, and she turned to her brother. She's coming to see you too, Zeus. I think that's a big part of this for her.

Connie got out of the truck, stiff and a little rattled by her mother. She laced her fingers and stretched her arms into the air. Hannah and Zeus followed, and the three of them began to walk towards the church.

A few people sat at the picnic tables, drinking coffee out of takeout cups. Hannah noticed a woman with a small canvas propped on her knees, painting another starburst Jesus, brown-bearded and lily white as a New England hippy, nothing of the Galilean left in him. I'm not sure I can do this, Hannah said, suddenly feeling the full force of her resistance to organized religious movements, and Connie turned to her sharply.

Just for a little while at least, she pleaded. Her eyes looked panicked, almost pathetic. Come in and see what the place looks like, Hannah. Then you can go. I don't want to walk in there alone.

A sudden compassion overwhelmed her, and Hannah thought, whatever she needs, whatever she's come for, God, *please* let her have it.

Are you coming in too? Hannah said, turning to Zeus, who gave a resigned *I guess so*, and all three of them walked in through the yellow door.

The reception area was so businesslike they could have been walking into a furniture warehouse. Worship music pulsed out of an open set of double doors to their right, through which they could see into a room with a low ceiling, rows of padded metal chairs, maroon industrial carpet, and walls the colour of mushroom soup. In front of them, a young woman sat behind a counter, typing into a computer. Nearby on the left, a man with a red rose tattooed on the back of his neck stood cracking his gum and reading something from a large rack of pamphlets.

The receptionist looked up, and Connie put her bag on the counter and leaned forward. We just arrived and wanted to know if there was any accommodation we could get for the weekend. My mother's been here before, and she said she stayed in some kind of accommodation?

Did you make a reservation? Because I'm afraid the dormitories are booked solid. It's a big weekend for us, and we've already got our six hundred.

Connie glanced at Hannah, who had joined her at the counter. But we just drove here all the way from Toronto, *Canada*, Connie said.

A delegation of eighty people just arrived from *China*, the receptionist said. But there's a Comfort Inn on the highway, and if you tell them you're with the Kingdom, they'll give you the conference rate. I think it's about seventy-five a night for a double.

The receptionist took a photocopied map of the area and made a red circle where the Comfort Inn was and slid it across the counter. The weekend service will be held across the street, she said, in our big hall. And if you want to hear Chad Dorian, that's where he'll be preaching all weekend.

Hannah noticed that Zeus had wandered over to the literature, his hand resting idly on a pamphlet. He was staring at the tattooed man beside him. The man checked his watch and walked towards the music and disappeared through the doors. Then a pretty woman in blue jeans came out of another door down the hall and started walking towards them at a quick pace. A moment later, a happy young man followed, running after her and putting his arm around her shoulder, and said, Martha, Jesus is going to bless you for those numbers! And they laughed at the good news of it and also disappeared into the room with the music.

You can buy tickets for the service at the door tomorrow morning, the receptionist said.

And what about the prophetic ministry? Connie asked. You have counsellors here who specialize in prophetic ministries, isn't that right? Rose had told her not to miss this.

Oh yeah, the receptionist said, brightening up for the first time. That's just awesome. You'll love it. You can sign up for that in the morning as well. Just ask someone where.

But we can go in there without paying or signing up, right? Connie pointed towards the open doorway where the music was coming from.

Oh, for sure, the receptionist said. That part of the Kingdom is always open and there's no charge. There's usually a worship band playing or a prayer team on the go.

Well, Hannah said, pushing herself off the counter, I hate to be indoors on a day like this. You go on in, Con, if you want. Zeus and I'll go get us a room at the hotel and we'll meet you there later.

I think I'll stay, Zeus said, coming over with half a dozen pamphlets. Why not? We can take a cab to the hotel when we're ready, right?

There's a shuttle bus you can take, the receptionist said.

Well, there you go, Connie said, and Hannah nodded slowly and said, Okay, and marvelled as she watched her liberal, ex-upper-middle-class sister enter one of the treasured sanctuaries of the American Christian right with her adopted brother, a bereft, gay ex-clown.

~

All manner of people were scattered around the worship hall. Young and old, from all walks of life. Some were praying, some reading, a few chatted softly. There were chairs enough for a hundred more. Up at the front, on a low stage, the band played a powerful, hypnotic song on drums, electric keyboard, and guitar. A young woman in a moss green V-neck sweater swayed behind a microphone, alternating between song and the spoken word. Her prayers sounded improvised and sensual, like requests beseeched in the intimacy of passion. Beside her a man played guitar, echoing every supplication with a phrase of confirmation, spoken or sung in harmony.

Zeus leaned towards Connie and whispered, Are they flirting with us? The man with the red rose tattoo was up near the front.

Kiss me with the kisses of your word, the young woman sang. Tenderize my heart. For you are the lovesick God, who delights in me, even in my selfishness.

Connie stood with Zeus at the back of the room. Eventually, she sat on the floor and rested her back against the wall, and Zeus walked over to a row of chairs and took a seat and removed his shoes. You could do that here. It was okay. Connie admired his ease. I'm too uptight, she thought, always have been. She had a lot of disappointed dreams. Things she hadn't managed to do. One of them – to become a missionary, like her mother's mother, who used to travel in convoy around the Canadian prairies in the 1940s. What were they? Nazarenes. Gathered under the canopy of a striped canvas tent in a farmer's dusty field. Hymns slipping out from the shade to drift and burn up in the sun. Her grandmother sang and played the ukulele and stood beside the preacher and illustrated, on a large sheet of paper pinned to an easel, the stories he told as he conjured up the Holy Spirit.

Connie had wanted to go to Africa as well, dig a well and worship with the beautiful people there. Her kids supported a foster child in Namibia through World Vision. His picture had been on the fridge at home. They paid the small maintenance fee out of their own allowance and wrote letters once a month and received a regular update. Nelson Bundha would graduate from grade school this summer. They had bought him two bunny rabbits last year for his birthday. It was part of a community program. The boy's letter afterwards had been ecstatic. He did not like to see his mother kill the new rabbits, but he understood. They were so soft. He had names for them, Mandela and Winnie.

Connie looked over at Zeus and in her mind took him home and put him to bed. In one of the kid's beds. Simon's bed. Zeus would love her house. But then she remembered it was gone. How much had she loved her house. That was her brace of bunnies. She'd loved her garden and the young magnolia tree. Harlan had planted that tree as a gift, in the middle of the night, so she'd see it in the morning when she went out to get the mail.

And the varsity rowing team. Connie had loved that too. Three mornings a week at five in the morning, down to the silent misty harbour, the undisturbed water like polished steel. Sometimes the mist was so thick it closed everything in, made the world small, even after the sun rose. Then the fog glowed white. It looked so solid and yet it could disperse in an instant, showing itself thin and wispy like a vandal, slipping out from between you and the tall grey hull of a sailboat, a mere twelve feet away. The caw of a seagull could take her back. The light boats the team carried down like surfboards to sploosh into the sea, nose first, then slicing through the water, the dip and drip of the oars, and the quiet, sleepy strokes before the coxswain began her drill. How high they sat in their shallow husks, as if it wasn't water they were on at all.

A young man in an orange t-shirt came out of a door at the far end of the room and began soundlessly vacuuming the floor with a kind of cylinder on his back, walking slowly between the rows of chairs like a beekeeper smoking out the hives. There was something comical about how he was doing it so intently that it made Connie think of Zeus. She looked at him from behind, his small shoulders, his shaved head, his vulnerable back. The band was playing something rhythmic and soothing now. She felt a sadness for him that was a lot like love. He seemed all alone. And yet here she was, his *family*.

A man stood up from his chair and raised his hands in the air, cobwebs tattooed onto his elbows. Another man stepped up to the mike and prayed for Wichita to become the first transformed city. He prayed for change, for mercy, for the relief of suffering. Then he called for an end to abortion. Why did they always have to be so militant on this point?

Connie got up and moved towards one of the tall black speakers, supported on what appeared to be the legs of a card table. She put her hand out and felt the puff of the drumbeat and bass guitar. I made it, she thought and pulled a chair over and leaned forward into the music. I'm so exhausted, and I've been faithful for so long. But now, God, I want something from you. I feel like I've done my part, but you've never really spoken to me. I need you to show me that you care.

Connie felt lonely and overlooked, and yet she knew you couldn't force God into a measly human corner. She'd never had a powerful religious experience, if she was honest about it. A woman on stage was praying into the microphone. She was speaking in tongues. Would she always be so unremarkable? Some kind of talent like that would have made her feel special.

She felt her own mouth with her tongue. Felt her teeth and how smooth they were. Had she grown hard? Was she incapable of vulnerability? She closed her eyes and prayed.

⇝ ⇜

Zeus felt porous, full of holes, holes and swallows, swooping and darting from nests built into his rib cage, out into the bright big room and back again. He understood that this place was a refuge, a room crammed full of music, windowless, where the rest of the world just fell away. And what bloomed at the front of his head was a feeling of space he didn't recognize.

What was it going to be like, meeting his parents again? What if he'd got the story wrong? What if he had to change all the ideas he'd told himself over the years, things he'd believed to be true about his past. What then?

Zeus felt so tired, he could barely keep his eyes open. He stretched out on the row of chairs and curled his wrists and tucked his hands under his chin. Through the frame of an empty chair in front of him, Zeus could see, about ten rows ahead, the back of a girl. She had a red dress, and she wore her dark hair in a thick braid. She reached up to scratch her ear and she was wearing a white plaster cast from her knuckles to her elbow that was covered in stickers and signatures.

She reminded Zeus of a girl he'd met when he was eleven years old, at a summer camp the Crowes had sent him to in Ontario. She had a brother who was older than Zeus by a year and was the first boy he ever fell in love with. They were staff kids and sort of hung out on the periphery of camp. They had created a restaurant out of a few empty packing crates and a red-checkered tablecloth. The name of the restaurant was painted on two crossed canoe paddles nailed to a tree that marked the path leading down to the river, where they caught the small rainbow trout they'd fry up with a strip of bacon and serve to the campers for twenty-five cents apiece. The sister had a crush on him. People called her Radish because of her rosy cheeks. One day she invited Zeus to the restaurant and met him at the top of the path, looking shy and embarrassed. Radish wore a daisy chain on her head and a white dress and told her brother to shut up when Zeus arrived. She placed herself deliberately beside him, and they walked down the narrow path together and she had a solemn way of walking. Her brother was humming the bridal chorus. When they got to the bottom, he declared them man and wife and laughed so hard he had to sit down on a big rock. Radish pulled her skirt wide, like opening a fan, and said, I'm happy now, and she was, until her brother's mirth grew a mocking edge. Stop laughing, Radish said. We're on our honeymoon. But he wouldn't stop laughing. Radish slapped her brother on the side of the head so hard he fell over, and Zeus ran away while they were still fighting.

The next day, the camp alarm bell started to ring. It was an old school-house bell and had to be rung manually, and it could mean there was a fire and everyone had to congregate in front of the mess hall. Radish's brother had fallen off the balcony and broken his leg. He was sitting up and his leg was bent wrongly and the cracked end of his shinbone was sticking out through the skin, clean and pale, like a branch with its bark peeled off. There was only a small trickle of blood. Most of the campers had gathered and there was a loud and jostling crowd, but the boy saw Zeus and waved him over. His eyes were shining with a kind of silver light. Tell me a joke, he said, and Zeus panicked to remember one. What do you call a scared dinosaur? The boy shrugged. A nervous Rex, he said, and the boy laughed. Zeus told him another joke, then another, and soon the ambulance arrived. The boy reached out and held Zeus's hand and, for a second, looked terrified, then two paramedics in blue uniforms took him away.

Zeus never saw him again but for months was haunted by the boy's look of fear, and as if he'd wanted something – and to be singled out like that, from a crowd. It had made Zeus feel anointed. It gave him the warmest, cosiest feeling to remember it now, and it made him want to be a child again – all that promise, and mystery and delight. But being a child was a treacherous place to be as well. It doesn't take much to make an orphan. One natural disaster and we'd all be children again, wandering the ragged earth with all the other orphaned children.

Look, there's a parade of them now. Coming down the road in their filthy, threadbare clothes, broken shoes. There is a village and they ask for shelter, but are politely denied. The orphans move on, burnt trees like black capillaries against the sky. They come upon a modern convoy of UN peacekeepers. We refuse to help you, the commander announces cheerfully. And the children don't mind. They accept these refusals graciously, innocent of any alternative. They walk until they come to the edge of a bright green lake, on the other side of which, an ancient white city is being bombed. Black fighter planes in the air like dragonflies, but the children are happy. Some of the orphans are taking off their clothes. They splash into the murky water in their thin underwear, shouting and laughing.

H

annah pushed the curtains aside and stood at the window of the hotel room. Suburban traffic eight floors below. Highway construction. Late-afternoon sun warm through the glass. Hannah lay down on one of the two double beds and thought about Norm. She loved him so much. Why didn't he want to have a baby with her? Sexy Norman Peach. He really knew how to thrill her. She touched her belly and moved her hand further down. Every forbidden thing rose to the surface. A woman arrives at her door. Hannah turns her around and presses her up against the wall, feels her tits, slides a hand up between her legs. Then she's being fucked, with the quick, sharp thrusts of a dog. Then a horse cock, like Catherine the Great, and rough-looking stable hands crowding around and jerking off. Norm at a distance, proprietorial. That was Norm's fantasy first, guiding the horse cock into her. He could be like that. A shocking, confident, liberated imagination.

When Hannah sat up and looked around, she felt smug, a bit self-conscious. The theatre of the mind was unpredictable and lawless, but life was good if you could enjoy the company of your own thoughts, take a little dirt in what felt good. Then she thought about Caiden Brock. Now resident of Wichita. She found a phone book in a drawer and looked him up. There he was. Listed. She raised a skeptical eyebrow, then dialled the number. As soon as it started to ring, her palms rushed into a sweat.

Hello? Julia's voice.

Is Caiden there?

Just a moment, please.

He was! And delighted to hear from her. You're here for what? Are you insane? You have to come for dinner. It's Friday night. We eat early because of the kids.

Will Julia be okay with that? Hannah said.

Of course she will, he said. Don't be silly. I'm going to swing by and pick you up right now. You need rescuing.

We're at the Comfort Inn, near the Kingdom of Salvation place. Are you sure it's not out of your way?

We need a few groceries. It's a thirty-minute drive. Meet me at the entrance.

And that was that.

Hannah went into the bathroom. Okay, she said. All right. And then she remembered his wife's voice. She looked at herself in the mirror. I'm thirty-six, she said, and I like the way I look. Then she noticed a small white pimple near her mouth and didn't mind. So Caiden could see it and think, she doesn't care about appearances, isn't here to attract me. She's here as a friend, to inquire about my life and wish me well with Julia and the boys. She left it there as a little white flag to her virtue.

Hannah left a note for Connie and Zeus on one of the beds and went downstairs. Caiden Brock was a married man, had been for twenty years. Hannah had been to his engagement party when she was sixteen years old. Caiden's parents were hosting a barbecue in honour of their son and his Michigan beauty-pageant fiancée. The pool in the backyard, potato salad on paper plates. Hannah was coming out of the bathroom and there was Caiden. He pulled her into his old bedroom and shoved his hand down her pants. He slipped a finger into her hot young body. He was breathing heavily and they both heard Julia through the open window, laughing at her new father-in-law, something he said about a watermelon on the side of his head. Caiden's desire was overpowering, and then he was embarrassed, and that made Hannah feel embarrassed too. I've got to get back out there, he said and left. On the window ledge was a model Ferrari. The sheers stroked it. Hannah looked down and saw Caiden bend for two beers out of a cooler. Hey, he was saying to his father. That's my wife you got there.

Caiden's SUV pulled up to the hotel entrance. He was still attractive, still had that dazzling roguish smile. He was wearing a navy blue sweater with the stars and stripes across the front.

Nice sweater, Hannah said.

I'm wearing it in honour of the fact my citizenship just came through.

You're an American now?

Oh say can you see, he said and saluted the sun visor. Do you know how long I tried to get a business off the ground in Canada? It was impossible. They take fifty cents on every dollar you make. There's no love-loss there.

So you like it here.

The States, he said, has been very good to me.

It's made you rich, Hannah said.

He laughed and slapped the leather wheel, then joggled it to make the SUV shake a bit. Things have been going like gangbusters, he said. In all respects − financial, spiritual. He counted these off, using his pinkie and ring finger. I have three sons now and another baby on the way. Pray with me, will you, that I get a daughter?

You want me to *pray* for that?

Prayers are all I need, he said.

Caiden had maintained his Christian faith – had not lost it apparently, or rejected what he was brought up to believe. It still surprised Hannah. To have such a materialistic definition of success and to feel entitled to God's blessing, as if worldly success was what God wanted for all of us. So your dissolute youth, she said, the drinking and the womanizing, have you renounced those along with the maple leaf?

Caiden gripped the wheel a little harder, then released it. My faith, he said, is compatible with sinful behaviour. It has to be. Because I'm a sinner. I'm capable of embracing the contradictions between belief in Christ and un-Christly acts. You're more of a purist, he said. Always have been. You'd throw the baby out with the bathwater.

Speaking of which, tell me the names of your sons.

He took his eyes off the road and turned to her. Mitchel, Chad, and Abraham, Caiden said. For a moment, he had that old look of knowing and risk and daring and sensuality, and Hannah's pelvis responded to that look.

There's a story in the Old Testament, he said, about Mishak, Chadrak, and Abednego. Three brothers who survive the fiery furnace. I always had a vision I'd have three sons.

There's a camp song, Hannah said, about those boys.

Maybe that's where the seed was planted, Caiden said and gave a boisterous laugh. You know, Hannah, some amazing things have been happening in the church, here in the States. Have you ever heard of the Vinyard? Well, they had a revival, a number of years ago now. I first went to one in

California and caught the laughing syndrome. You ever hear about this? Whole congregations coming over laughing. Even the Anglicans caught it. In fact, I think it *started* in England. Can you imagine? Prim little country ladies, in their Sunday best, laughing like drunkards. When I was in California, this preacher touched my forehead and I fell over. They have bouncers there to catch you, and I lay on the floor and laughed and cried and was totally paralyzed but full of the Holy Spirit. It was so powerful, Hannah. It was like being on acid, only I felt totally lucid.

Hannah envied Caiden's ability to be so easily transported. She would have liked to have had an experience like that. They were passing brick-and-glass bungalows on wide lawns with three-car garages. The air was windy, the sky full of contrast. Big white clouds steamrollered across the blue, strobing the sunlight, making the world loom bright and large one moment, then recede into the shadows the next.

God has been using me in amazing ways, Caiden said. I feel called, at times, to say things to people. I don't know why I'm saying them or what their relevance is, but it ends up being exactly what they need to hear at that precise moment.

Hannah had forgotten what it was like to talk to Caiden. How egotistical he could be. They had never really talked. Maybe it was the age difference. But he'd always seemed more interested in the potent physical effect she had on his body than in anything she might have to say. He liked her wordless, daredevil willingness to try anything – and she liked the electricity his presence sent through her body. But then, there had always been a lot of women.

How's your wife?

She's a strong, virtuous woman, he said. Well, she'd have to be to keep a man like me in line. I've made love to that woman thousands of times and I'm still not tired of it yet.

He indicated and they turned into a vast parking lot in front of a Walmart.

Remind me to get brownie mix for the boys, he said, and milk.

In the canned goods aisle, as Caiden was taking down a can of chickpeas, his cell phone rang. He said, Okay, honey, whipped cream. I'll go get it, Hannah said, and as she was walking off, she heard him say, I love you too. A slightly wincing tone. Check up on your husband and use whipped cream as an excuse. That was the Christian way. Appear at all costs to have grace. It made Hannah want to get drunk and swear, make a porn film on the cold linoleum floor of an American box store.

They drove west to a wealthy neighbourhood with houses set so far back off the road they had their street addresses nailed to trees. Flagpoles marking the driveway entrances.

I hate patriotism, Hannah thought, and felt a sudden deep craving to see Norm. They were so compatible. They wanted the same things. There was no desire to emulate the trappings of success. They sought inward, intangible rewards – surges of feeling, intellectual achievements. They liked their rented apartment, the art on the walls they'd made themselves, the duets they sang together, Norm on guitar. They liked the fact they'd never had Cheez Whiz growing up, or juice boxes or store-bought cookies, and how ashamed they'd been by their hand-me-down clothes, and how they'd both had paid jobs by the time they were fifteen and what that did for character. Maybe she could live without a child. There were other considerations.

At the door, Julia was beautiful and ripe with her fourth pregnancy. She was wearing an apron and her hair was shiny brown, her skin glowing. A box of pasta in one hand, her other hand affectionately resting on the back of her son's neck. Two more boys came around the door, curious and enthusiastic as puppies.

Hi, Julia said in a flat tone, and Hannah understood this visit was a mistake. She suddenly felt like an emblem, a symbol of Caiden's reform and fidelity, and a concession to forgiveness on Julia's part. Hannah might as well have sent a cardboard cutout of herself, or a blank screen onto which they could have projected their new better selves, void of those lawless and inappropriate joyful urges.

But just as quickly, Hannah summoned up a generous spirit and held out her hand, and Julia shook it politely. Then Hannah said to the children, Okay, which one of you is the troublemaker.

☲ ☴

It was five-thirty in the afternoon when Rose arrived in Wichita. She'd made two flight connections and been travelling for nearly ten hours. She walked out past the baggage claim to where people were being met by their families and friends. A child ran into the arms of a joyous grandparent. Two young people embraced, his hand inside the back of her sweater, an exposed crescent of pale skin. Rose felt tired and hungry. She stood beside her compact wheelie suitcase and felt like a fool. What was she doing here, really? She should never have let Tim convince her. Now she was dreading calling her daughters. And how was Zeus going to feel? She had to get a cab, and to book a room near the church. Off to her left was an airport bar and grill – first things first. She wheeled her suitcase over and sat down in a dark booth and ordered a porter house steak and a glass of red wine.

What was she expecting to accomplish by making this surprise appearance? She told the waitress she was stressed. I just flew out to drop in on my kids unannounced.

The waitress gave a quick snort and said, Oh, they're gonna love that! Well, maybe your family is different, I don't know. You want a baked potato or french fries?

Rose was humiliated. Fries, please. If she had called them first, what then? Would she even be here? Perhaps she was just caught up in her own needs, after all. Rose picked at her steak and sipped her wine and finished neither of them.

In the taxi, she looked out at the lights of Wichita city, all the young people heading out for a Friday night on the town. Perhaps she was trying to create a little adventure for herself, however selfish she was being. She felt like she'd been looking after people all her life, propping them up behind the scenes. She thought back to when her husband was first ordained and assigned to a parish in Montreal. He was out nearly every evening, attending one meeting or another, visiting elderly or dying parishioners in the hospital, rushing off to help a poor family being evicted or immigrants in a panic because they couldn't read their utility bills. They had met so many people, their stories so compelling. There was that drug dealer, Teddy, who'd grown up Hassidic but had converted to Christianity. He started bringing his associates to prayer meetings at the church. They'd take a seat in the sidechapel and their pants would slide up past their ankle boots to reveal the butt of a gun or the handle of a knife. Rose had had to ask Tim to talk to them about their hardware. He made a gentle request, and after that, they left their guns and knives in the silver collection tray by the door. Teddy was so fond of Tim he invited him on a fishing trip with his buddies. When Tim fell asleep in the boat, Teddy and his friends hooked a fish to the end of his line, then tugged on it and jostled him awake. Pastor! Pastor! You caught a fish!

But those were hard and exciting times for both of us, Rose thought as the taxi turned off the highway into an industrial section of the city. There was that soup kitchen she'd started in the basement of the church, that took up so much of her time and energy, where she sold secondhand clothes, and taught sewing and cooking classes to single moms. It's where she'd met that frightening homeless man, Hunter, with whom she found herself doing spiritual battle.

Hunter had a messianic complex and a small following of disciples. One day he walked right into her soup kitchen and tossed the plywood tables into the air. The coffee urn exploded in a brown spume, and a boxful of sugar cubes went scattering across the floor. He tipped over the racks that held the donated clothes she'd so painstakingly cleaned and labelled, then he threw a black taffeta ball gown in her face – the same shiny blue-black as a raven's feathers. The ball gown seemed to swirl around and engulf her head. He said, I know that your father died of a heart attack four years ago, and that he never approved of you. She'd run to the phone and called the police.

He came back again on a Sunday morning before the service and Tim had to escort him outside. It was in the middle of a snowstorm, and Rose could remember how the snow had swirled around Tim's black cassock while Hunter towered over him, shouting obscenities. You motherfucking hypocrite! You parasitic dog-fucking son of a whore! It was terrible, but Tim had shown such courage. He'd stood his ground, even bursting into song at one point, belting out 'Onward Christian Soldier' at the top of his lungs. It almost seemed funny to her now. But then she recalled that awful vision she'd had of Hunter lifting Tim up by the armpits and throwing him backwards, impaling him on the spiked, wrought-iron fence in front of the church. She'd squeezed her eyes shut and begged God to protect her husband. When she opened them again, Hunter was crossing the street with his hands on his head, like he was being arrested. Twenty minutes later, composed as anything, her husband was leading the morning service. How had he been able to do that? He never complained about a thing. He just went on about his business with a quiet and dignified confidence. He was such a private man, and it meant they never talked about all that stuff.

It was that same year he got possessed by an evil spirit. It was that Ida woman, after a Bible study, complaining about the flowers on the altar. Tim had tried to interrupt her, and then Ida stood up and loomed over him like Hunter had done. She said a few words that Tim could never recall, and a coldness like a grey fog, with a foul sulfuric smell, rose up out of her and swept down onto him and covered him like a lead apron. Ida walked out of the church and Tim struggled to make it from the chapel to his office. This time the girls were there, doing their homework. He collapsed into a chair, pale as a corpse, and told them to call home.

As soon as she heard Connie's voice, Rose knew something was wrong. She arrived at the church fifteen minutes later and ran into her husband's empty office. Tim's watch was on his desk, next to his priest's collar, his cardigan on the floor. She called out his name and ran back into the cavernous church and down the stairs into the basement. She came around the corner to where the washrooms were. The door to the men's room was open. Connie and Hannah stood in the bright fluorescent light, in that white tiled room, thirteen and fourteen years old. They looked terrified. The door to one of the stalls was open, and Tim was sitting on the toilet, pants around his ankles, vomit on the floor, crying like a child. Why had she and Tim never tried to talk to the girls about what they'd witnessed? There hadn't been any talk about that either. These were the kinds of mistakes she'd go back and fix, if only she could.

Tim stayed in bed for two weeks after that while a procession of priests came and went through the house, sprinkling salt and holy water in all the rooms, even the bishop with his miter and staff. The bishop had a warmth that Rose had appreciated. He was the only one who took the time to ask the girls about school. Eventually, Tim got better. Meningitis was mentioned by a visiting doctor, but everyone knew it was the work of the devil.

The taxi had stopped and she was in front of The Global Kingdom of Salvation Center. It was dark outside. Things didn't quite look the way she remembered. She was starting to feel anxious again. It was her effort to do the right thing and her insecurity, clanging like gongs against each other. Her hands were cold and clammy. She paid the driver and stepped out onto the sidewalk. She yanked the handle up out of the top of her suitcase. Oh, but it was good to be here again, at this holy place of worship. She'd go inside and ask about accommodation. When she got settled, she'd call the kids. It wasn't wrong of her to have come, so what if she was nervous. It was probably a healthy sign, a good kind of nervousness, even if it was making it hard for her to breathe. Her breathing was getting shallow. She swung her purse off her shoulder and started digging around in it. Lord, just let me get inside first. Her throat was constricting. Her chest too. Where was her inhaler? Is it possible she'd forgotten to bring it? She had the urge to cough. She unzipped her jacket, hooked her hands around the collar of her sweater and dragged the neck down. Please, Lord, don't let this happen to me. Not right now. She had begun to wheeze. Two people standing nearby turned to look. Asthma, Rose whispered. She was buried in sand with only a straw to breathe through and starting to panic. The more panicked she felt, the harder it was to get air. Silver spots flared and fizzled in front of her like flakes of magnesium. Dizziness. Oh God, Rose said, and then she passed out on the sidewalk in front of The Global Kingdom of Salvation Center. She went down sideways and didn't get her hands up in time. She sliced her head on the base of a metal garbage can and lay unconscious on the ground, bleeding from her hair. A small crowd quickly gathered. Someone call an ambulance! a woman shouted and ran into the building.

◻ ◻

You okay? It was Zeus. He had walked over to Connie and was crouching beside her chair with his hand on her back. I fell asleep. Do you know what time it is?

It's late, Connie said, sitting up straight and bending her spine from side to side. She turned to Zeus and looked at him imploringly. Why is the Bible, she said, full of stories about favoured children singled out for greatness, when most of us will never be? There's this constant feeling of falling short. And a great pressure to conceal it, by keeping up appearances. I know my mother found it very difficult being the wife of a vicar, but talking to her, sometimes, was like talking to someone on TV.

Yeah, but you can't just tell someone like that to drop the act, Zeus said.

I know, Connie said, because if you persist with it for long enough, the person behind the act just shrivels up from neglect and disappears. They turn to dust – that's all that's left. Connie brushed her hair back with both hands. No, that's wrong, she said, speaking very slowly and deliberately. What's left is the awful but acceptable murder, of a beautiful if flawed and ambiguous life. I even know how a thing like that starts, I'm just not sure how you stop it.

Connie knew that her mother carried a wound at the heart of the very thing that saved her – her faith in God – because her father had refused to go to her baptism when she was fifteen years old. He thought a church that would deign to baptize his spirited teenaged daughter was a church incapable of wisdom. Rose ached to serve God. She, too, had grown up with the dream of becoming a missionary, like her mother, but her own father thought she was unworthy. It gave Rose a feeling that would infect the rest of her life, that she was a sham Christian. It was the worst blow to her confidence – to be accused of fraudulence when she felt so sincere. Connie knew all this because Rose had told her daughters this story and it had made them so sad, but it was the kind of sadness that drives a wedge into closeness.

When you're a child and your mother's sad and you can't help her, Connie said to Zeus, you have to run away.

I know about running away, he said.

We all did, in our own ways, run away from Rose and Tim. I think that's why she's coming now. She knows it too. And this time she wants to make sure we all make it home, wherever that is exactly.

⅀ Ɛ

Caiden dropped Hannah off back at the hotel. Before she got out of his suv, he said, I'm sorry if I was an asshole all those years ago.

233

You weren't an asshole, Hannah said.

I mean, all that groping and stuff. I wouldn't want you to feel like I'd –

Hannah shook her head.

You know, it always surprises me, he said, but the more I get to know you, the more I like you.

Why should that surprise you? Hannah thought. What should have surprised him was how little effort he'd made to get to know her in the first place. Hannah wanted to say that it seemed the opposite for her, that she liked him less, that he would never know her, that she'd played devil's advocate in the car, had only told him about what wasn't going well in her life in reaction to his exaggerated claims of personal fulfillment, his smug self-satisfaction. She'd asked him if God had a message for her, seeing as he had this ability, and he'd said that it didn't work that way. I never ask for it, he said. It just happens. And Hannah looked out the window, annoyed at herself for having fallen for it in the first place, having caved into her curiosity.

Now, standing on the curb, she felt a quick, ferocious gallop of disappointment. She'd wanted Caiden to say that he was still in love with her, would always be, though there was nothing to be done about it now. That would have redeemed everything. To make exuberant desire the cause of his behaviour, not turn it into something depraved. That's what sullied the memory. It was the idea of sin. She'd had no regrets about it until now. Until now, the memory was pure. She'd been irresistible to Caiden. She'd had that power over him, but now he'd taken that away from her by apologizing and turning his desire into a weakness. Desire wasn't shameful. It was Jesus who made sinners of us all.

Hannah watched Caiden drive away, then covered her mouth. An overwhelming need to cry was coming to the surface. She moved away from the hotel entrance. All through dinner, she'd been repressing this sad, new, painful knowledge that had revealed itself to her, that he'd never really loved her. She walked around behind the building and stood beside a dumpster, put her hands on her knees, bent forward and sobbed. It was more like vomiting than crying, and it passed soon enough, and afterwards she felt purged.

In the lobby, Hannah spotted a payphone, went over, shoved her credit card in the slot, and dialled her number in Toronto. Norm was home.

I'm sorry about our last phone call, he said.

Me too, she said. I miss you.

Hannah told Norm about arriving here, the church, and how Zeus had stayed with her sister and gone in. She could see Norm shaking his head with that knowing grin of his. I think I've realized something on this trip, she said.

What, an epiphany? Norm said. On the road to Damascus?

I'm happy with you, Norm.

I'm glad to hear that, he said.

We're sort of made for each other, don't you think? I don't want to be with anybody else.

I love you too, Hansky Polansky.

I know you do, she said. And that's the funny thing. I've never really felt that with anyone before, or believed it, or trusted it, or whatever. And I don't question it with you. Let's just be with each other and see how things turn out, okay?

You know, we're going to be all right, he said, you and I.

When she got up to the room, Zeus was unpacking. Thanks for bringing our bags up from the truck, he said, and Connie came out of the bathroom holding two glasses of water.

So how was dinner with Caiden Brock? Connie said, her tone full of innuendo. *That* was fast.

Can you give it a rest?

Sorry, she said, putting the glasses down on the bedside table. How'd it go? Connie was taking off her sweater. Seriously, she said.

It was awful, Hannah said and collapsed onto one of the beds. Apparently, the more he gets to know me, the more he likes me.

Well, that's nice, isn't it?

Not really, Hannah said, because I kind of feel the opposite. I don't think he's ever really been interested in *me*. He's just been fascinated, all this time, by all the things I made him feel about himself.

Sounds a bit adolescent, Connie said and her cell phone rang. It was Rose. When did you get here? Why didn't you tell us you were coming? We had to hear it from Dad. She paused. Then, What do you mean, the hospital? What happened? Connie took the address down and said they'd be there right away. She hung up, shaking her head, and explained how Rose had had an asthma attack, passed out, cut her head open, and had to have stitches.

What *is* it with her? Hannah asked in wonder.

The sisters were amazed at how often Rose's drama overtook anything else that might be going on. This is, like, *so* the last thing I want to do right now, Connie said, pulling her sweater on again.

Hannah was digging in her bag for the keys to the truck. It's so typical the way Mom's just totally managed to hijack this entire trip. And as usual, irritation got the better of whatever concern they may have been feeling about their mother.

I'll go get her, Zeus said, and the sisters looked at him, then at each other.

Connie said, If you want to.

Hannah said, Will you recognize her?

It hasn't been *that* long, he said. So Zeus went to get their mother, and Connie and Hannah were thoughtful and a little repentant as they got undressed and ready for bed. Maybe we should've gone with him, Hannah said in the doorway to the bathroom. Do you think she'll mind that we didn't?

No, it'll be good for them to have a little time together, Connie said.

I suppose, Hannah said and went in to take a shower. When she came out, Connie's blue cashmere sweater was arranged on the table so the cuffs of both sleeves were soaking in their own glass of water. What's with the sweater? Hannah asked.

Connie looked embarrassed. Sometimes I soak my sweater cuffs before going to bed at night, she confessed. So they're tight again in the morning.

Hannah let this sink in like the marvellous thing that it was. Then she said, You know, the best thing a family member can give another is the privilege of not having to worry about them. When you tell me something like that, for some reason, I don't worry about you, Con. I find it reassuring.

You're so weird, Connie said, but you can make my heart feel light and happy.

That sounds like a direct translation from the Chippewa.

Connie smiled and wrung out her cuffs and hung her sweater over a chair.

Sitting alone in the truck, Zeus thought of the day he'd driven Fenton to the lake. His death announcement. Where are you now, Fenton? Where did you go when you died? Zeus felt a movement like the stroking of a thousand soft, tiny feathers down the front of his torso. I don't want to cry, he thought, and out came a mournful *hoo hoo hoo*. It was dark outside and there was no one around, but he felt exposed. He took out the directions the guy at the reception desk had drawn on a piece of paper and put it on the seat beside him. Pull yourself together, he said out loud, and began driving towards the woman who'd adopted him fourteen years ago out of the sheer goodness of her heart. His stomach was in knots.

The hospital, when he pulled up, was bright as a spaceship. He parked near a neon red cross, got out of the truck, and walked into Emerg, activating the enthusiastic welcome of the automatic doors.

Immediately there was a ruckus around a gurney as an old man was pinned down and sedated. A nurse lifted an IV bag into the air, filled with silvery liquid. A woman was being held back by a strong-looking male intern and asked to let the doctors do their job now. The antiseptic smell had its own encoded memory bank, and it made Zeus feel a little panicked.

He walked into the Emergency waiting room. It wasn't very crowded. On a row of seats sat a woman with greying hair, reading a magazine, wearing a mask attached to a portable compressor, a faint mist coming out of the side ports, like she was bubbling. At her feet a small red suitcase on wheels.

Zeus walked over and sat down beside her. She turned towards him with a polite reaction, and he reached out and pulled the mask away from her face. Rose leaned backwards, the mask taut at the end of its elastic. For a moment, neither of them moved. Then a recognition dawned on her face and she look embarrassed, then said, Some pickle I got myself into, eh?

Zeus gently replaced it and leaned forward in his chair with his elbows on his knees.

Rose checked her watch and pushed the mask up onto the top of her head. How are you, Zeus? I wasn't expecting *you* to come get me, she said. I didn't recognize you at first. You've got no hair.

It'll grow back, he said and sat up again. For a moment, he was distracted by a noise on the TV. Some protest at an election rally.

Are the girls here? Rose said.

They're at the hotel, Zeus said.

Did they send you here on your own?

They were going to come, but I offered and –

It's so good to see you, she said and pressed his knee briefly with her hand. I'm very pleased you're here. And she started to blink, as if her eyes were welling up.

Zeus looked up at the chemical mist rising from the mask on top of Rose's head. It's hard, he said, being back in a hospital.

It must be, she said. I'm very sorry about your friend.

Rose removed her mask and turned off the compressor. That was my last dose, she said and rubbed her face where the mask had been. Her face was older and had a more vulnerable quality.

Zeus took a deep breath and said, So what about you? How are *you* feeling?

It's been a long day, she said. I'm sorry, causing all this trouble. She turned her head to the side and lifted her hair to show him a shaved patch of white skin with six stitches.

We should get you back to the hotel, he said.

Rose gave a sudden shiver and tossed her magazine onto a nearby table. They had to bring me here in an ambulance, she said, laughing gently. I've never been in an ambulance before. She leaned towards him and put her hand on his knee again. The good thing about travelling at my age, she whispered, is that you always travel with health insurance. Can you imagine how much this would've cost me?

She seemed different somehow, Zeus thought. And he wondered if she had changed. People get older, and they can change. He liked the idea. Strangely, it made him feel safe.

Rose suddenly grew serious. I didn't die, did I? She touched the wound on her head. I feel like maybe I died, and this is all some strange episode in the afterlife. It feels like a dream to be sitting here beside you.

It's not a dream, Zeus said. Dreaming comes soon. Do you want me to take you to the hotel now?

Yes, as soon as they let me go here. She looked at her watch again. I'm waiting to see the doctor. They need to check my oxygen levels before they can release me.

Just then a woman walked over and moved the compressor and sat down beside Rose as if she knew her. The woman was big. She was dressed in black, with a black wrap slung around her neck, and her skin was very white and smooth.

Oh my *God*, she said, opening her purse with a small metallic click and taking out a pack of Nicorette. How much is one person expected to endure? She cracked a tablet out of the pack, pitched it into her mouth, and started chewing furiously.

Who's this? Zeus asked.

The name's Esperanza Saks, she said and held out her hand.

How do you do, he said. I'm Zeus.

Oh, what a great name, Esperanza said. Her eyes were on fire. A white light brimmed around the edges and her pupils were deep black.

We met out in the hall, Rose explained. Her mother was out there on a stretcher for a very long time, poor thing, before anybody would come and see her.

She was screaming her head off, Esperanza told Zeus. You see, my boyfriend, Marty, he just had a stroke. That was two weeks ago. Then today, my mother collapsed and had to be brought in — and now *this*? She turned to Rose. This news about my brother? I mean, it's just insane! I don't understand it! She sat rigid for a moment, then covered her face and sobbed soundlessly into her hands.

Zeus looked at Rose. Her brother just died, Rose said softly, and Zeus nodded. Why was he drawn, again and again, to these mournful scenes in hospitals? Did he, in fact, have a hand in all this suffering? Was he supposed to know what to do? What to say? Because he didn't. If someone else could be here instead of me, Zeus thought, somebody *else* inside my shoes —

Let it out, sweetheart, Rose said and put her hand on Esperanza's back.

Now this was the Rose he knew, Zeus thought. Attending instinctively to the pain of others. Esperanza took a kleenex out of her purse and wiped her eyes and blew her nose. She looked out across the room.

The awful thing is, she said, my *dad* just died four months ago. My mom and I were mourning him like a family of elephants. We helped him to die like a midwife helps a woman give birth, stroking him with our trunks. I've learned so much recently about being human. Or being an elephant – I don't know which one! And there he was – my dad, Nigel Saks – in his music satchel under the piano stool. He'd been cremated and he was back home. Suddenly, the thing you can't accept becomes beautiful and you *want* it. We toasted him in a circle, and there he was, on the floor in his briefcase.

I used to know a man once, Zeus said, who got into suitcases.

Rose turned to Zeus and looked as if she might laugh.

Esperanza spat the gum into her kleenex, put it back in her purse, and clicked it shut. Zeus wasn't sure if there was more. She tossed her long dark hair over one shoulder, then the other.

We had asked my brother, *Donny*, to come to the funeral, she said. So he came, but his eyes were rolling back into his head. Boy, did I ever fake him out though. Jollying him into position at the back of the church. You were there when it counted, I told him afterwards, but you were *stoned* and it's only going to get worse.

It was nearly eleven o'clock, and Zeus was getting impatient, though Rose was showing no sign that she wasn't interested and sympathetic to Esperanza's story.

I have a gay Catholic friend from New Orleans, Esperanza said, called Romeo?

She was lightening up, Zeus thought, that was a good sign.

Well, she said, Romeo told me he had an order of Carmelite nuns *praying* for Marty. I wanted to know, are they wearing *panties*?

Esperanza laughed, and Zeus saw a small muscle of irritation flex along Rose's jaw line. She had quietly taken offence, perhaps even made a private judgment, and this was also something he recognized. She could rush in to help, but she would only go so far.

I used to make fun of his spirituality, Esperanza said, but guess what Marty told me this morning? He said that, in the middle of the night, he felt people *praying* for him. I'm telling you, if you've got spiritual friends, use them if they have access to nuns. I still have this beautiful image of all these nuns with their panties off, down on their knees. I got Romeo to light one of those candles. Did you know they can burn for three days straight? If there was a Christ, he'd be *Romeo*.

Rose had started to gather up her things, she was pulling on her coat.

But, oh *God*! Esperanza said. I can still remember kissing my dad, day after day. Until an hour before he died, he could still pucker!

I'm just going to go over there, Rose said, and talk to the nurse about getting released. She stood up. Excuse me, will you, for a minute?

Esperanza put a hand to her throat, straightened her posture, and lifted her chin. She looked proud and wounded. She turned to Zeus, and there was a quality in her look that made him feel as if he knew her, the kind of person she was, maybe even some of what she'd been through.

After my dad died, she said, my brother came back and helped himself to what was left of Dad's medication. He took all his morphine. He said he just wanted to kill himself, and I didn't speak to him for months. So then I thought, he *must* be dead. I *wanted* him to be.

But then? Esperanza said, and her eyes seemed to shine again. After Marty had his stroke? I realized my brother's an animal, a drug-taking animal, a fox in a hen house. He behaves exactly the way he's supposed to behave. I felt so much compassion for him. We're all becoming more of what we are, Zeus. He acts the way he acts. A crow eats its baby bird. That's what they do. You can't blame the crow for that, she said. We're all becoming *more* of what we are.

When Zeus and Rose left the hospital, it was almost midnight. They were delirious with fatigue. The three of you drive all the way here in *this* thing? Rose laughed outright, getting into the truck. When Zeus had closed his door, she said, That woman in there, I thought she'd never stop. I got the feeling she comes from a very *theatrical* family. Something of the chaos of her life reminded me of you and Hannah. The sordid messes you could get yourself into, living outside the church like you do.

Zeus felt that feathering again, like the front of his body was fizzing up with carbonation. He refused to show his feelings. They drove to the hotel in silence, Zeus half waiting for Rose to apologize. They cruised the parking lot until he found an empty space.

When the truck stopped, Rose said, It's not like you're the same as me, Zeus, or *have* to be. I understand that now.

Zeus got out and slammed the door. He felt an old anger coming to the surface. A strip of light peeled off the back of the building and a man stepped out of a door and, standing beside a dumpster, lit a cigarette. I'm going to go over there, Zeus said and started walking towards the hotel. Sometimes it seemed all religion did was make people worse.

The man didn't see him at first and yelped at somebody coming out of the darkness. Sorry, Zeus said. I didn't mean to scare you. Could I bum a cigarette?

Yes, the man said, of course. He was wearing a brown cleaner's uniform.

Zeus bent towards the man's lighter, inhaled, and got a head rush. He sat down on the curb that bordered the narrow lawn surrounding the hotel and let the cigarette burn down between his fingers. Rose caught up with her wheelie suitcase and asked Zeus gently, Are you coming inside?

Zeus ignored her and turned to the man, Where are you from?

I'm from Libya, he said. My name is Zoher.

Zeus, he said, and they shook hands.

The man turned to Rose and she raised her hand at the wrist. Rose Crowe, she said in a sad voice. Do I detect a British accent?

Irish, he said.

Was she going to pretend that everything was fine? Zeus wondered.

Many years ago, Zoher said, my country send me to Oxford, but in Oxford they keep me for twelve hours at customs, then tell me I have to leave. This is just after Lockerbie. There is embargo on Libya. I am suspect. But do I know anything about the bombing? So I go to Dublin. I learn English and computers. My government, they pay for everything. Libya was *socialist* country. I knew the two men accused of bombing. They had nothing to do with it. We refuse to release them and there is blockade. You know this? All traffic coming from air and sea. You can only trade by desert. So now Libya is poor like Cuba.

Are you saying you knew the men who did the Lockerbie bombing? Rose asked.

University friends, Zoher said. Libya is small country, not like here. Qaddafi? He lived in same house like us. You could become great doctor in Libya, very famous, but you cannot make money. So maybe you leave. Go to Germany.

But they were found guilty, weren't they? she said.

Zeus flicked his cigarette onto the ground. Was she seriously interested in this right now?

Many people claim responsibility, Zoher said. Islamist jihad revolutionaries. Hezbollah. Maybe even Mossad, Israeli intelligence service. So much fear, always the enemy is invisible. That's how it will be from now on.

He dropped his cigarette and twisted his shoe over it. I miss my country, he said. I miss my friends. I used to play soccer with Qaddafi. Always his jersey was number ten. Always he played in goal. He loved fresh dates with camel's milk, just like my wife. I miss her. I miss my children, my mother.

Zoher raised his face to the dark sky. I like it here at night, behind the Comfort Inn. I smoke a cigarette. I look up at the stars. Same stars over Tripoli. I blow smoke out of my mouth and it carries my prayers to Allah and I wait. I wait for peace. Sometimes I wait for revenge. That is life. Islam teaches us about suffering. When we suffer, it does not surprise us as much as you westerners.

Our disappointments undo us, Rose said, reaching out to lean on the handle of her wheelie suitcase.

And our disappointments, Zoher said, lead us to a greater devotion. In that, the Arab resembles the Jew. You are never so close to yourself, as when you are staring your enemy in the face. A man without enemies learns nothing.

Rose shook her head. These are not my beliefs, she said almost inaudibly and put a hand on her wound. My head is throbbing, she said. The painkillers must be wearing off. I need to sleep now.

Don't we all, Zeus said and continued to look out across the parking lot as Zoher helped Rose towards the door. There was mist around the lampposts, the sound of highway traffic, like a manmade river surging across the land. The orange logo of the Comfort Inn hummed like a futuristic moon and the pavement, so expansive and familiar, seemed like the natural state of things, as if the earth was really made of concrete. Not built up, Zeus thought, but uncovered. After years of clearing and sweeping the debris of nature away, this is what the world was meant to look like. The artificial is real. It was, perhaps, a strange, new, magnificent landscape, if you could give yourself over to it.

I n the morning, Hannah woke fresh and well rested. Zeus was just leaving the room, already wearing his trench coat and scarf. I'll wait for you guys downstairs, he said and closed the door.

Connie came out of the bathroom with her hair wet and her jacket on. You're not dressed yet? she said to Hannah, going over to the hotel phone. She called the front desk and got her mother's room number, then she called her and woke her up. Rose didn't want to get out of bed. Connie asked her if she needed anything, some breakfast maybe, but Rose declined. All she wanted to do was sleep.

The sisters took the elevator down to the lobby, where Zeus was waiting on a black leather bench, studying something in his hands. Connie went over to the front desk to see about getting some food sent up to her mother, and Hannah took a seat beside Zeus. What's that? she said, and he handed her the coloured photocopy Fenton had given him.

It's a recent picture of my parents, he said.

Oh my *God*, Hannah said. These are your parents? Wow,

you look so much like your mother. They're so good-looking. They look pretty young.

My mother's only two years older than you are, Zeus said.

Really? Hannah said and stared at the wall in amazement, her mouth slightly open.

Connie returned and checked her watch. Come on, it's already nine o'clock, and I want to get a spot with the prophetic ministry before it fills up.

Look at this, Hannah said and showed her the picture. It's Zeus's parents.

You're kidding me, Connie said and looked at it intently. That's *crazy*. Oh, *Zeus*, she said, handing the picture back and giving his shaved head a maternal stroke.

The three of them walked out of the hotel and into another clear day. The sun was so vivid, cars on the highway flashed like diamonds on a long conveyer belt. They got into the truck and Hannah turned out of the parking lot.

I think it's going to be a really good day, Connie said. Have you decided what you're doing, Zeus? Are you staying with us for the weekend? When are you hoping to get to Chimayó? Do you have any money?

That's too many questions at once, he said. I haven't decided anything yet.

Is there anything we can do for you?

He shook his head.

Maybe you'll find the service interesting today.

Or maybe he's had enough religion to last him a lifetime, Hannah said.

I don't think he needs you to decide that for him, Connie said.

What I *am* enjoying, Zeus said, is listening to the two of you squabbling over what you think is best for me. It's kind of heartwarming. Why do I have to do anything? Why can't I just follow you around like a little brother?

Well, *I* might go in, Hannah said. I'm sort of curious to see what the Christian right is up to in America these days.

Really? Connie sounded more annoyed than skeptical.

Don't I get any credit for keeping an open mind? Hannah was speeding up between the stop signs and braking abruptly.

Your mind's so open, Connie said, I don't know how anything makes an impression.

They drove back to the church and this time turned towards the big hall. Both lots looked full, and they stopped in front of a young man wearing an orange vest and holding a baton. There were still a few spaces left on the far side, he told them, so they drove slowly across the busy lot. It was Saturday morning and people were filing into the hall, locking up their cars with licence plates from Kansas, Missouri, Texas, Colorado, men tipping their baseball caps, women pushing up their sunglasses to talk to one another. Hannah parked the truck facing a large vacant lot behind the building, overgrown with scrub and a dense thicket of young trees.

They all went in. There was a crush around the registration table and a lawlessness to the way people cut into the line. I'll go get the tickets, Hannah said, and meet you at the entrance.

Behind the registration table, two teenaged girls in jean miniskirts and tight t-shirts leaned against the wall. They had the ease and idleness of staff kids. One of them started to sing a worship song and the other one cut her off, Don't pretend you know how to sing.

I'm not the only one around here who can't sing, the other one said. Why do you think they turn your microphone down every time you get on stage?

The woman in front of her was buying seven passes for

the weekend. She was wearing a loose, hand-sewn cotton dress, and her brown hair, streaked with grey, was pulled back into a bun and held in place by a white, elasticized doily. In contrast, the woman seated at the table wore heavy makeup and several gold rings on her fingers. She closed the lid on a black tin box and said, Next, please?

Hannah bought three tickets and then it occurred to her, this is *simony*. The crime of paying for religious advice. It was a word she'd learned in an undergraduate class on James Joyce. She'd never thought of it in any context until now. She joined Zeus and Connie at the entrance, and together they followed the general flow into a huge auditorium, cavernous and acoustically absorbent as an airplane hangar, noisy and hushed at the same time.

They stood inside as if spellbound. On the left was an elevated carpeted stage, behind which were long, draped lengths of yellow and purple cloth. On either side of the stage were two white projection screens that hung suspended thirty feet in the air. Microphones and music stands and two drum kits on stage, and endless rows of grey metal chairs arranged on the floor. At the back, a hillside of bleachers. Let's go sit up there, Hannah said.

That's Hannah for you, Connie said to Zeus. Prefers to sit above the proceedings, instead of down on the ground, in the thick of it.

Okay, so we'll meet up after the service, Hannah said.

What about the prophetic ministry? Connie said.

Sign-up table's at the other end, a man said in passing.

Thank you, she said.

You seem really determined about this, Hannah said.

Well, it's half the reason I came here in the first place, Connie said.

Maybe we should all go, Hannah said. I've never got a reading from a Christian psychic before.

It's not like that, Connie said. But I guess you can find that out for yourself.

The three siblings walked through the crowd, gathered like factory workers before a shift, the air thrumming with voices, abuzz with spiritual industry. Some people sat, while others wandered or paced or prayed. Some reserved chairs with their jackets and purses, greeted old friends. A young woman sat cross-legged on the floor beside a garbage can, rocking back and forth, braiding her hair.

They got in line behind a small Chinese couple who moved forward tentatively, as if unsure of their right to be there. Before the couple reached the table, a woman with a booming voice cut in front of them. She made no apology, her large behind sheathed in an expanse of faded blue denim. Is this where you sign up for the prophetic ministries?

The young man behind the table nodded and handed her an appointment card.

She read the card and complained, But my husband and I wanted to go this morning.

Two o'clock is the earliest I can give you, he said.

Well, that's just dandy, she said, when we've come all this way.

Her husband leaned in around her. We'll take this afternoon, he said and led his wife towards the stage.

When it was their turn, the young man gave Connie and Hannah both a small blue card with an appointed time of two-thirty. You'll need these to ensure your spot, he said.

Hannah turned to Zeus. Do you want one? And he shook his head.

Just follow the arrows, it's on the second floor, the young man said. Enjoy!

Together they moved away from the table and passed two men standing together with their hands on each other's shoulders and their heads bowed. They passed another small group of men praying together, younger than the last two. They looked like farmers' sons. One boy had his fists clenched in front of his face and was saying, Yes! with such passion and ecstasy, it was almost sexual.

Through the crowd, against the far wall next to the stage, Hannah could see three young women dressed in pale blue leotards and wraparound skirts, with long hair and supple bodies, stretch and prepare themselves for some kind of dance. She tugged on Zeus's sleeve and pointed with her eyes.

I feel like I'm at a circus, he said. The anticipation before a show. It's the same anything-could-happen kind of atmosphere.

They had arrived at the back of the central aisle. Connie headed for a row of chairs and Hannah decided to stick with them. They all sat down, Zeus in the middle.

I feel like something's heating up inside of me, he said. It's like a vibration, or a tingling, like I've got a light bulb in my stomach or at the back of my throat. He stretched his mouth open. My palms feel like they're giving off a kind of light. Zeus turned his hands over and stared at them.

Don't you dare go getting all Holy Spirit on me, Hannah whispered, and the service began with a crashing sound from the electrified worship band on stage.

There was cheering and clapping. People started to lose themselves in the ecstatic mood. Down in front of the stage, a woman ran in circles to the music, with her arms thrown out in jubilation. She was running backwards in a tight circle, with a circumference so small it looked as if she was spinning around at the end of a string. Then the dancers came out on stage, to sway and undulate to the music. A plump, middle-aged woman in a white turtleneck and a long green skirt jumped out of her chair and ran across the floor. Her glasses bounced on her nose as she ran, her bright yellow hair pulled back by a sky-blue handkerchief. She was very plain and yet the rapture on her face made her beautiful.

There's a spirit of something here that I approve of, Hannah said. Despite the politics, the gas-guzzling culture, the moral conservatism, the fear of outsiders.

It's like the release of a good drug trip, Zeus said, and God knows we all need to get high sometimes.

The fact that it's communal, Hannah said, I think that's key. People getting emotional in public, looking out for each other.

It's a rock concert, Zeus said.

My heart and flesh cry out, sang a man at the microphone. I've tasted and I've seen. Come once again to me.

An older woman pranced like some kind of bird across the floor, dainty on her toes. A man in a baseball cap fell to his knees while the woman beside him stood up, suddenly rigid as if electrified, her back arched, face raised to the ceiling, one fist clenched at her tailbone, the other in front of her mouth, like she was holding a pole through her body.

Better is one day in your house, than thousands in a house of gold!

The whole congregation was moving now, swarming like a hive. A woman sitting at the edge of the central aisle, a few rows ahead, was crying. It was the movement of her shoulders. She got up, knelt in the aisle, and lay face down with her arms straight at her sides. Free at last, Hannah thought, with a sentiment that swung between sympathy and scorn. It was total surrender. Other people were still on the fighting side of that surrender, still needed to shake and flail the resistance out of their bodies, spasm like epileptics. I guess those people have the hurdle of their *pride* to get over, Hannah thought, before they can let go.

Praise Adonai! a voice shouted over the loudspeaker and a cheer was raised, as if a field goal had been scored. Then a Jewish-sounding song with a fast tempo began, and the frenzy and the emotion rose so swiftly and slammed so hard against the rafters, Hannah thought the roof was going to blow right off the building.

Come let us go to the house of the God of Israel! the voice called out. It was Chad Dorian, the star pastor. He had come up to the central microphone and was calling for intercessors, full-time Annas. We need to raise up, he shouted over the music, a lot more Annas! Faithful women of God to intercede on behalf of the church and of this great country of ours, to pray for its leadership in the world, especially as we gather this coming week on Tuesday to elect a president.

A woman, sitting in the row in front of them, jumped up – a biker chick with bleached and feathered hair, tanktop and jeans, a leather jacket on the back of her chair. Two friends on either side of her put a hand on her lower back and bowed their heads. The woman started to shake. When she sat down again, she rubbed her thighs and ran her feet on the ground. She was so excited, she'd been anointed!

The music gradually faded and the congregation, exhausted, subsided in their seats, like a wave sinking into the sand.

Chad Dorian said, Today I want to talk about the battle of Jerusalem. But I want to lay down a pretty extensive foundation.

He said, I know you're all trying to get to heaven, but, my friends, heaven is just a holy holding pattern until the end times. At the second coming, all the people in heaven are gonna get physical bodies. And after the earth is redeemed, heaven's gonna be brought to earth and made material.

You see, the pastor said, heaven is a supernatural spiritual realm, while the earth is a material physical realm, involving human emotion and physical sensation. The millennial earth, that Jesus is going to establish after the second coming, will bring the two together – but! – you must have a resurrected body. When Jesus came back after the crucifixion, it was to show how he was both spirit and body. He could walk through walls and yet he still needed to eat and drink. I'm not saying I understand how he did this, I don't know the details. I'm just painting a broadstroke picture for you here, folks.

Sounds pretty specific to me, Hannah whispered to Zeus, and Connie leaned forward to give her a questioning look.

Chad Dorian called for a theocratic government. Boy, I don't know how this is gonna happen either, he said, but there are so many chapters about this in the Bible. Go ahead and read them, you'll be, like, wow.

Blessed are the meek for they shall inherit the earth, he said. I'm sure you've all heard that one before. Well, that was Jesus talking about the millennial earth. Jesus was the first millennial theologian, and he was talking about ruling the government of the economics of the earth. What that means is, we, the meek – instead of the wicked! – will rule the world in a theocratic and moral way. And I know I'm stretching minds now, but we can't dumb this down, folks!

Connie bent forward, with her elbows on her knees, and stared at the floor. Hannah looked at her sister and her heart broke over the shape of her head, the curve of her shoulders.

Satan hates it when somebody's happy! Chad Dorian shouted. But what he's really trying to do is keep himself out of hell. He's been enjoying his freedom. He doesn't want to give it up. But if Jesus rides back into Jerusalem as the king of the Jews and establishes the kingdom of God on earth, then Satan is locked up in prison and thrown into the lake of fire. Can you see why he might want to prevent this from happening?

The congregation was captivated, drinking it in.

But the kingdom won't come until the battle of Jerusalem is won!

Chad Dorian joked about the temple. I don't want to know everything about it, he said. I want *some* things to be a surprise. I only want to know what's in the scriptures. People come to me with theories, and I say, I don't care. I only want to know what the scriptures say.

He talked again about the paradox of heaven and earth becoming one. The throne in the temple, and the temple and the earth being in the place underneath the soles of our feet. And the room where Christ resides, he shouted, is further inside, than even the centre where Ezekiel was!

He had the congregation in his sway. The mood was rising. There were shouts of approval – amens and hallelujah!

Jerusalem is the vortex of God's end-time drama, he said. I don't know the exact definition of the word *vortex*, but it's this fuel, this energy. But friends! he shouted. The kingdom will not come until the leaders of Jerusalem accept Christ as their Messiah! Because Jesus chose Jerusalem – the physical bricks and mortar of that holy city – as his home, the future seat of his government, when he will finally make heaven and earth meet, to fulfill a prophecy foretold even before there were people on the earth.

Someone nearby shouted, Praise Yahweh!

Chad Dorian's voice grew softer, more confidential. Satan has a special rage against the Jews, he said, because if he destroys them and Jerusalem, then Jesus can't come back to earth and claim Jerusalem as the new kingdom. Now, I'm happy to be a gentile. I don't want to be Jewish. God didn't make a mistake there. But will I die, if I have to, for the battle of Jerusalem? You're darned right, I will.

In the new millennial world, the pastor said, fear will not dominate your spirit, faith will. If fear dominates, the anti-Christ has won. The Bible says, Jerusalem will be the throne of the lord. *The throne of the Lord*, he repeated. This must be the devil's most hated verse in the whole Bible. He wants to sabotage the apocalypse, and that's why there's so much terrorism focused on Jerusalem. That's why all the wars in the Middle East – the Israeli-Palestinian conflict, the war in Iraq, 9/11, even Nazi Germany – they're all predicted in the Book of Revelation. It's all in here, friends, and I don't enjoy saying this, believe you me, but if you're not seeing it when you read the scriptures, it's because you don't *want* to see it.

We are approaching the vortex! he shouted in a hoarse voice. There is no time for apathy. Things are going to get much, much worse before they get better. Many more righteous men and women will die before they get resurrected. We must prepare ourselves for battle. We must prepare ourselves for the second coming because Jesus Christ is coming back to restore the kingdom of heaven – the Global Kingdom of Salvation – here on earth, folks! This place under your feet, this body of Christ in the community that surrounds you here, this is a taste of what the rapture will be like!

There was a roar of cheers and whistles. People stood and clapped with their hands over their heads. Chad Dorian took a handkerchief out of his pocket and wiped his face. He held his Bible in the air. I want, he said in a quiet, exhausted voice, all of you who are visiting us today from Israel to come to the front. Let us pray in Christ's name for the strength of our Jewish friends, that they might have the fortitude for the task that lies ahead. And while we pray, Crystal Carter, if you will, will come up and lead the worship band.

A young woman with an acoustic guitar walked humbly with her head bowed over to a mike at the side of the stage and swung her guitar forward across her belly and started picking out some gentle chords. The drums hooked into the beat and then the electric guitars buzzed in like allied aircraft. A flute fluttered high over the music. People surged forward. Chad Dorian prayed into his microphone. He called on his intercessors, and two more women and a man appeared, plucking microphones from their stands, and began to pray on stage. A whispered cacophony of voices over the swelling music. Then the intercessors began speaking in tongues.

It's ironic, Zeus said, but when they speak in tongues like that, it sounds Arabic. Close your eyes and you could be in a mosque in Tripoli.

But we're not in a mosque, Connie said. We're in an ugly aluminum hangar, in the middle of America, with a thousand charismatic right-wing Christians. But I've got to go forward. I came here for prayer and I'm going to get prayed for. Are you coming?

Hannah shook her head.

Zeus stood up and said, This is bullshit, and he wandered off.

Connie watched him go. I can't help him right now, she said to Hannah. I need to think of myself, and she stood up and walked towards the stage and the crowd swallowed her up.

This was madness, Hannah thought. And Zeus was right. If you closed your eyes, it *could* be a mosque. And Tripoli sounded like an exotic bird. Or a famous blue sapphire. Maybe the medievalists got it right. Maybe the mass should be recited in Latin, with incense and bells. In a language you can't understand. To remain a mystery, Hannah thought and opened her eyes. Her sister was right as well. Here was ugliness and an appetite for the divine. And what did the Jews think of it all? Had the Jews come? Or were they racing for the exits?

Hannah lost the truck in the parking lot, then found it. Zeus was lying on his back in the truck bed. I thought you might be here, she said. Is everything okay? He was staring at the elaborately sculpted clouds in the blue sky overhead. Do you want to go for a drive? she asked and Zeus sat up.

Where are we going? he said.

I don't know, and Hannah tossed him the keys. Check on Rose first? Then I thought we could go into town. Grab a beer or something?

When they got to the hotel, Zeus waited outside by the truck and Hannah took the elevator up and knocked on her mother's door.

Rose opened it, then headed straight back to bed. Her hair was vertical and waving around like grass. Her eyes were puffy. Her skin a little shiny.

Come out with us, Hannah said. Come have lunch and see the city.

Rose shook her head, then yawned so violently it seemed to come from another source that overpowered her. Hannah sat down on the edge of the bed. There was a bottle of pills from the hospital on the bedside table, next to an inhaler. How are you feeling?

Like an idiot, if you must know, coming all this way and look at me. I just need to rest and I'll be fine later. She lay back down. Hannah noticed a small spot of blood on the pillowcase next to her head. Maybe it was the tetanus shot, Rose said. I just can't get out of bed.

Though it was ridiculous, childish really, Hannah felt mentholated with hurt, some stupid feeling of rejection. That's okay, she said, I understand. Do you need anything? Do you want me to get you some tea or something?

Rose grunted, Uh-uh.

Connie said the front desk would get you something to eat, Hannah said, if you called down for it.

As she was shutting the door, her mother called her back. I forgot to tell her this morning, Rose said, I was half asleep, but I have a letter for Connie, from Harlan. Can you give it to her for me? I don't think it's urgent, but I told him I'd give it to her right away.

Sure, Hannah said, and her mother pointed to her purse. Hannah opened it up and beneath the kleenex and keys and lipstick found an envelope addressed to *Connie Foster*.

Hannah went back out to the truck, where Zeus was waiting in the passenger seat. You drive, he said, and they headed downtown. A man in an open-air Jeep, wearing a turtleneck under his sweatshirt and mirrored aviator glasses, passed them while talking on a CB radio. At the next red light, he was stopped in the lane to their left. Hannah watched him lift an enormous insulated mug to his face, the size of a small, tightly rolled sleeping bag. From his rear-view mirror dangled a black wooden cross. The most religious, she thought, always have the darkest dispositions. That's why they're the ones most in need of rescue. It's why Jesus spent so much of his time with the prostitutes, murderers, and thieves. And lead us not into temptation. But why not? So many of the things prohibited in her youth were not as scary or carried such negative consequences as had been forewarned. People were so easily chagrinned. When someone said, Have you no shame? Hannah wanted to say, No, and why should I? Shame was the invention of nervous people.

But then, some people had nervous *upbringings* and scrambled all their lives to manage with the rules they were taught. When she was nine years old, Hannah had given her mother the finger. Rose had looked so shocked. Do you know what that means? she said, and Hannah shook her head. There were no words for it because it meant fuck you, which she didn't want to say out loud. She already felt embarrassed and didn't need to be punished. It means, Rose said, that you want to put your finger in my vagina. It still made Hannah shudder to think about it now. But it was what her mother thought was the appropriate thing to say at the time. It's what she *knew*. What's wrong, Hannah wondered, with the way *I* think things ought to be now?

The closer they got to the downtown area, the more opulent and bigger the buildings became, as if wealth was the fertilizer that made lifeless things grow. The streets were clean. Things gleamed. Election posters cluttered the windows.

There's so much shit you have to put up with when you're gay, Zeus said, and for a moment Hannah was silent.

But that's why you're so great and compassionate, she said. Because you know what it's like to be excluded.

I don't think Rose will ever look at me again as just myself, he said. Just Zeus, the person.

You can't listen to her about certain things. You can't listen to *either* of my parents when it comes to anything that isn't traditional or conservative. I love them, they're my parents, but they can be totally narrow-minded. Whatever she might have said, I'm sure she didn't mean to hurt you. She tries so outrageously hard to be irreproachable. I mean, what's *that* all about?

You belong to her, Zeus said. You never have to doubt that. You know she loves you.

Oh, I know she loves me, Hannah said. I'm just not so sure she's ever really *liked* me. Hannah had never realized how true this was, but instead of opening her heart to the pitiable fact of it, she quickly pushed it away. Whatever, she said. It doesn't matter.

Hannah almost ran a red light, braking hard at the very last moment. Zeus grabbed the dashboard. Sorry, she said, as a very pregnant teenager waddled across the intersection. She was wearing a t-shirt that said, *I'm not with stupid anymore!*

Zeus sighed and said, What if people started caring? The sun was just coming out from behind a cloud and the light was travelling towards them at a stately pace, making things emerge as if for the first time. What if people *actually* started to care about all the things they pretend to be indifferent about? he said. What difference would that make?

People don't feel important, Hannah said. They don't feel like they matter. I mean, I never really felt like *I* did, you know, growing up.

The side of a building went orange as the sunlight moved across it. Cars across the intersection flared and the bright boundary of the sun slid across the pavement and up over the white hood of the Ranger and soaked the windshield and made it go milky. Hannah's hands on the steering wheel felt warm in the light.

Once, that may have been true, Zeus said, raising his head. But I kind of see you surrounded by people who tell you all the time how much you mean to them. But maybe you can't hear them. This Norm guy. Your mother. Your sister, even. Would you believe me if I said I really cared about you too?

Hannah turned to look at him. Someone behind them honked, and she drove on. In a minute, they passed a billboard that read, RAMADAN — 1.5 BILLION CELEBRATING — FIND OUT WHY against the backdrop of a blurred and rippling American flag.

You know, this country is the mirror image of ourselves, Zeus said. We're all so divided. Did you know that the Christians, the Jews, and the Muslims all come from the same family through Abraham?

Did I know this? I'm not sure I do. The problem with being a rebel, Hannah said, is that you disinherit a lot of your education. There's so much about the Bible I've forgotten.

Fenton was sort of obsessed with this stuff, Zeus said. Apparently, Abraham had two sons. The first one, Ishmael, leads to the Muslims, and the second one, Isaac, leads straight to Mary and Joseph.

Why isn't this talked about more often?

Their mothers didn't get along, and that's why they went their separate ways.

So they're not enemies at all, Hannah said. They're siblings.

Exactly.

They parked the truck and asked a man in a wheelchair where they could get a beer. Try Frankie's at the end of the block.

Frankie's it was.

The bar was small and dark. They sat down at a round plywood table and both ordered a Bud Lite. Hannah took a swig and fell back into her own element. The TV above the bar blurted out more election coverage, a campaign ad, Obama shaking hands in a crowd, looking confident and relaxed. You know, Hannah said, this is where you'd find Jesus, if he were alive today.

I *am* alive today, Zeus said.

Hannah gave him an indulgent look. What people don't understand, she said, is that Jesus was one of the original shit disturbers, a revolutionary. He went after the establishment. He believed in the redistribution of wealth, that everyone should get a fair share. Jesus wasn't a republican, he was a democrat.

Zeus wasn't interested in a rant. It was the middle of the day. At the bar, two women in cowboy shirts were having a drink. One of them said, People in the south, they smile with their mouths but not their eyes.

Zeus went over to the bar and started up a conversation with them, Beverly and Sandy Lanache, and soon they joined Hannah at the table. After half an hour, Sandy invited them to stay at their place. With me and my wife here.

You're married? Hannah said. That's so great.

We have a king-sized bed, she said. You guys can sleep in the middle.

The come-on made Hannah feel bashful.

I'm just joking, she said. Sandy was a dentist and explained that she did free dental work on the weekends for the poor of Wichita — she was used to taking in strays. As she talked, her silver bracelets clinked. She had soft-looking hands with long, slender fingers. Hands you wouldn't mind having in your mouth, Hannah thought.

For a moment she considered the possibility and regretted the circumstances of her life that sometimes made her feel constricted, slightly uptight. My dentist in Toronto, she said, just lost two fingers in a car accident and had to shut down his practice.

I hope they were insured, Sandy said, leaning back in her chair and putting her hands behind her head.

They ordered another round of drinks and talked about the upcoming election and the Republican Party, the Arab Spring, and the old war in Iraq. They talked about the economy and how bad the recession was, and how Kansas seemed to be at the centre of it all.

Forget that people used to be successful farmers in this region, Sandy said.

Or that we have a rich local history of religious and political dissent, Beverly said. Now all the farmland is owned by multinational corporations, and we're under the thumb of right-wing evangelicals. Beverly took off her baseball cap and put it on the table. She pushed her hands through her thick grey hair and massaged the back of her neck. There's still a big deception afoot, she said. Four years ago, good Christian working-class people heard his moral rhetoric and thought McCain had their best interests at heart because they're on the same page when it comes to abortion. But the Republican Party hasn't changed. It's still an exclusive party representing the interests of the wealthy elite. Only they don't like to talk about that anymore because being rich isn't the proud mark of superiority it once was.

If it was up to the state of Kansas, Beverly went on, Obama would never have won in the first place. McCain would have got into the White House, and the lies and misinformation perpetrated after 9/11 would never have come to light. But it's not over. There's still a lot of crap flying around, what with the right-wing media and bullshit from preachers like this Fred Phelps guy we have here.

Oh, my God, Sandy said. He's so horrendous!

This guy, Beverly said, rounds up a group from his church whenever he hears that somebody's died of AIDS. They go and picket the funeral with signs that say, God hates fags. They chant *faggot* at the top of their lungs near the graveside, right in front of the grieving family and friends. Can you believe that?

Zeus shook his head. He was clawing the sticker off his beer bottle.

Sandy squeezed his arm gently, in sympathy. She said, This morning I was reading about the latest university campus shooting, and recognized in the list of victims the name of one of my professors. He was a prominent biomechanics researcher. Maybe one of the top five researchers in the country. He was working on movement dynamics in cerebral palsy. I saw him a few years ago at a conference on socialized medicine. A good man like that gets shot, while the Phelps of this world seem protected.

They're protected by the people they can bully, Zeus said. His fury seemed barely contained.

It's true, Beverly said. Look at how *cowed* we all are. Where are all the free thinkers, willing to put themselves at risk? Why aren't we all more outraged, all of the time? Like that Chinese student who stood in front of the tanks in Tiananmen Square. That's what we should all aspire to be. As brave as that solitary, determined student, with his white shirt sleeves rolled up, carrying his briefcase.

Connie started to eat a damp tuna wrap she'd bought at the snack bar in the lobby. The eating area was full, so she wandered outside, where she chucked the rest of her sandwich in the garbage and thought about going back to the hotel to see how her mother was doing. She looked at her watch. It was ten past two. After the service, she'd been prayed for and it had left her feeling tired but thoughtful. She must have written in her journal for over an hour. It was coming up to her appointment time with the prophecy team and she didn't want to be late for that. What would it be like? she thought. Would God speak to her through the agency of a prophetic counsellor, and would she recognize it if he did? She so badly wanted to feel, on this trip, like she'd got some irrefutable proof, beyond her own decision to believe in him, that God existed. Other people spoke with such certainty about hearing the voice of God, but she'd never even gotten close. She wondered where her sister was, and if she'd make it on time.

To her left, a small group of people were gathering around a van. The back doors were propped open and a girl of about ten, in overalls and a sweater, was standing there, clacking a pair of metal tongs. There was a steel coffee urn in the van and a tower of styrofoam cups. A woman held out a white paper napkin, and the girl used her tongs to pluck a cinnamon bun from a sticky metal tray and hand it to her.

You gonna have one? a man asked. He seemed to have magically appeared at Connie's side. I recommend them.

They smell good.

My wife makes them.

She must be a good baker.

She's the best.

The man extended a hand the colour and texture of a worn baseball glove. But then I did marry her. The name's Dashiel Flander.

Connie Foster.

You're not from around here, are you.

Vancouver Island.

God seems to have called people from the four corners of the globe to come here this weekend. He pushed back the crown of his trucker's cap. You're smack-dab in the heart of the United States of America, here in Wichita.

I can feel it, Connie said. I take it you live around here?

Dashiel turned a little and pointed beyond the big hall. We're about thirty-five miles southwest. My wife and I run a residential detox centre. We've been hearing about Chad Dorian and his ministry for some time now. Got wind of this here jamboree and thought we'd check it out. See if we could help. See if anyone needed hot coffee, he laughed. Cinnamon buns are a real ice-breaker. My daughter and I call them my wife's ministry muffins. You got kids?

Three, Connie said. One girl, younger than yours, and two boys.

Bet the boys are a handful.

Emma has her way of keeping me busy too, she said. So what do you make of this here jamboree?

Well, I had a poke around inside, Dashiel said, and I think we'll take part in the service tonight. But this here is what I'd call some large-scale evangelicalism.

There's something about a crowd, Connie said.

Oh, yes, there's powerful energy in a crowd.

And support.

You hit the nail on the head there, Connie. Now *that's* something there just ain't enough of in this world. That's why I opened up the detox centre. Had a little stint with the booze myself when I was younger. Booze and pills. Wound up on the streets in Fort Worth. Oh, it was the best of times, Dashiel said and his delivery was comical. It was the worst of times. You see, I had no support. There ain't two ways about it. My parents had both passed away and you never think you're gonna end up one day without a friend in the world to help you get by, but you'd be surprised how many people find themselves in that position.

When I finally crawled back home, he said, with my tail between my legs, I knew what it was like to be homeless and rebuked. Dad's farm was still in the family name, but it had fallen into disrepair. I wasn't up to the new farming methods and that's when God must've looked down on me and thought, Okay, now there's a sinner I could use. I found myself in the Salvation Army building one night, sitting in a little circle of men. They were all chain-smoking and sucking back this terrible black coffee, and every time a man raised one of those soft white styrofoam cups to his mouth, his hand shook so bad the coffee would spill all over his knuckles. When I took a sip from my own cup, I realized I was no different from those guys. I'd turned into one of them. That night, I accepted Jesus Christ as my Lord and Saviour and was born again. Three months later, I opened the farm to some other addicts who wanted a chance to get clean, without the hassle of the streets, you know, pushers and other addicts.

The neighbours were less than thrilled, but they've come around. We started offering volunteer manpower at harvest time and try generally to keep our guests productive. That's the best therapy. We now have about forty residents. Two barns converted into dormitories, one for the women, one for the men. Six extra beds in our own home, for residents with children.

Sounds like you're doing a terrific job, Connie said.

Oh, you know, Dashiel said, it's not me. It's really the people who come and get clean that deserve the credit.

I'd like to be involved in something like that.

Connie, the need is great. These people are so poor. Last month, we delivered a baby. The mother didn't have any medical insurance. She's a recovering heroin addict. Well, the baby, you should have seen her. Came out yellow as a Chiquita banana, so we called her Chiquita. She's as healthy as a peach now.

Connie smiled and said, not self-pityingly, but with true humility, You make me feel like a fraud. I've never done a good generous thing like that in my whole life.

Connie walked back inside and followed the arrows for the prophetic ministry, up a set of stairs that led to a small second storey, the kind of floor where a boss might look out over his factory workers, safe above the thundering sound of a thousand industrial sewing machines. At the top of the stairs, a woman sat behind a desk collecting appointment cards. It smelled like air freshener, a bubble-gum smell. Can I keep mine? Connie asked and opened her bag and showed the woman how she'd already stuck her card into her journal. The woman said, Oh, you're good. Look at you. Aren't you good.

She directed Connie down the hall towards what looked like a classroom. There were rows of wooden chairs and about fifteen people sitting around, some talking in low voices while others read their Bibles or simply sat and stared. The sound was of a hushed expectancy. Connie took a seat in the third row, and a woman with brassy dyed hair came in wearing a dark green wool wrap, which she flung over her shoulder before pointing to a row of four people and saying, Come with me.

A man at the back said, What about the people who've been here since one-thirty?

Who's been here for more than an hour? the woman said.

Half a dozen hands rose into the air.

Okay, sorry, folks, she said to the first group of four, who sat down again, looking disgruntled, and led the other six people out of the room.

It doesn't usually take this long, Connie heard a woman say.

A man mumbled, What is this, the gates of heaven?

Connie felt as if the room had suddenly turned into a gypsy tent, with paper lanterns and strings of red chili-pepper lights. What was she doing here? What was she after? She wanted a mystical experience of God, but is this where she was going to find it? In this assembly line? The tone was so crass, it made the whole thing seem ridiculous.

Now a man was taking an informal census of the people in the room, trying to figure out who had waited the longest and who should go next. I used to be a crossing guard, he joked, directing a few people to get up and sit near the front.

Another man laughed and said, You have the gifts of administration and provenance.

Connie closed her eyes. When it was her turn, she followed the lady with the brassy hair out of the room and passed Hannah on her way. You came! she said, holding back nothing of her relief. Come with me, she said and grabbed her sister's arm. Have you been drinking? she whispered.

We went into town, Hannah said.

Where's Zeus?

He's outside somewhere.

Connie shook her head and led her sister into the prophecy room. Inside, there were two circles of chairs, one on either side, tape recorders on some of the seats – the kind with the flip-up cassette slots – and maybe twenty people.

What are the tape recorders for? Hannah asked.

You get a recording of what they say to you, Connie said and suddenly realized she didn't want Hannah to overhear what the prayer counsellors might tell her. This should be private, she said, for both of us. We should probably separate.

Fine, Hannah said and headed off, seemed to remember something, came back and handed Connie a letter. It's from Harlan, she said, and Connie quickly pressed it against her chest with a look of panic.

Don't read it now, Hannah said. It'll colour your experience.

I guess so, Connie said.

It's not urgent, Hannah said. It's a letter.

You're right, Connie said and slid the envelope into her Bible.

Hannah made her way across the room and, as she slipped between two chairs to take a seat, turned and gave Connie a goofy wave, as if they were both climbing into different cars on a rollercoaster.

Connie felt such affection for her sister then. She loved it when Hannah was funny. Two women on her right stood up and put their hands on a man's head and started praying over him. Another man was kneeling in front of a black woman, in a pale blue business suit, and prayed while holding her knees. It's loud, Connie thought. It sounds like the sea. All those susurrating voices. She tried not to stare as four people prayed in a muscular, energetic way over a young man, kneeling on the floor in the corner of the room. He was bent forward with his forehead on the carpet and Connie heard someone say, God loves you, Kurt. And it reminded her of Harlan's description of his own conversion, twenty years ago, at a Leighton Ford crusade.

Across from her, a Chinese woman sat with an older couple who must have been her parents. An attractive couple, with kind, gentle faces – even their posture had a cheerful grace about it. The father in a pressed white shirt and olive-green, high-waisted slacks. His wife in a navy blue windbreaker. Their daughter had her arm in a sling, and a bearded man was praying for her.

I see a town crier, he said.

The young woman didn't know what he meant.

That you will cry Jesus to the people, the man explained. Tell people all about him.

As if jolted by an electrical current, she rose up in her chair and cried out a sustained musical note, like a ribbon pulled across the room. It was joyous and painful, as lonely as a train whistle, and then it subsided and she sank primly back into her seat, as glassy-eyed and limp as if she'd just had an orgasm. A moment later, she cried out again, singing her one ardent note, oblivious to anything else, carried out of herself by some divine power.

I want something like that to happen to me, Connie thought, and she looked across the room at Hannah. Already a woman had sat down with her, to impart a message. Connie started to feel sorry for herself. Even here, she wondered, in this place, am I to be overlooked? I want, she prayed, to feel blown away by you, Lord. Crush me, if you have to. Devastate me. Just don't ignore me!

When she opened her eyes a woman was sitting beside her, pressing with the first fingers of both hands the record and play buttons of a tape recorder on her lap. What's your name, honey?

Connie, she said.

Well, Connie, what I got was, um − oh, I get pictures? And I saw the word *jewel*, and I believe God considers you his rare and precious jewel. And I just saw this treasure chest, and there were all these jewels in there, but *you*? God looked in this chest and you just shone the brightest.

I mean, you *sparkle*, she said, and that's how he sees you. He delights in you. He has adorned you with his beauty and you carry that. He calls you beautiful, he calls you precious one. I see your heart, and I see that there's been some, like, electrical wire that has been put around it, of *defence*, and I see that the Lord is just breaking that wire. I see him coming in with such a fire for you, that he's coming in and he's saying, no wire! I desire you! It's like this passionate burning flame that wants to capture every corner of your heart. And it's not like you've done anything wrong because you *haven't*. But I see that he's just breaking in there, in such a way that he's actually surprising you. It's like, nobody could ever love me this much, and he's saying, but I *do*.

The woman's voice was mellow and reassuring. Connie felt herself softening too. The woman patted Connie on the knee, then turned to look up at another woman who was waiting to pray for her. She handed over the tape recorder and said, She's all yours, Doris.

Doris sat down beside Connie and arranged the tape recorder and put her hand on Connie's shoulder. She said, I'm getting a powerful sense that you are a mother. I sense that you have children, am I right?

That's right, Connie said and a powdery bomb like a bag of flour went off at the base of her spine.

You have a girl, I think.

Yes.

And two boys, is that right?

How do you know this?

And your daughter, Doris said, squinting as she talked. She's the oldest, and she's a very strong and independent girl.

Connie started to cry and Doris handed her a box of kleenex from a nearby seat.

And the two younger boys, she said, maybe you worry about them a little more? Perhaps they seem a bit more vulnerable, out in the world?

Connie sucked in a jagged lungful of air.

You worry about their safety. And maybe about their spiritual welfare as well. The kind of role model their father's been to them, and whether or not he's been modelling good Christian values. Doris paused to give Connie a sympathetic look. You've had a bit of a rough time, haven't you?

Connie was nodding and twisting the kleenex into a tight strand.

You've been carrying around a real specific burden of concern, and God is telling me, he's saying that, by the grace of his son, Jesus Christ, and the power of the Holy Spirit, today he's going to lift that burden off your shoulders.

Doris lifted her hand off Connie's shoulder and Connie felt lighter.

What I'm feeling in my heart, Doris said, what feels really obvious to me right now is this certainty that your children, all three of them, will come to know God. I sense that you've been troubled about this, am I right?

It frightened Connie how accurately Doris could read her. *And from whom no secrets are hid.*

All I know is what Jesus permits me to know, Doris said. And he's saying have faith, Connie, that your children walk in righteousness.

How could this woman know these things about her, the things she needed to hear? When Connie opened her eyes and looked around, Hannah was gone. Have I been here a long time? she asked.

What's a long time, Doris said gently, when you're spending it with the Lord?

Connie thanked her and took the tape and sat holding it in her lap. She had been longing all her life to hear God's voice, hear him speak to her, and she wondered now if she had. But regardless, she felt a confidence that was palpable, that was having a deeply relaxing effect on her body. Think of it as a holiday – wasn't that what her mother had said? She opened her bag to put the tape inside, saw her Bible, and remembered Harlan's letter. She opened it calmly and read.

> Connie,
> Just wanted to let you know that the kids and I are okay. I know you don't like them being here, but at least Jodes been smoking out on the balcony since they arrived. Last night, I made fishsticks and mashed potatoes and it reminded me of my own childhood. The

kids had been out in the street earlier, in front of Jodie's
building, playing in the rain. It was one of those really
windy days, I know how much you love that. The
ocean all covered in white caps. Around four o'clock,
there was a huge downpour, with thunder and lightning,
which is totally out of season, I think. But you know
what the weather's like these days. Well, I went out
with an umbrella and stood with them. They were
hugging my legs like they do, and within minutes, the
gutter was like a river. We all sat in it while the water
rushed around us, spraying in an arc off our bodies, and
they were having a blast, laughing their heads off. I
thought, is this what I've been afraid of all my life?
What have I been running away from? When we came
in, we were all soaking wet, but Jodes had warmed up
three towels in the oven like our mom used to do. I just
wanted to write you and tell you that we're all good. I
don't want you to worry about me. I mean, I'm totally
ashamed of myself too. But I want you to know
everything's going to be okay. And we really miss you,
me and the kids. We can't wait for you to get home.
    Love, Harlan.

Hannah left the room like a spy. When she'd arrived with her
sister, she'd felt curious and open to what might happen but
also guarded. It all came back to her, how she used to feel, sitting in church, ashamed of how detached she felt. Was it really
a sin? The sin of being unconvinced? Wasn't God powerful
enough to overwhelm her doubts? There was Thomas in the
Bible. He was a disciple, but he got proof. That's all she wanted

too. A little wound oozing with blood and water that she could slip her fingers into, to lay her doubts to rest. Was that too much to ask for? Hannah looked around the room. The scene laid out before her – the ministrations, the whispered urgencies, the sudden distressing noises of agony, or ecstasy – it put her in mind of a temporary field hospital, at the edge of a battle, taking in the maimed.

She was waiting for someone to approach her. Did she look like a hard sell? She felt her body heat up with self-consciousness, then a woman with malformed hands sat down beside her. The woman's knuckles reminded Hannah of antique, nickel-plated taps. What's your name? she asked. Then she pushed the buttons on a tape recorder and started talking about a net, how Jesus was mending it, how Hannah was going to reel in a lot of fish. As she prayed, the woman's eyes kept darting towards her. The effect was imploring, uncertain – as if she was seeking her approval. Hannah felt like she was dealing with an amateur, a novice in the prophetic ministries business. She looked across the room at Connie, who sat alone with her head bowed.

I see you out in a boat, she said. And just like the disciples, when he told them, they'd been fishing for a really long time, but the Lord said, cast your net on the other side, and when they did that, the net just became so full of fish. And I believe that God is *calling* you to this. All the pieces of the puzzle may not be there yet, but it is a time of mending and when it happens, you're just going to cast your net out into the sea and it's going to reel in a *lot* of people.

The woman stopped, and Hannah, out of consideration for the woman's feelings and affected by her physical handicap, gave a gentle pushing gesture with her head to signify that it had, indeed, been meaningful, and thanked her. The woman pressed eject on the tape recorder, but the slot was empty. Oh dear, she said. Another woman hovering nearby said, You'll have to do a recall, Margot, and handed her a blank tape from her pocket. Margot, blushing and stammering slightly, repeated her story about the fishing net, into the machine.

When she was done, a man came over to Hannah and knelt in front of her with a look of heartfelt urgency. He was a good-looking guy, about her own age, with brown hair and hazel eyes. He was kneeling close to her and Hannah felt a stirring within her that meant she was in the proximity of the possibility of sex. Not in a literal sense, but alive to the possibility. It was distracting. It made her feel excited and shy and a little seedy, but she felt it must be undeniable to him too. There was acknowledgment in his eyes, some flirtation.

The man said, Jeremiah 29, verse 11, says, *For I know the thoughts*. And I'm just going to, for I know the thoughts I think towards you, Hannah, says the Lord, or Adonai. *Thoughts of peace, and not of evil, to give you a future and a hope*. I just felt that you're a woman who he's – you've – I'll just put it plainly. He's just madly in love with you, and he has a wonderful plan for you.

The man had a golden voice, the warm chestnut accent of the southern states. I know, he went on, I just believe, in the beginning of your life, the word *rough* wouldn't begin to describe the kind of things you went through. I think you've had a long season of roughness. I still think you keep having these long seasons of roughness, but I hear him say this, Hannah, I am so in love with your heart for me and for other people. You're an overcomer, you're someone who is going to help many people see Jesus. There is, he says, there is thousands without hope, and you're going to bring hope to thousands.

How? Hannah thought. How is this going to happen?

I just felt him say, just let her know this, that I know the thoughts that I think towards you, and that they are thoughts of peace. The man licked his lips and ran a hand through his thick hair and shifted sideways off his knees. He pulled a leg up and rested his Bible on his knee, close to his face.

An overcomer, Hannah thought.

The man found a new page. Psalm 56, verse 8, he said, glancing up at Hannah, and this will be a big one for you, because it is for me too, and I think we're the same. There was a flash of masculine power in his look that quickened Hannah's heart.

I think we've had the same kind of past, he said. Psalm 56, verse 8, says, he knows every wandering, which means every step we've ever taken, and every tear we've ever cried. He's collected them in a bottle and recorded it in a book. He is going to, he is coming so *near* to you, and you're a woman who literally has been snatched away from the enemy's hands, to a woman of grace that you are right now, right here today, and you are a woman that he delights in and there is, um, there's a treasure inside of you that's going to be released to other people. Like there's parts of Jesus that people will never know until they meet you. And they'll say, hey, I never knew that about Jesus after talking to you. God's restoring you. He's totally restoring you. Okay, I'm done, and he sank back towards the floor, as if sapped of energy.

Hannah found herself crying a little. It felt good to be praised and she was crying a little out of gratitude, because she was flattered, and out of consideration for his feelings as well. She was crying a little out of politeness, out of a wish to conform – at which point, he whipped out a small pack of kleenex and Hannah felt shabby. Tears were the goal, and this whole business an indulgent theatre of sentimentality. I'm the big stuffed bear at a shooting gallery, Hannah thought. Won and handed over to this guy who just shot down another sliding row of tin ducks for Jesus.

But then Hannah felt oppressed by her own cynicism and noticed that she *was* feeling moved, somewhere within her rib cage, high up in her chest, underneath the clavicle. There was a definite feeling of shelter in this room. They could be survivors from a plane crash and the Red Cross had just arrived. The raw, unspoken intimacy of being in a room with twenty strangers in various states of exposure or breakdown or joy. She experienced a similar, affecting intimacy during her cooldown exercises at the Y. She would drape her body backwards over a large rubber ball and stretch her stomach and a feeling would rise from her belly, and maybe it was muscle memory, but it was the same kind of grief or sadness that accompanies vulnerability, and she'd lie there without self-consciousness, surrounded by people she didn't know, listening to their soft grunts, and the half-nakedness of being in a t-shirt and shorts, and the exhaustion of having pushed herself, and knowing she was safe and had a common goal, often gave her a feeling of being spiritually at one with those people, and filled her with a melancholy peace.

The man lowered his head for a moment, his Bible closed on the floor. Then he looked up again with his bright brown-green eyes and said, I also see where you had to paddle upriver and fight upstream and you were every single day just getting to be like, no way am I waking up and having to fight again. But there's going to be a grace, there's going to be a grace to just go with what God has brought you and you're, you're a *leader*. You're going to learn to prophesy life into people. You're going to learn to prophesy grace into situations. And he says this, I'm going to bring *young* ones to you. And I'm going to let the young generation come to you. Because you're safe. You're very, very safe.

Young ones, Hannah thought. Because I'm safe. An overcomer. She liked that, who wouldn't be drawn to this reality? It was self-aggrandizing. It reminded her of Caiden Brock. His important life. All that *significance*. The handsome man with the golden voice was standing up. Thank you, Hannah said, but he was already distracted, gathering himself for the next encounter, as if they hadn't made a connection. Some of the excitement that had been ticking over inside her began, already, to peter out. Hard sell, all right. Time to pack your bags, girl, and move on. So Hannah turned back to what it was she knew without a doubt existed and belonged to her, things that made her happy, were reason enough, her sister over there, her brother, Zeus, hanging around somewhere outside the building where she'd left him, half drunk on beer, the wind in the trees, the sun on her hands through the windshield of a rented truck. And *Norm*. She would tell him it was okay. She didn't need that much reassurance. Reassurance was deceptive.

Hannah left the prophetic ministries and went downstairs and out the main doors and stood in the fresh air and there was Zeus, on the other side of the parking lot, following close behind some kids who were crossing the street and heading towards the church.

When they'd got back from the bar, Zeus had wandered into the big hall and gotten drawn into that crowded intimacy once again. More stirring music in a minor key. The air seemed to rumble. The Lord is building Jerusalem! Great, great is the Lord! Greatly to be praised! Over the noise, a brassy boom. At one end of the stage, a man was blowing into a tapered horn, it must have been about fourteen feet long. It was a call to prayer. The congregation went quiet and Zeus suddenly realized he didn't want to be there anymore. Sorry, he said. Sorry.

A man in a yellow sweater said, Are you all right, son? Where's your seat?

I need to get out of here, Zeus said and pushed past him. He rushed out the main doors and stood outside, the light silvery, a misty quality in the distance. It was getting colder, he could feel the damp. Two women sat on a bench drinking coffee. They didn't know he was there, but Zeus could hear them talking.

Yes, but what experience do you have of death?

I knew a guy who was killed in a motorcycle accident. And all my grandparents are dead.

But have you ever suffered the death of a child?

No.

Because that's the worst.

So they say.

Who does?

The death experts, of whom you must be one, you wear it so well, the trophy of it.

The breeze was picking up. Zeus tightened his red scarf and buttoned up his coat and walked the length of the building. He turned the corner and already it was quieter. A shock of lawn. The overcrowded parking lot behind him. He continued to follow the building, tracing the wall with his fingertips, close enough to hear a faint voice preaching on the other side of the aluminum. A cricket in a cage. Behind the building was a low stone wall, a wooded lot, overgrown with weeds and the stalks of something gold, now broken and bent into triangles, then a screen of young trees, pinkish grey and nearly leafless. Bordering the lot, a mechanic's garage, open for business, a service road, and more of what looked like industrial warehouses.

He was ready to move on. He'd had enough of this Kingdom of Salvation place. What was he doing here anyway? He was a day or two away from possibly reuniting with his parents, if that's what he wanted, but he wasn't even sure of that anymore. Seeing Rose had been kind of upsetting. Would it be the same with his own parents, only on a more devastating scale? If he did go see them, he didn't want them to know he was coming, he wanted to catch them by surprise. Maybe that was cruel, but he had to see what he'd missed, or what it was that he'd been spared. He felt his skin shiver, as if the air was full of static electricity. A gust of wind blew up as he came around the back of the building and his knees went soft and he buckled just a little.

There was Fenton.

Standing with his back to Zeus, his dark red hair on fire, balanced on the low stone wall, looking out over the wooded lot, with his arms held wide like he was flying, or crucified.

Fenton! Zeus yelled, but his voice got lodged in his throat. He raced towards him, did a handspring off the wall, and landed on one knee in front of him. Fenton leapt backwards and fell over. Jesus Christ! What the hell's your problem!

Zeus stood up. Sorry, he said. He felt like his heart was exploding with every beat. I thought you were someone else. Zeus looked away and stared into the distance, then sat down on the little wall and put his head in his hands. He wanted to cry.

The boy was recovering from the shock, brushing the dirt and dead leaves off his jeans. After a while he sat down too, facing the other way.

You look a lot like, Zeus said by way of an explanation but couldn't finish his sentence. Now that he had a closer look, the boy didn't resemble Fenton at all. His hair was brown and he was wearing a grey sweatshirt and jeans. He couldn't have been more than fourteen, fifteen. What had he been thinking? You here for the service? Zeus said, his voice unnaturally high.

The boy shook his head.

You live around here?

No.

Just hanging out?

I guess so.

By yourself?

I'm here with my dad, he said. He's across the street right now, in this ugly little room at the back of the church. It's where I'm supposed to be right now too, getting *purified*, but I don't know. The boy looked over his shoulder at the trees, I'd rather be out here, looking for birds. There are tons of birds this year. Their migratory paths are all off because of the weather. I heard a whippoorwill yesterday. I've never heard a whippoorwill around here before. And a woodpecker. There's lots of starlings, and red-winged black birds. I saw a falcon last week. It was either a peregrine falcon or a red-tailed hawk, I couldn't tell for sure at the time.

Sounds like you know a lot about birds.

It's just stuff you know when you live in the country.

So you're not from the city?

The boy shook his head. I'd rather go hunting and fishing than go to a mall. I like being outdoors. I used to set rabbit snares all the time, but I'd only do that now if I really had to, like if I needed the food to survive. The boy reached down and picked up a thin stalk of something dry and put it in his mouth. I still go fishing, though.

I've never killed an animal, Zeus said. I don't know if I'd be able to do it.

Last winter, the boy said, me and my dad set a whole bunch of rabbit snares. The next day I went out to check on them, and even from far away I could tell there'd been this big commotion. All the snow had been brushed away in a wide circle around one of the trees we'd put a snare on. It wasn't until I got close that I saw the bird. We'd caught a grouse by mistake and the copper wire was this perfect straight line away from the tree, it was so tight, and the bird was lying just beyond the circle. The wire had cut through its neck, right down to the bone. You could see from how the snow had been swept away and the flecks of blood what a terrible struggle that bird had had before it died. After that, I didn't want to set another snare, which is kind of sad because it was, like, one of the only things my dad and I really enjoyed doing together. We ate the grouse, but I didn't like the way it died. My dad said, that's life. But I don't know anymore.

A squirrel rustled through the dead leaves on the ground. There's a lot of stuff I don't know anymore, the boy said and let out a frustrated growl and kicked the wall with his heel. The squirrel scurried away. Someone's probably out looking for me right now.

Who's out looking for you? Zeus said. He was still feeling the warm sluggishness of the beers he'd had in town with Hannah.

It doesn't matter, the boy said.

Zeus was thinking the boy seemed older than he looked, or maybe this was an effect of growing up in the country.

That was a pretty impressive flip you did, by the way.

Thank you, Zeus said.

Where did you learn to do that?

Oh, I used to do a little acrobatics, but I'm totally out of practice. Fenton would have liked it, though − that guy I thought you looked like, who's not even alive anymore.

You thought I looked like a dead guy?

Yep. Zeus adjusted his coat.

A friend of yours?

He was more than a friend, Zeus said and brought his feet up and sat cross-legged on the low wall. I really miss him.

The boy looked confused. Are you gay?

What is it with you people around here?

The Bible says −

Fuck the Bible, Zeus suddenly said. He wanted to be back in a place where being gay wasn't a big deal. Not in the country, but in a city − a *big* city. And yes, he said, Fenton was my boyfriend, so I guess that makes me gay. But there was nothing sinful about it. He was my best friend. And he also happened to be very beautiful to me. We just really seemed to satisfy a need in each other.

What, to get bum-fucked?

Zeus dropped his head, then stood up to leave.

Sorry, the boy said. I don't know why I said that. Sometimes people wonder if I'm gay too.

Well, are you?

The boy shrugged and Zeus sat down again. It's okay if you are, Zeus said, I won't tell anyone.

Even if I was, it's not like I could do anything about it.

Why did it have to be so hard? Zeus thought. Couldn't it be easy for just one kid?

A dark blue van came out of the mechanic's garage and drove away. I got into bed with my boyfriend once, Zeus said, at the hospital before he died. I curled up beside him and realized I'd always felt safe with him. He always made me feel at home. And for someone who's never really *had* a home, well, that meant a lot. And now that he's gone, I don't really know where I belong anymore.

You don't have a family?

I've had two families so far, Zeus said. But it didn't really work out with either of them. I was adopted when I was eight years old, but I left that home when I was fifteen.

That's how old I am, the boy said. Sometimes I think about running away.

What's your name? Zeus said.

Enoch.

Well, Enoch, you might look back one day and realize your parents aren't doing such a bad job.

How do you know that? You sound just like everybody else.

Why? What have they done that's so bad?

They can't think for themselves, Enoch said. All they do is what they're told. They've got no feeling, or intelligence, beyond what they think they're supposed to do.

Zeus dragged his hands over his stubbly head. He was a smart kid.

And now they want this woman over at the Global Kingdom, Enoch said, to perform this stupid exorcism on me.

What? Zeus couldn't believe it. He looked out at the trees and a little black bird dropped off a branch and spread its wings and it appeared to be wearing a bright red cape on its shoulders. It swooped past them and off over the big hall. Look! he said, but the boy ignored the bird. Zeus felt sorry for him. I wish I had some advice for you, kid. Honestly, sometimes I think I'm the most clueless person.

There's nothing wrong with being clueless, Enoch said, flicking his hair back as if it was wet. How's anybody supposed to know anything these days?

They sat in silence for a while. The sound of a plane flying overhead seemed to match the brief brightening of things as the sun came out, then hid again. Zeus said, Have you ever – I mean, have you ever even kissed a boy?

Enoch shook his head.

Zeus could remember what that was like. All the fear of getting over that first kiss, the thing that would make it all real. Do you want me to kiss you? he said, and the boy baulked, but only for a moment, then seemed to grow smaller.

Zeus held his breath and squeezed his hands together in his lap. He understood that the proposition was a little risky, maybe even wrong – and yet the small bud of a desire was growing inside his belly, pushing up from some bleak place, an adolescent place, somewhere half rotten and forbidden but satisfying in the way revenge, or anger, can be satisfying.

Okay, the boy said slowly. His voice was quiet. Kiss me then.

Zeus inched his way along the wall and sat very close. The boy was warm. A ripe, syrupy smell. He had a nervous look on his face that Zeus didn't want to see, so he closed his eyes and thought about Fenton and felt Enoch's rough, slightly chapped lips touch his own, and a sweet, heartbreaking sensation bloomed inside him.

There he is! It was a girl's bossy voice.

Zeus leaned back again. A boy and a girl, Enoch's age, were running towards them. Zeus couldn't hear them, just the roar of dry leaves as another gust of wind swept across the ground. They were teenagers, and wore teenagers' clothes. The girl had her hair up in a bouncy ponytail. Enoch had stood up and was now giving off a terrible blank passivity.

We've been looking for you all over the place, the girl said. What are you doing back here?

Who're you? the boy asked Zeus.

I'm nobody, Zeus said. I'm Jésus Ortega.

Come on, Enoch, the girl said. Let's go back to the church.

Everybody's waiting, the boy said.

Don't pressure him, the girl said, then she turned back to Enoch. Delilah told us to come and get you.

So let's go, Enoch said and led them away.

Zeus watched him go. He wanted to stop him, tell Enoch that whatever they were going to do to him in there would only make things worse. Trust me, he thought, you'll end up hating yourself.

Hannah was standing at the edge of the parking lot. Somewhere in the distance a muted boom went off, like a dynamite blast, and she felt a hand on her shoulder. She swung around and there was Connie, her face beaming.

Well, Connie said, *I* just got what I came here for.

Great, Hannah said.

Maybe we should go check up on Mom. Where's Zeus?

He just followed some kids into the church over there.

Really?

He looked like he was on some kind of mission.

So let's go get the truck, Connie said. We can drive over there and wait for him.

There was something about the way he was heading in there, Hannah said. Looked like he was about to break something.

What, like a window? Connie said lightly and recalled how Harlan had thrown that garbage can through the store window not so long ago. She told Hannah about it now, and it shocked her. At the time, Connie said, it had shocked me too. It was a side to him I'd never seen before.

They had arrived at the truck and Connie was waiting for Hannah to get in and unlock her door. They got inside and Hannah said, So what did Harlan's letter say? Is everything all right?

He wants us to go back to the way we were, Connie said and gave her sister a helpless shrug.

Hannah started the truck. Remember that time at camp, she said, when we were kids and you broke that window? They'd been in a cabin after dark. It was at a family camp, and their parents were in the dining hall with all the other parents, having an evening worship service. There was only one baby-sitter, walking between the cabins, checking up on all the kids. Dad overstuffed the woodstove, Hannah said. The lid blew off and flames shot out, remember?

That's right, Connie said. I forgot about that.

How old were we? Hannah said.

Five or six?

Remember how terrified we were?

Well, *I* was terrified. I thought we were going to die. It seemed like the whole cabin was on fire. I couldn't get the door open, Connie said, so I ran straight to the window.

And put your fist through it, Hannah said. Somehow you managed not to cut yourself, but you shattered the whole pane of glass.

And *you* just walked calmly to the door and opened it, Connie said.

Well, it was a tricky knob and I had a knack for it.

I was your big sister, Connie said. I felt so responsible.

You've always felt responsible for me, Hannah said.

Yeah, and a whole lot of good that's ever done.

Well, you're brave. And you have the courage of your convictions, Hannah said, parking the truck in front of the church. Remember how convinced we were that God was watching over us? Because we ran all the way to the dining hall in our bare feet, without even getting a single scratch. We didn't trip or fall, and there were lots of tree roots across that path.

Running through the woods in our little homemade nighties, Connie said.

Sometimes I feel like we're still running through the woods, Hannah said, in our little homemade nighties.

You know, Connie said, all this time I've felt so vulnerable to danger. And yet, imagine how many disasters we've actually averted? She nodded towards the big hall across the street. Am I like that, do you think? I mean, am I like these people? Connie looked genuinely concerned.

You're not like that, Hannah said. You're something else. *I'm* something else.

∋ ∈

Zeus stood to one side of a small room at the back of the church, next to an old-fashioned, elegant wooden coat stand that seemed out of place in its surroundings. He watched as a group of about thirty people, men and women with kids, mothers with their babies, pressed in around Enoch. They had begun to pray, calling out shouts of praise and exultation. The room was painted an ugly shade of green and felt claustrophobic. He felt sick about the kiss. Had he given Enoch a burden? Would it make him suffer?

A tall, blond woman he heard referred to as Delilah seemed to be leading the ceremony. The congregation was closing in on her, and he couldn't see Enoch anymore. The woman raised her Bible in the air and leaned forward and started shouting at the floor. What is your name! What's your name!

Zeus hated the tone of her voice, how angry it was. He moved closer to the edge of the group and saw that Enoch was now face down on the floor and being pinned there by two big men. One was pressing down on his shoulders while the other one knelt on the back of his legs. Beneath them, Enoch was twisting and writhing.

Zeus started sweating. They're going to hurt him! he thought. He despised what was happening. He crouched to look through the legs of the people and tried to get Enoch's attention. For a moment, Zeus bowed his head and covered his eyes, then Delilah shouted, Clear the space! Nobody talk!

The room fell silent and Zeus stood up again. Delilah's arms were thrown wide open and all Zeus could hear was Enoch's exhausted panting and thumping under the weight of those two big men. Delilah leaned forward again and demanded, Who are you? What is your name, evil spirit?

Zeus winced. There was no healing going on here, only a battle of wills that would require so much defiance, it would take Enoch years to soften his heart again. And where were his parents in all of this? He suddenly forced his way through the crowd, to where Delilah stood with her Bible, and shouted, *Stop!*

Everyone froze. The men leaned back and lightened their grip. Enoch glared up at Delilah from the floor. There was the watery sound of many people catching their breath. Zeus didn't know what to do next. You should be doing this to *me*, he said. *I've* committed graver acts than this boy.

The congregation was murmuring now. Delilah turned to Zeus and said, What do you want here? This is not your business.

I'm a repentant sinner, Zeus said.

One of the men who was holding Enoch stood up and straightened his shirt, and Enoch bolted to his feet. His face was red and wet with tears and snot, his eyes were puffy. He looked proud and hateful and victorious.

I'm the one who needs purification here, Zeus insisted. You can't refuse me, can you?

Folks, Delilah announced, this man here is requesting deliverance.

Hallelujah! someone called out halfheartedly.

By what name, she asked, does the demon that torments you go by, brother?

Delilah spoke with such composure, it was almost as if she'd been expecting him all along.

You can speak openly here, Delilah said, brushing her hair back with her fingers.

I will, Zeus said, but first I'd like to take off my coat. He pointed to the wooden coat stand and the congregation parted. Zeus walked towards it slowly, unbuttoning his beige trench coat. A single hanger dangled from one of its curled stems. It reminded him of something. It was the beginning of a mime Fenton had mastered and performed many times. He'd never attempted to perform it himself, and wondered now if he could do it unrehearsed.

∄ ∈

Connie left Hannah waiting in the truck and walked into the church. She looked around the worship area but couldn't find Zeus, so she headed past the reception desk. She came to a corner where another hallway started, heard a voice shout, *Stop!* and got a jolt of fear. It sounded like Zeus's voice. She hurried down the hall and opened a door to a room that was empty. She opened another one. Two people sat in an office, working at their computers. They turned to Connie and she apologized. At the end of the hall was another door, and when she opened this one, Connie saw a crowd of people, standing motionless, watching rapt as Zeus arranged his coat neatly on a hanger. She stood there perplexed.

He brushed the coat off with the back of his hand and a man went towards him, but Zeus held him off with a gesture. Wait, his hand said, and the man waited. Zeus tugged at the shoulders of his coat and straightened it up. He tilted his head as if inspecting the results, taking stock of the coat. It was a good coat. A decent coat.

Behind him, the audience was being patient and watchful. Even from the back, you could tell a transformation was taking place. Zeus seemed no longer himself but a charmed, enchanted being, transformed as if by magic into a character capable of funnelling down and distilling into a kind of concentrated moonshine all the pathos of the world. And he was pouring it into a cup and asking you to drink it. He untied his red scarf and wound it twice around the neck of the hanger. There was a good suggestion of a person in just the coat and scarf. Zeus dusted it off some more, then thrust his arm into the coat's sleeve and pivoted to face the room, his back pressed up against the coat.

Okay, this is ridiculous, a tall, blond woman said.

A teenaged boy shouted, Leave him alone! and people turned to look at him.

A few young kids had come out of the crowd as if they knew something was about to happen. Of course they did, Connie thought. Suffer the children.

Zeus held up his arm for more meticulous dusting when suddenly it froze. It had come to life! The arm belonged to the coat, and Zeus was leaning away from it suspiciously. He didn't dare move. He looked up over his shoulder at the coat stand, then back at the arm of the coat, its hand open and hovering in the air. The hand made a move towards him, and Zeus recoiled. It inched forward, and Zeus shrunk back an inch.

The room had grown quieter. Everyone was watching him now. What would he do next?

Zeus's expression was one of alarm, eyebrows arched. His eyes darted one way, then the other, as the hand moved closer. It touched the front of his t-shirt, felt the fabric, tidied it up, then swiftly, with one stiff finger pressed to his jaw line, swung Zeus's face towards its own. Zeus gave the coat a nervous, obsequious smile. The audience laughed. Then the coat began to brush him off, reciprocating with the same fussy care and attention Zeus had shown it earlier. The coat dusted off his arms, his shoulders and chest, and then, with a sudden flicked upswing, it had Zeus by the throat.

Connie was amazed and found herself smiling.

He hung suspended in terror, chin in the air, until the coat released him, and stroked him in one tender, sensual caress, from his neck all the way down to his belly. Zeus grovelled and swooned, in an agony of submissive pleasure, his face drawn into a grimace of longing. He looked slavishly, irrevocably in love.

How does he *do* that? a child's voice asked.

And then, abruptly, Zeus pulled out his arm, extracting himself from the coat and shuffling off to pick up an invisible suitcase. He hesitated. This was going to be a classic, heartbreaking farewell. He turned, rushed back to the coat, shoved his arm in, and they embraced again, facing the audience, cheek to cheek, with all the tenderness in the world. I will never let you go. The coat reached up and lovingly traced a lazy circle on the tip of Zeus's nose, making his whole head follow fawn-ingly. Zeus closed his eyes and his eyebrows peaked in the centre. His mouth, hanging open slightly, started to blubber. He turned to bury his face in the coat's chest and his hand flew up to the coat's shoulder, floating up through the final distance very slowly, leading with the wrist like a piano player lifting his hands off the keys. His hand, having finally settled on the coat's shoulder, gathered up a fistful of material and clung to it.

Together they rocked one way, then the other. In unison, they rose and sank on the wave of a powerful sigh. Stillness again. Then they jumped apart. Zeus grabbed his head. He was late! It was time to go! He shuffled away from the coat, bent to pick up his suitcase, straightened up, then stopped. He looked back and waved. There was applause.

So *this* is what he did, Connie thought. He didn't even need a costume, he was so thoroughly a clown. What a lovely, remarkable thing to do. If anything, she had underestimated him. They all had. It wasn't Zeus who had needed their pity, it was Zeus who could have rescued *them*, if only they'd been open to the possibility.

At dinner that evening, they were subdued, drained by the excesses of the day. They'd found a tavern near the Comfort Inn and were sharing a large plate of nachos.

You should have seen him, Connie told Rose and Hannah. Had the whole room eating out of the palm of his hand. I couldn't believe how good you are, she said, turning to Zeus. You could have your own show.

Zeus was picking the black olives out of his nachos and putting them on the edge of his plate. I still can't imagine clowning without Fenton, he said.

But you were *born* to be a clown, Connie said.

Entertainer to the charismatics, Hannah said dryly. Do I see a new character emerging?

Fenton used to say the art of clowning was all about the search for love and acceptance, Zeus said. Clowns like to pretend they're happier than they are, but it's usually because they're trying to avoid something dark.

Avoid it or *illuminate* it? Rose said.

They illuminate human suffering the way falling down the stairs can cure you of a headache, Zeus said.

Rose reached across the table, held Zeus's wrist for a moment, and said, It takes some of us a long time to learn new ways of thinking about things. I'm not saying I didn't mess up. I did, I know that, and I'm sorry. But it's easy to fall into the mistake of waiting for other people to make up for theirs. Even if they do, it will never feel like it's enough, because the only meaningful change comes from within.

The waitress came over to ask if everything was okay, and Hannah nodded thank you.

What I'm trying to say is, you've just got to ignore everything that's outside of yourself at some point in your life, Rose went on, and be entirely faithful to *you*. And then, you know what will happen? You'll suddenly come into contact with the rest of the world. At least that's what it seems to me, although I'm not there yet myself. I'm still working on getting to know Rose Crowe.

I think I understand what you're saying, Zeus said, but what means the most to me is that you're here. I mean, you came all this way. That's what nobody ever did for me, and I wouldn't want you to think it went unnoticed.

In the morning, they checked out of the hotel and drove Zeus to the bus station, where he bought a ticket to Chimayó. You sure you don't want us to take you there? Rose asked, and Zeus confirmed that he did not.

This is my final leg of the journey, he said. And I want to do it solo.

Rose asked him if he had enough money, and Zeus told her about Fenton's twenty thousand dollars. She said, I remember when you were about nine years old, you came to me one day with this tin box. It had a map of New Mexico you'd cut out from a magazine, I think, and some fruit roll-ups and things you'd been saving to make the trip back to your parents' place. You also had eighteen dollars in there, saved up. It made me so incredibly sad to see how homesick you were, but that you had made a plan, and come to tell me about it? I realized then that you had a kind of determination, and I knew you were going to be okay, that your heart was open.

Zeus nodded and looked down at his feet.

Rose put her hand on his face and said, It would make me very happy to hear from you sometime, Zeus Ortega. She said goodbye, then went out to wait in the truck.

Connie and Hannah walked him to the bus and Zeus turned to his sisters. They looked so full of apology.

Connie hugged him and said, We'll stay in touch, okay, little brother? Good luck in Chimayó.

I love you, Hannah whispered into his neck as they hugged goodbye.

Now go, Zeus said and watched them walk out and turn at the door, one last time, to wave.

The bus was slow, and Zeus had to make a connection in Oklahoma City and then take the overnight bus to Santa Fe. In Amarillo, in the middle of the night, he woke up and saw in the yellow haze of a lamppost a family of seven, standing beside a mountain of suitcases and striped woven bags, like they were moving house, or on the run. It reminded him of a day Tim and Rose took him out shopping and let him get a red varsity jacket with black leather sleeves and a felt patch of a bluebird carrying a ribbon in its beak like a tattoo across the back. He'd begged them for it and they'd let him have it, and he'd loved that jacket with his whole being, wearing it until the cuffs were threadbare and the bluebird patch was so frayed it had lost all its features. It took the driver fifteen minutes to load all the family's luggage, and then they boarded noisily and took seats all over the bus beside the other huddled, sleeping passengers.

At dawn, Zeus woke and from the window of the Greyhound bus watched the landscape of his childhood come into view again for the first time, unimaginably beautiful – the sky its distinctive blue, behind an endless pattern of white clouds, and the red hills spotted with the dusty green pompoms of sagebrush and mesquite. The bus stopped in Santa Fe, and Zeus bought three tamales in tinfoil at the plaza and carried them onto another bus that would take him to Chimayó, though when he tried to eat, he realized he was too nervous. The bus wound its way through hills and past cliffs that seemed to him both to reflect the magnitude of his emotions and make them feel puny. They carried on towards Chimayó and passed the famous pilgrimage church, so much smaller than he remembered it, like the toy model of a church, its rounded corners giving it a soft, spongy look.

Zeus got off at a stop a little further after that and followed the map Fenton had made for him.

As he approached his parents' house, he began to panic. There it was. A single-storey adobe, old jalopy up on cement blocks, evidence of children. Toys in the yard. A stray dog sniffing around under a window. His feet wouldn't slow down. He just kept on walking. I can't do this, he said to himself.

He found a shady spot on the other side of the road and sat there, staring at the house for what felt like an hour, trying to imagine what their lives were like. What would he be interrupting? As he sat there, a car drove up and turned into the drive. It was the same car his father had owned when he was a boy. A bit faded and a little rusty in places, his 1978 Ford Thunderbird. The car stopped and the doors opened and two young girls jumped out of the passenger side and started running towards the house. A man got out and shouted at the kids to come back to the car. It was his father. A thin, wiry man, with tattoos on his arms. He opened the trunk and lifted out some bags of groceries and gave one each to the girls. He carried the rest inside and the door closed behind him. Another car started to come down the road, music blaring, windows down, two guys about his own age in the front seats with their black hair slicked back. They slowed down to look at him as they passed. Zeus grabbed his duffle bag and hurried away.

He headed back out to the highway and started hitchhiking. It was a long time before anyone picked him up. He was heading north, and at dusk he got dropped off at a crossroads and started to walk. The sky was denim. In the west, a thin band of yellow flared briefly above a bank of violet clouds, then went orange, pink, and finally blue, the dark hills like hunched shoulders, growing blacker and bulkier on either side of him as the light drained out of the sky.

Zeus walked through the dark countryside. Occasionally, a car or a truck would pass, one lit up like a casino, with a neon blue cross on the grill. Its headlights showed trees to his right, tall Ponderosa pines growing out of the sandy ground. Zeus wandered off the highway and started walking into the woods. A half-moon rose. Tomorrow was election day. He thought about his country and the world. He came into a small clearing surrounded by trees, dropped his duffle bag, and sat down. He felt exhausted. He opened his bag for something warmer to wear and as he was getting a sweater out noticed the edge of Fenton's white clown suit. He put his sweater on and pulled the suit out and laid it on the ground, where it seemed to soak up whatever light was left in the evening until it was a glowing thing. It had a human shape, but it struck him now as empty, just a piece of clothing that Fenton wouldn't want him to be dragging around with him wherever he went. He caught it by the wrists and swung it over his head, and it hung down his back like a long cape. He tied the arms around his neck, crouched to dig out Fenton's slippers and stood up, wearing the slippers on his hands. He felt like a confused superhero.

Someone drove by on the highway and the strobing of headlights against the trees gave what he was about to do an almost criminal aspect. The wind was picking up. Fenton's clown suit rippled like a flag. Zeus tucked the slippers under his arm and got a lighter from his duffle bag and a map he'd picked up at a motel and twisted it into a wick and lit the tip. He cupped his hand around the flame and held the wick upside down to encourage the flame to climb up the map. He took a few blind steps away from his duffle bag. He couldn't see anything beyond the flame.

Zeus dropped the slippers and crouched to arrange them in a V, the way Fenton used to stand in them, then he untied the silk knot at his throat with one hand and laid it on top. He was rotating and waving the twisted map, trying to nurse the flame without scorching his wrist.

The wind was threatening to blow it out, so he used his body to shield it and tried to think of something to say, but now his fingers had begun to burn, so he flicked it on the ground and kicked it on top of the white silk, which gathered and rushed as if sucked towards the flame. What was left of the map unfurled to expose its breast, a fragment of intersecting highways, then started to shrink around the edges in a tightening noose of orange cinders.

He grabbed some leaves and twigs and laid these down on top. The fire exhaled a lot of grey smoke, a foul smell, then the whole thing caught and there was a sudden burst of flame and firelight, illuminating a cathedral of branches vaulted over his head.

Zeus was poking at the fire with a stick, it was burning well now. He stood up and tried to think of something to say. Your death was like a grand piano falling out of the sky.

He thought he saw a flashlight through the trees. A dog barked.

He poked the fire again. There was more barking. He looked out into the darkness. A furious male voice shouted from somewhere off in the distance. Now Zeus could see lights from a farmhouse, then a gun went off.

He tore off through the woods terrified and ran until he couldn't run anymore. Breathless, he turned to look and saw, through the black pillars of the trees, a dome of pale light and a ghostly vine of smoke rising up into the night sky where a few early stars had opened up their eyes. Then the black figure of a man obscured the light, his shadow rising into the trees. Sparks flew up and darkness again. Zeus didn't dare go back for his duffle bag. There was nothing in it he strictly needed, his wallet was in his pocket. He decided to keep on walking, without possessions, without ties, alone under the night sky.

After a while, he found a little hollow beside a fallen log and lay down with his head on his arms and looked up at the stars. Same stars over Tripoli.

That night he dreamt of arriving at his parents' house in a white pickup truck. He got out and stood across the street as a car drove up and pulled into the drive, loud music coming from behind its closed windows. It was his father's Thunderbird low-rider with a portrait of Zeus and his mother painted on the side and the words *ámale por siempre* on a ribbon above their heads. The passenger door opened and the music got louder. Two little boys who looked just like he used to sat patiently in the front seat. His mother came out of the house then, braiding her black hair. She paused for a moment and looked in his direction, then called her children inside. His father opened the trunk of the car, lifted out a thin grey dog, and put him on the ground. When he straightened up, he noticed a young man standing next to a shiny pickup on the other side of the street.

He could see his wife's face in him. The young man started to walk towards him, and José Ortega felt as if someone had punched him in the chest. He never thought he'd have the good fortune of seeing his son again. He moved forward with his arms outstretched. Jésus, he whispered, his heart seized hard with joy and pain. My sweet Jésus.

ACKNOWLEDGEMENTS

For being my first intrepid champion, heartfelt thanks to my agent, Ellen Levine.

For her amazing skill, generosity, and commitment to this book, I owe a debt of gratitude to my editor, Ellen Seligman. Many thanks also to Kendra Ward at McClelland & Stewart, and Heather Sangster of Strong Finish.

To my friends and readers – who all gave more sustenance than they could possibly know – I would like to thank Natalie Loveless, Michael Redhill, Claudia Dey, Alison Pick, Kathleen Winter, Erik Rutherford, Sheila Heti, Liz Unna, Michael Helm, Laura Repas, Carle Steel, Lisa Moore, and Carole Galand.

To the independent cafés of west-end Toronto, thank you for offering friendly public space in which to work. May the revolution continue!

I would like to pay a note of tribute to the outdoor chapel at Pioneer Pacific Camp on Thetis Island, where all my religious sentiments began.

The skit that Zeus performs at the end of the book was inspired by an act created by the masterful Russian clown Slava Polunin, which he performs in his eponymously titled Slava's Snowshow.

To my parents, Michael and Elaine Pountney, and my sister, Michelle Troughton, for their love and support, and everything they know, I am very grateful.

Lastly, love and thanks to Michael Winter, for enduring faith and countless hot dinners, and our son, Leo, for being himself a clown of such tender wisdom.